MIRACLE GIRLS

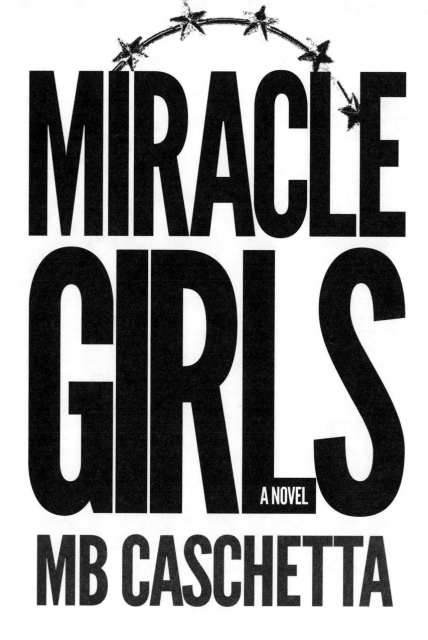

MIRACLE GIRLS

A NOVEL

MB CASCHETTA

Engine Books
Indianapolis

Engine Books
PO Box 44167
Indianapolis, IN 46244
enginebooks.org

Also available in Hardcover and eBook formats from Engine Books.

Printed in the United States of America

10   9   8   7   6   5   4   3   2   1

ISBN: 978-1-938126-15-4

Library of Congress Control Number: 2014935318

For Meryl and
for miracle girls everywhere

In memoriam
Mary Mastroianni
(1912-2007)

And Thou that art the flower of virgins all
Of whom Saint Bernard loved so well to write,
To Thee at my beginning do I call;
Thou comfort of us wretches, help me indite
Thy maiden's death, who won through her merit
The eternal life, and from the Fiend such glory
As men may read hereafter in her story.

—Geoffrey Chaucer
Prologue to *The Second Nun's Tale,*
The Life of St. Cecilia

THE FIRST

Soon Cee-Cee Bianco will climb into the back of the family station wagon stalled at the end of the driveway. Her puffy down jacket slung over pajamas, bare feet wedged into a pair of red plastic cowboy boots from Woolworth's.

Fingers pink from the cold.

When she faces forward, presents are stacked in the passenger seat, bits of red ribbon still half hanging on. When she looks behind her, the driveway runs into a stretch of endless highway, a bright swirl of sun and snow.

Clutching her little bottle of medicine, she thinks about Frank's advice. *Drink this when you feel one coming on, honey.*

The doctors blame her visions on asthma and allergies. Nonna's priests say it's all in her head.

With one hand in her pocket, she shuffles a miniature deck of cards, practicing. Ta-da!

For a minute, nothing happens. Nothing but snow.

Then her brothers come out of the house, kicking onto the front porch, elbowing and calling each other names. They pound on the car window until Cee-Cee unlocks. They jostle for space, shoving her over so they can pile in the back, and sit oldest to youngest: Anthony, Roadie, and Baby Pauly.

Cee-Cee is always last.

"Move it over, stupid!" Anthony says.

She is named for the virgin martyr who survived a burning

bath and three bloody whacks to the neck, then refused to die for three days. To be a saint, Cee-Cee knows, you have to be tough.

Pressed to the door, she feels a purple bruise blossom on her arm.

She closes her eyes to shut out the noise and does not open them again until Baby Pauly is shouting in her ear, pointing to Glory who is about to leave again.

No one ever thinks of calling Glory Mama.

But for now Cee-Cee is still just a regular girl—ten years old—on Christmas morning, her favorite day.

It's the same every year.

Glory gets mad at Frank and throws a shoe. "You think this junk buys love?" she shouts, stumbling over boxes of toys. "You think it makes you a better father?"

Frank always ducks. "Watch it, will you?"

Baby Pauly and Roadie stop hitting each other with their new Bobby Orr hockey sticks still wrapped in plastic. Anthony looks up from a box of chocolates.

Cee-Cee sits in front of the color TV and sings, "*Happy Birthday, Baby Jesus…*" to the tiny baby in the manger that Nonna gave her. She rocks back and forth, making the figurines hop around so the Wise Men do a dance.

"Cut it out," Anthony says, throwing a raisin-nut cluster at his sister's head. "We're not that religious."

Glory stops yelling at Frank long enough to shake Cee-Cee by the shoulders. "I swear to God, Cecilia Marie Bianco—" But music from a special report comes on the TV.

Suddenly everyone is staring at the screen.

A photograph shows a girl with wavy red hair, freckles, and a gap in her smile where Cee-Cee can see the faintest flash of tongue. *Eileena Brice Iaccamo*, the newscaster says in a somber voice. *Kidnapped*. She was last seen wearing a pink sweater.

"That girl goes to my school," Roadie says.

Frank says. "Another one?"

"More kids go missing in Romeville than anywhere," Glory says. "I read it in the paper."

Frank shakes his head. "Sickos."

A bunch of Vietnam protesters with long messy hair come on the TV next. They shout, holding up two-finger peace signs and shaking them at the camera.

"Look!" Baby Pauly points at a pair of nuns carrying signs.

Roadie nudges Baby Pauly aside with his foot. Now everyone can see the nun shout into a reporter's microphone about the terrible war.

"Hey, it's Sister Bertrille," Frank says, the Flying Nun. She's wearing a full habit.

"What is wrong with those women?" Glory says.

"Damn holy rollers." Frank can't stand God or Nonna or Nonna's friends, who are mostly nuns and priests, especially when they show up on the news. "They think prayer is what's saving them from communism?"

Glory switches off the TV. She kisses the top of her daughter's head. "Take a stab at normal, baby. Do it for me."

After Frank goes to work the next morning, Glory pulls everyone out of bed to pack it all up and put it in the car: even the toys that aren't broken, even the sweaters that fit. Cee-Cee puts a new doll in the pile, eyeing G.I. Joe still in his box.

Now he will never get to kiss Barbie.

Glory confronts Baby Pauly. "Who's going to teach you to skate?"

He pulls a hockey puck from under his pillow and hands it over.

"Everything's closed today!" Anthony warns. "Snowstorm's coming!"

Anthony watches TV in his underwear. He is failing the ninth grade again. Everyone else is dark with ink-black hair, but

Anthony has a jagged line of reddish-brown bangs framing his white face. His skin is so veiny and blue it makes you think of skim milk. Even his eyes are blue. His fingers and toes are always flinching like there's a colony of ants burrowing under his skin.

Even at night when everyone is asleep, Cee-Cee can feel her brother twitching.

Spurred on by Anthony's bad attitude, Glory stacks the repackaged Christmas gifts by the front door, ordering Roadie to pile them in the front seat of her car.

"Nowhere to go, Glory!" Anthony says. "You're out of your mind."

Glory grabs an armful of coats from the closet. "You think you're the last Pepsi in the desert, Anthony Gerard?"

Cee-Cee pulls on a random jacket over her pajamas. She feels Anthony's eyes on her, like always.

"St. Agnes married Jesus when she was only thirteen. And they chopped off her head," she tells him. She can see Agnes' headless body in a blinding white wedding dress, the happy look on her face as it rolls to the floor.

Anthony won't stop watching Cee-Cee.

Over his shoulder the clouds roll past the window; they look like giant fluffy cats. Finally he turns and follows Glory into the hallway.

"Doesn't look like the desert to me, Glory! Looks like a blizzard."

Glory herds her children toward the door. "If you're so smart, Anthony, then why don't you try being the grown-up?"

The bank where Glory works is closed, and probably most of the roads. Still Cee-Cee does what she's told, escaping out the front door.

"Trust me, people!" Glory says. "J.C. Penney's is always open."

IN THE BACK SEAT of the station wagon, Cee-Cee keeps her eyes closed, listening to the sound of her own heart beating above the noise of her brothers settling. The driver's side door slams shut with a waft of perfume, followed by the sound of Glory's fists pounding the dashboard.

"Damn you, Franco Bianco!"

Out of gas is nothing new.

Most mornings Frank shaves and puts on a tie. Sometimes he lets Cee-Cee lather her face too; she pretends to shave with a butter knife. Before he leaves, he and Cee-Cee go around the house for a quick game of hide and seek, but they don't look for someone who is hiding. They look for Glory's hidden money.

No matter where she stashes the extra cash—zipped in a pillow, taped under the toilet tank, squirreled behind a loose panel in the basement—they always find it.

While Frank puts on his shoes, Cee-Cee acts as lookout, spying through the front window for her father's ride, the only taxi in town. She gives Frank the high sign when *Il Duce* arrives, cutting his lights and coasting up the driveway. They listen to the engine softly humming.

Right on time, Frank always whispers. *Just like the real Mussolini.*

He gives Cee-Cee a wink and puts an index finger up to his lips. It's no secret Frank's lost his job, but everyone plays along.

Cee-Cee knows his first and only stop is Blanche's Iron Door, an old Marine Midland bank converted to a bar. *'Cause that's where the gin is flowing,* Glory likes to say. After Blanche's husband died, Blanche changed the name and got Frank to hang an old vaulted bank door on the wall in the far corner above some tables, securing it with rusty wire.

In the car, defeated, Glory rolls down her window. "Bastard!" Frank is famous for leaving an empty tank.

Cee-Cee imagines the white puff of Glory's curse clouding

up and rolling out the window in all directions as if her voice might reach Frank, who is by now long gone.

Sometimes when the school nurse calls to send Cee-Cee home with a fever, Frank pays *Il Duce* to pick her up and drop her at Blanche's. At the bar, he bunches up his coat for a pillow and makes her lie down on an empty pool table. Blanche covers her with a red-and-white checkered tablecloth, plastic on one side, fuzzy on the other.

"My Norbie will sure be glad to see you lying there like a princess," Blanche will say.

Norbert Sasso is huge and sweet and especially slow when it comes to thinking. He shows up eventually with his big moony face and his tongue unfurling like a flag. Sometimes he's alone and sometimes he's fast on the heels of a girl with ponytails and scraped knees, which is how Cee-Cee met Mary Margaret in the first place.

"This is my best friend besides you," Norbert said. "Her name is Mary Margaret Cortina."

The girl focused her sharp eyes on Cee-Cee. "What if someone wanted to play and knocked you off the pool table with a cue stick?"

"Hasn't happened yet." Cee-Cee propped herself up on an elbow, feeling her fever lift. "Do you play pool?"

Mary Margaret shrugged.

"Cee-Cee's protected by angels," Norbert said.

Mary Margaret scrunched up her nose. "Do you believe that crap?"

Norbert rubbed his hands together at his forehead.

Cee-Cee shrugged. "Why not?"

Later Blanche said they should give Mary Margaret a break for being in a bad mood because her mother keeps having babies that die.

"We could be friends," Mary Margaret said, making Cee-Cee's heart ache with happiness.

In the car, Roadie, fourteen, produces a wrinkled twenty-dollar bill from his coat.

He has wiry hair perched on his head with a life of its own; from the side he looks like a bird about to take flight.

"Where did *you* get money?" Anthony says.

Glory sounds excited: "Who cares where! Why didn't you say something, honey?"

"Found it in the lint catcher," Roadie says.

"Good place!" Glory snaps her fingers.

Cee-Cee stashes the information away for the next time she and Frank play hide and seek for Glory's money.

Now Glory leans into the back seat and gives Roadie a wet kiss. Roadie's black eyes come alive when Glory pays attention to him, making him look soft and watery, more like the father he's named after: Franco Christopher Bianco Jr.

Glory shakes Cee-Cee's arm. "Snap out of it! You boys make sure she doesn't have a problem. Nobody leaves this car but me!"

Before Cee-Cee can get a quiet moment to think about the latest missing girl, Baby Pauly is jostling her, pointing. Cee-Cee opens her eyes. She follows his finger past the front yard where the highway meets Route 177.

All four Bianco children turn to watch Glory as she steps into traffic. They see her in flickers: crisp green parka, black flyaway curls, brown suede boots with the fringe hanging down.

On the broken shoulder of Route 177, she leans into a cop car as if God were not watching.

"Who?" Baby Pauly asks.

Cee-Cee wipes her coat sleeve against the window, watching white flakes chipping away from the sky. "You know who."

Glory sways a loose hip into the wind.

"That cop that's always flirting with her, stupid," Anthony says.

"*No gas, no flow, no go, man.*" Roadie mimics what they can all imagine Glory saying to the cop.

Baby Pauly presses his face against the rear way-back window, where Glory keeps a spare tire and jumper cables, then drops back into his seat next to Cee-Cee. His cowboy boots are just like Cee-Cee's, but he wears them on the wrong feet.

He chews his lip. "Is Glory going to get arrested?"

"Wipe your nose, Pauly!" Anthony's mean voice makes Baby Pauly and Cee-Cee freeze, hearts beating in tandem. It's hard to say which is worse: Bossy Anthony telling them what to do, or Silent Anthony sneaking around the house at night.

Cee-Cee can feel fear bubbling up in Baby Pauly's chest.

They are not a family that's very lucky with cars. Frank is always crashing into lampposts and trucks. Once he ran someone over, but the lady managed to lie down flat in the grass between the tires. *Best magic trick ever* was how he told it. Glory only lets Baby Pauly and Cee-Cee ride bikes up and down the driveway.

Now Baby Pauly looks at Cee-Cee, panicking.

His soft sloping profile is the mirror image of his sister's face. Glory loves telling people that they're twins—identical—even though Pauly is eleven months older than Cee-Cee.

It's good to be the same, Glory tells them. *Then you never have to be alone.*

Frank hates when she dresses Cee-Cee and Pauly in matching outfits: a blue-suede cowboy and cowgirl suit, or bow-tie and shorts that match Cee-Cee's sash and skirt. Baby Pauly's eyelashes are dark and feathery, curling up at the edge like a girl's.

Frank thinks he acts too much like a baby.

The cop car pulls into the driveway, an eerie light pulsing out a red glow over the snow banks and the white house with its peeling paint.

"Don't worry," Cee-Cee whispers. "Close your eyes and we'll be invisible."

Baby Pauly immediately does what his sister says.

Their plan is interrupted when Anthony gets out of the station wagon and slams the door, letting in a cold gust of air.

Cee-Cee and Baby Pauly watch as the bright green arms of Glory's parka flap in the snow. She reaches out, but Anthony slips past her and stomps onto the porch, letting himself into the house with his key.

Glory bounds back over the snow toward the station wagon where the rest of her children are watching the cop park his car. He steps out into the snow, shiny boots glinting. They see his miniature reflection go gliding across the rearview mirror: slicked-back hair, dark blue uniform, bright metal badge pinned to his coat.

Baby Pauly can't take it any more: "KIDNAPPER!"

"Cut it out, Pauly," says Roadie. "No one's going anywhere."

Baby Pauly looks at Cee-Cee, then back at the cop, then once again at Cee-Cee.

"Save us," he whispers.

But there's nothing she can do.

At least it's not anyone they know, not somebody's father, or the janitor from school, not the boyfriend of one of the lunch ladies, or the cheating husband of Baby Pauly's favorite room-mother. This is just a guy Glory met at work, as if the only people making deposits at her bank teller window are men who flirt. They are always tall and sometimes loud with cigarette breath; they are never kind like Donny Osmond or Jesus.

Sooner or later the women show up, usually wives, but sometimes girlfriends. Glory calls them the Mrs. So-and-Sos. Sometimes they pound on the door in the middle of the night, or turn up at the movies and ask questions. A few of the nicer ones find Cee-Cee on the playground during recess or in the parking lot before school. They take her aside and button her sweater, tighten her braids, pull up her socks. Once in a while one of them slips her a baloney sandwich on the sly, or gives her some good advice: *Don't talk to strangers, honey; plenty of little girls get stolen that way.*

When Glory picks Cee-Cee up in the public school parking

lot, she wears giant dark glasses. *Look at those cows,* she says about all the other mothers who greet their kids with apples and cookies and smiles.

Once Glory found a garbage bag on the front porch, left by a particularly bold Mrs. So-and-So. It was filled with hand-me-down clothes and a handwritten note, which Glory crumpled and threw into the wind. *People have some nerve,* she said.

Somehow, though, Cee-Cee ended up wearing the tiny flannel shirt and green corduroy jumper, the cable-knit sweater with the matching skirt and the bright red tights. Glory laced her into a perfect-fitting pair of black-and-white saddle shoes.

Walk around, Glory said. *You look like a million bucks!*

Cee-Cee didn't want to love the pretty oxfords, but couldn't help it. The dark-black and shiny-white panels were like nothing she'd ever worn before. Just the same, she took the prized possessions off, then put them on again, lacing and unlacing. Later, she set them on a pillow at the end of the bed and got on her knees to ask for help.

Live a little! Glory said. *They're just shoes.*

Sometimes Nonna's church Sisters stop over with homemade jam or roses from their garden. They have questions for Cee-Cee about her visions because Nonna keeps them up to date. But Glory snatches their jars and bouquets and slams the door in their faces.

Old black crows, Glory says.

Watching through the window as they walk away, Cee-Cee thinks the Sisters are pretty in their short veils and dark suits, their sensible shoes. When they stop by Nonna's for tea, they are cheerful all the time.

Now Glory comes flying around the back of the car and stops abruptly at Cee-Cee's door. Snapping it open, she springs her daughter out of the station wagon and into the cold.

Using her best grown-up voice, she says. "This is my baby girl."

The cop nods hello.

"Vinnie's going to take us to the mall in his police car, honey. He's a real live Trooper. Aren't you, Officer Golluscio?"

"Oneida County. Safest traffic patterns in the state!"

Cee-Cee stares up at the cop, eyeing his shiny badge. "What about kidnappings?"

But Glory grips her arm tight, as if she were a tiny criminal who might try to flee, and gives her the stink-eye, which means she should shut up. Before she can decide whether or not to obey, Baby Pauly propels himself out of the station wagon with surprising force.

"STOP!" he screams, taking a lap around the station wagon. "YOU'RE UNDER ARREST!"

Shoving Cee-Cee into the cop's arms, Glory tackles Baby Pauly from behind. She manages to sit on his legs and cover his mouth with her hands.

Looking up at Vinnie, she tries to smile. "This will just take a sec."

Vinnie backs away, pulling Cee-Cee with him to the cop car. He helps her into the passenger seat, where the heat is blasting and a ham radio blares out static. Slamming her door, he jogs around the car and climbs into the driver's seat, rolling down the window to await further instruction.

Baby Pauly struggles under Glory's weight, kicking up snow in the space behind the station wagon, yelping and struggling. He tries to bite her, but Glory has the advantage of weight and size. She pins his arms and legs with her own.

"Get the boxes, Roadie," she yells.

Roadie springs into action, wrapping his arms around a stack of packages with stickers that say "Love, Daddy," and carrying them over to the cop car.

Vinnie unlocks the back seat. "You can sit back there if you want. I'll even let you play with the handcuffs."

Roadie unloads the gifts and heads back over to Glory, who

is still on the ground straddling Baby Pauly, trying to sweet-talk him out of his tantrum.

As if nothing out of the ordinary were happening, Vinnie yawns, revving the engine with his shiny black boot. He turns on the a.m. radio, switching stations, smiling nervously.

"Pretty soon they'll have astronauts orbiting the earth," he says. "Can you believe it? People—just like you and me—shuttling around up there like it's nothing?"

Cee-Cee does not answer. *Never talk to a cop*, Frank always says.

"Wonder what we'd look like down here from up there. Ever think of that?" He sighs, shaking his head. "Probably a lot better from that far away."

When Cee-Cee closes her eyes, she sees Vinnie without a uniform, peering into a pink bedroom and then coming across a small kid's single shoe under his sofa. One minute he's sitting at the dinner table with his wife and kids; the next minute they are gone. All the cereal bowls, crayons, peanut butter crackers, peas ground into the rug, homework, teddy bears, tears—packed and removed, divorced.

She feels how it always surprises him—an unexpected stab in the lungs.

Cee-Cee and the cop both take a sharp breath in. He looks at her knowingly. She doesn't meet his eyes, but instead watches Glory shaking Baby Pauly on the snowy ground near the station wagon in front of the cop car, Glory's messy hair and unzipped coat.

"Nothing's easy," Vinnie says, watching out the window. "But you seem no worse for the wear."

Cee-Cee can feel that sitting in this vehicle with her makes him feel better.

"Problem is, it only gets harder."

Cee-Cee concentrates on St. Lucy with her eyes plucked out.

"Ever see a pair of eyeballs on a silver plate?" Cee-Cee says, breaking her rule about talking to cops.

He seems uncertain. "A pair of what?"

Outside in the snow near the station wagon, Baby Pauly squirms under Glory until Roadie's dark hair, and Glory's dark hair, and Baby Pauly's dark hair are all the way white with freshly fallen snow. Roadie touches their mother's shoulder.

Then, just like that, it's over. Glory picks herself up, brushes herself off, and shakes out her long black hair.

She looks at the ground as though none of these children belong to her.

Through the windshield of the cop car, Roadie nods at Cee-Cee, who begins to inch toward the passenger door. Vinnie gets out to free Cee-Cee into the snowy air.

Roadie stands motionless in the driveway, waiting for his sister to catch up. His arms are full of Baby Pauly, who is whimpering quietly now.

Defeated, Glory heads toward the little patch of white snow next to the cop car where Cee-Cee is standing.

"Sorry, Glory," Cee-Cee says.

But Glory makes a wide circle around her daughter and climbs into the cop car, slamming the door without a word.

Baby Pauly pops his thumb out of his mouth. "Let's go watch *The Price Is Right*."

Roadie carries him toward the house. "C'mon, Cee-Cee. We're going inside."

The storm, too, has taken a sudden turn, dropping wet snow like apologies. Baby Pauly tips his head back on Roadie's shoulder and catches a few flakes on his tongue.

Cee-Cee doesn't have to turn around to know that Glory and the cop are backing down the driveway onto Route 177; she sees them in her mind. As they pull away in the cop car, Cee-Cee can feel them staring for just a moment at the back of her head, small and unhooded, a fiery orb barely detectable through the chalky white snow.

AMANDA WHALEN LOVES SNOW.

Mornings like this, she can almost catch a whiff of childhood: maple syrup and firewood. Walking across Our Lady's schoolyard, she takes a deep breath and closes her eyes. The vague lights behind her eyelids form the hint of her mother's face, the hazy outline of her father standing at the kitchen door. It always surprises her to find them still there after all these years.

Amanda's father worked on the railroad. Her whole young life people said he'd surely get run over by a train, the way he climbed around tinkering on engines, sometimes while the cars were still moving. But one night only a few hours after he'd come home from work, a wayward spark escaped from the wood burning stove while they slept; it set fire to the kitchen tablecloth, which spread to the drapes, sending flames up the wall.

Asleep in the front of the house, five-year-old Amanda was wakened by firemen sounding their sirens and calling to her from the street.

Jump, they said into a bullhorn. *Come to the window and jump.*

Instead, Amanda crawled to the hall and shouted for her parents. When no one answered, she rolled down the staircase to the open front door, where she stood up and walked right out of that burning building. More than half her body was covered in third-degree burns.

In the hospital, they peeled her blisters every day and scrubbed them with soap, a painstaking process that went on for hours and made her scream for her mother. She'd missed her parents' funeral, her chance to say goodbye. The next several years she spent in a blaze of white pain that obliterated everything and kept her apart from the world. When she was finally released from medical care, a cousin came and picked her up outside the hospital where she stood bracing herself against the cold air and sunlight; they seemed to make her scars tighten and hurt all the more. Against all odds, there she stood alone in the world for the first time with a handful of presents from the nurses and doctors who'd been her only friends.

For a while, Amanda was passed from relative to relative, until finally she was placed in St. Mary's Home for Wayward Girls, an orphanage in Montreal run out of an old Victorian house by the Canadian Sisters of Mercy.

To keep them safe, the Sisters tied their girls together with ribbons. At bedtime they told cautionary kidnapping stories, spinning out the tales of Little Benny Foster and the Lindbergh baby, wealthy boys snatched from their beds for ransom, as if something equally terrible might happen to them. You could spot a pair of St. Mary's girls a mile away by the purple bindings they wore on their wrists. They were never allowed to walk anywhere alone, not outside the orphanage, not inside—not even to go to the bathroom.

Where is your inseparable, Little Miss? A clever idea—instant belonging. *Why are you here on your own?*

It was an innocent time—a time before children routinely went missing—but the Sisters of Mercy were nervous as hens. They were all the more riled up when just a few short miles across the border from St. Mary's, a little girl named Sharon Hill had reportedly disappeared on her walk home from school. Her family waited with the police, praying for a ransom note that never came. It was a mystery: if Sharon Hill hadn't been kidnapped for money, then—what? The Sisters of Mercy speculated and prayed, tying their orphans together all the tighter.

Amanda's inseparable was a small but pretty one-armed girl named Carolyn Hayes, who was quick with a smile, sweet and blue-eyed. From the moment her wrist had been tied to Carolyn's—tricky at first for Carolyn—Amanda felt soothed, happy almost. It was an unexpected gift, having someone permanently near.

For the first time since her parents had died, Amanda's heart opened. The terrible burns under her clothing, strange shiny webbings that had formed from her chest to her thighs, seemed to ease a little. What did scars matter when she had the imperfect, beautiful, smooth-skinned Carolyn at her side? They slept in the same bed, bathed together, compared their physical deformities, and confessed their past tragedies. They dreamed of sharing a future as Catholic Sisters running their own orphanage in America, where children would be as loved as they were.

Amanda couldn't believe a world in which Carolyn existed a mere arm's length away was the same world in which she had lost so much. Everything had been up for grabs: her family in the fire, her grandmother from pneumonia, her relatives in Canada too poor to keep her. But at least she didn't have to worry about potential adoptive parents taking Carolyn away: *Who would want a one-armed girl?*

When the ribbon tying them together was abruptly cut one night while they slept, Amanda saw her mistake. Carolyn had contracted scarlet fever and was carried off to the hospital. When she died later that week, Amanda's question had been answered. *God* had wanted a one-armed girl, even if no one else did. God had taken her.

Months later, little Sharon Hill's mutilated body was found caught in a storm drain a few blocks from her home. The newspapers in Canada all quoted U.S. authorities, indicating that the crimes committed against the girl were unprintable, which meant sexual. The Sisters were convinced that Sharon Hill's murder marked the beginning of something awful and evil, a time of danger for children.

Now, all these years later, Carolyn's death and the tragedy of little Sharon Hill blur together for Amanda. She makes a point of treating each child passing through Our Lady as a precious gift, ephemeral but special, in need of rescue, yet as fleeting as the wind.

Through the snowfall, Amanda spots the bright green Pinto in Our Lady's parking lot. The driver's ebony skin is barely visible through the early dawn as he ducks into his car, then steps back out.

"Oh, it's you, Mother!" he says in his velvety Nigerian accent. "Dark out here."

Amanda winces at the day's first jarring reminder that she is no longer the lost and hopeful Amanda Whalen, but the serious leader of a Catholic order of teaching sisters with an equally serious name. "We'll have to keep an eye on the weather."

Brother Joe nods, tilting his head in her direction. He wears a dark sweatshirt and sneakers, not his usual attire.

"I was just thinking of my childhood," Amanda says. "How I was once just a girl named Amanda before I was anyone's Mother."

Brother Joe nods. "I think the rest would feel more comfortable if you went by your religious name."

She smiles at him. "It's good for them to stretch their minds."

No matter how hard she tries, Amanda cannot get a unanimous vote from the Sisters on abandoning their arcane male names and returning to their birth names. But on principal, she insists they call her "Sister Amanda," rather than "Sister Stephen" or worse, "Mother Stephen." She wants them to see that God loves her whatever she calls herself, that modernizing does not ruin faith. So far, though, no one else has followed her lead. They call her "Mother General" on principle.

Amanda would like to think she respects the sanctity of

tradition as much as anyone. Hadn't she observed years of silence and study and servitude? Hadn't she donned a crown of thorns and lain face down before the altar in the symbolic death of her worldly self? Just like every last Sister, she too had risen from the floor anew and emerged from the chapel as a Bride of Christ. She ate the sweet wedding cake and drank champagne. She had even been as convinced as anyone, if not more so, that her spiritual name, Stephen, would transform her into someone pious and wise, someone worthy of bearing the name of the very first disciple to be martyred. And yet in the end she'd discovered that she was, still and all, just herself—sometimes her better and more divine self, sometimes her weak and flawed self. But whatever anyone called her, she was still just Amanda Whalen, secretly deformed, raised by Canadian nuns, protester of wars and advocate for girls in trouble.

Amanda had to admit that she was also at times fierce and exacting, wrong-headed and stubborn. She had ideas and agendas. But wasn't that exactly why God had called her to service? Wasn't her fierceness the point, her ability to survive against all odds? She'd always meant to bring her whole self to her vocation—good and bad, wise and impetuous—damaged even. Surely God knew what He was getting Himself into.

Brother Joe takes her sack of supplies and puts it in the hatchback.

"Where are the others?" Amanda asks.

Brother Joe points through the dark past the schoolyard, through the snowy distance, to the three figures trudging toward them. Amanda opens the back car door for them, noticing one is wearing an arcane smock, long black skirts, a habit with a matching veil, and a box-style wimple cutting a square around her face.

"Again?" Amanda says. "You'll freeze!"

Sister Robert-Claude hikes up the heavy skirts to reveal red leggings. "Long Johns, Mother!" Hopping into the back seat, she sits next to Sister Eugene and Sister Pius. Like Amanda, today they are dressed in warm civilian clothing from the charity bin. Sister Eugene wears a down coat and matching scarf. Sister Pius, standing no taller than 4'3", is decked out in a child's red snowsuit.

Amanda herself has on a pair of small round blue sunglasses, a warm brown turtleneck with boots and plaid bell-bottoms. This morning she brushed out her hair and parted it in the center, smiling at herself in the dark window. It's the one thing she misses most since having donned the veil as a Bride of Christ: her beautiful blond hair.

Amanda settles into the passenger seat as the rest of her party slam the back doors.

Brother Joe pulls out of Our Lady's parking lot.

"You don't think the habit is a bit much?" Amanda says. "You were already all over the news this week."

Sister Robert-Claude unearths a tobacco pouch from deep inside her gigantic woolen sleeve and rolls a cigarette. "If we're going to get arrested, I want the public to know who I am: a Catholic Sister with an ax to grind for peace! The only way anyone recognizes us is in these old getups, Mother. Our newfound subtlety of dress is lost on the public."

Sisters Eugene and Pius chuckle.

Earlier in the week the three had accompanied Amanda and Brother Joe to a protest where getting arrested was a distinct possibility. Together the five of them joined the Valley's most well-known war protesters, mostly peaceniks from Utica, a few parishioners, and members of the region's notorious Radical Peace Circle. Leading the protest was Daniel Flannigan, an extreme philosopher and activist, best known for being the first American priest to be arrested for civil disobedience.

On the railroad track, no one had gotten arrested. They'd lain their bodies down on the cold rusty tracks and held hands to form a human chain. The idea was to stop the 5:33 a.m. train from delivering munitions to the Caxton Air Base where they were to be loaded onto planes and flown to Europe, then to Southeast Asia. Amanda and the others had recited the Rosary and sung peace songs, staring up into the sky. The snow formed a fine white blanket over their bodies, but Daniel Flannigan's hand was warm. Amanda followed the steady sound of his reassuring breath.

Over the years, he'd been the one friend she could turn to for advice when her own peace mission posed challenges and obstacles.

She had just become Mother General when they first met. She and the handsome priest had struck up a conversation at a peace conference, the first one Amanda had ever attended.

From that day, Daniel—Father Dan, as he was widely known—has signed all his letters to her familiarly: *How I delight in you, beloved Amanda. —Your Daniel.* He has gone so far as to compare his chaste love for Amanda to that of St. Francis for St. Clare, St. John of the Cross for St. Teresa of Avila. Of course, Amanda has heard rumors about him—everyone has. Despite herself, she is flattered. Once when he tried to caress her cheek, she told him, "I have dedicated myself to Christ and no one else." She thought about her deformed body, about how it would never belong to a man.

In the end, the munitions train was a no-show. It was diverted either due to the threat of their demonstration or a mechanical problem somewhere near Rochester. There were whispers that the conductor had gone AWOL.

Dan didn't wait for confirmation, but announced their protest a victory. He spoke commandingly through a bullhorn: *Congratulations on stopping this train! To stop this war, we will move mountains if we have to.*

Everyone cheered.

The national news cameras trailed his every move while local reporters interviewed as many protesters from Romeville and Utica as possible.

Now, in the back seat of Brother Joe's Pinto, the Sisters relive the protest, recalling Sister Robert-Claude's interview on the local news.

Amanda interrupts them: "No protests this morning, Sisters; we're canvassing."

"Again?" Sister Robert-Claude says.

Amanda frowns; they didn't used to question her authority.

After a moment, Sister Robert-Claude cracks her window and lights up. She takes a long deep drag and adds a final sigh: "Well, you're the boss." Toughest of all the Sisters, Robert-Claude is often the most critical, which Amanda has been able to use to her advantage.

"I needn't remind you that we're trying to keep a low profile," Amanda says. "It can't be all fun and news reports."

The backseat three answer in unison—"Yes, Mother General"—then fall silent.

At thirty-seven, Amanda is the liveliest of Christ's Most Precious Wounds and the youngest Superior the order has ever had. She is well aware of the irony that she who is so orphaned should be called Mother by so many. It's something she's learned to live with.

Naïve and overambitious when she first became the Mother General, she'd made some embarrassingly grand statements to Father Giuseppe. *I am who I am,* she'd said initially, *an activist and a proponent for peace, and I am not about to change.*

Father Giuseppe was amused, but supportive: *Good for you, Mother! And good luck! You've got some cranky Sisters on your hands.*

It was true that the Sisters of Christ's Most Precious Wounds wore long black robes with full veils like the one Sister Robert-Claude unearthed as a sight gag for protesting. It was as if Vatican II hadn't happened at all. In her first year as Mother General, Amanda made a point of changing all that. She introduced less cumbersome garb. She overhauled the educational system at the school. She encouraged a more modern policy of taking on projects out in the world, attending teaching seminars and religious conferences, working in soup kitchens, tending to the neighborhood poor and sponsoring community works.

Her colleagues didn't think much of her at first.

She was green, they said, overly eager. She had big shoes to fill, replacing the previous and much beloved Mother Augustus, who had died gracefully and beautifully before everyone's eyes. Behind Amanda's back the community petitioned Father Giuseppe, complaining that their new superior was much too radical to bring any of them closer to God.

You can't push the river, Mother, Father Giuseppe said over a glass of wine. *It'll go better if you ease Our Lady into the twentieth century.*

She smiled as he poured more wine: She hadn't even started making the big changes yet.

Brother Joe whizzes them past mills and canning factories, soap and iron works. Past the grand old train station perched at the end of decrepit Main Street with so many businesses now on the verge of bankruptcy.

When at last dawn breaks over central New York, the neon Paul Revere buzzes to the end of his electric ride atop Revere Ware Copper Works. The sign arrived after the factory opened in Romeville during the Industrial Revolution. And there he rides every night until sun-up, never minding that Romeville is hundreds of miles west of the place where the original event took place. It amuses Amanda to find the Revolutionary War hero here in this sleepy town of all places, flashing and buzzing above them. The sight is as familiar to her now as the trains rattling by and the dilapidated Town Hall with its crumbling bricks.

The wheat fields and farms shine with silver snow in the distance. Beyond that, daybreak is glinting over the mountains. Brother Joe parks the Pinto in an empty lot above the old railroad tracks, a kind of graveyard where abandoned train cars sit empty and abused, most with busted wheels and rusty holes in their aluminum frames. On their doors, faded lettering announces the cargo each once carried: Romeville-Turner Radiators, Erie-Canterbury Coal, Dryden Oil Drums, Pope's Fuel & Propane.

"Just one quick stop; then we canvass." Amanda gets out of the car, hauling her supplies from the hatchback. "I'll be right back."

The Sisters scramble to join her.

"You think she ran away, don't you?" Sister Eugene says. "The missing Iaccamo girl, you don't think she's dead!"

Sister Pius chimes in. "I always felt something bad was going on in that family. Have you met the father? You must think she could be one of ours."

"Let's not get excited," Amanda answers. "I don't think anything yet."

"The news reported that the girl was spotted around here," Sister Pius adds. "They found a piece of her sweater down on one of those fences."

"Needle in a haystack." Sister Robert-Claude is the only one who remains unruffled.

"Back in the car, please; this is a solo job," Amanda says gently. "Joseph, keep an eye out, and only come down if there's trouble."

She walks the gravel path down to where a fire is burning in an old barrel. No one is huddled over it, keeping warm. She walks straight to the last rail car, Wystan H.A. Livestock, and knocks. The door slides open, revealing several men in dirty clothes. They stand on the lip of the train car glowering at the visitor. One of them pulls out a shotgun and points it at her.

"What do you want?"

"I've brought food and dry clothing from the Catholic church." She smiles, aware that with her scars covered by a turtleneck and slacks, she could be any pretty young woman delivering help. "And I'm looking for a child."

A murmur goes through the train car.

One of the men laughs. "You got a *child,* Sister?"

She smiles. They know who she is because only religious personnel bother with them at all.

Another man takes the sack from her. "There's no one here but us. If you're looking for the Boogey Man, then it's the Romeville Snatcher you want, and he ain't here. We're an exclusive gentleman's club."

A few men laugh.

Amanda hands the nearest man a folded note. "Give this to the girl if you see her."

He frowns. "We're not messengers, Sister."

"We're all God's messengers, gentlemen." She flashes a smile, not unaware of her charms. "If you hear anything, I trust you'll get word to me."

They look down at their shoes, considering the request.

"Enjoy your breakfast." She backs away, heading up the gravel path.

The Sisters are dozing when Amanda settles into the passenger's seat. Sister Robert-Claude's head rests on Sister Eugene's shoulder.

Sister Pius rouses as they pull away and pass back through town. "No luck, Mother?"

Amanda looks between the buildings for glimpses of the wide-open wheat fields surrounding the town. "Not yet, Sister. But let's see what we can find."

Each time Brother Joe makes a stop, the five missionaries get out and search behind buildings, in alleyways, all the cracks and crevices of Romeville. They sit for a while in the cold car at the end of the Iaccamo dairy farm until Sister Robert-Claude's snoring begins to irritate Amanda.

"With all respect, Mother," Brother Joe says. "It's probably too late anyway."

With Glory gone, the days pass like a slow string of Sundays. Cee-Cee and Baby Pauly are left behind, and they know it.

"Bet she went to Canada to visit the cousins," Baby Pauly says. "Bet you a million doll hairs."

People drift through the house, but nobody cheers anybody up. Nobody knows where Glory goes when she's gone like this. Usually by now there's talk of getting shipped off to Nonna's house, but since Anthony's gotten older, Frank says no one's going anywhere.

Still, Nonna's like a train when it comes to her family, and Frank does not put her off at all. He says, *Marina, she's taking a break, that's all,* but Nonna knows the score. She arrives on the sly, forcing a bath on anyone in her path, doling out kisses even if you don't want one. She makes Cee-Cee and Baby Pauly put on clean pajamas and sleep in their own beds. She cooks up a storm and leaves instructions for Roadie about what to put in the oven when.

Like magic, she always manages to leave just in time. No one is ever the wiser.

Grandma Bianco, Frank's mother, is the opposite of Nonna. Grandma Bianco never shows up unless it's someone's birthday and there's going to be cake. She sends Uncle Moonie over instead to make sure no one burns anything down.

Mrs. Patrick is the only one who makes regular daily visits.

Every other morning she brings groceries and sits at the kitchen table drinking Sanka with Roadie. Mrs. Patrick has been friends with Glory forever; she's Roadie's godmother. Everyone is still pretty careful around Mrs. Patrick because Glory says she doesn't have both oars in the water.

"I know Gloria Petramala like I know myself," Mrs. Patrick says. "She'll be back...mark my words. She likes her time alone. Got those nice friends in Syracuse from bank-teller training. She's probably having a little visit."

Today Mrs. Patrick delivers Jeremy Patrick, her son, and Roadie's one friend, with an overnight bag and his dirt bike.

"Hello, pumpkins!" She pulls Cee-Cee and Baby Pauly onto her lap. "Smells like Nonna gave you two a good scrubbing."

The storm, she says, will veer and hit Canada. Cee-Cee and Baby Pauly like the sound of the word *veer*.

Mrs. Patrick is resolute. "Storm or no storm, Jeremy can't stay if no one is here."

"*I'm* here!" Anthony yells from the living room.

When Mrs. Patrick leans forward, Cee-Cee and Baby Pauly go with her. "And I don't mean *him*. I mean an adult like Frank, or one of your grandmas."

Cee-Cee loves the way Mrs. Patrick smells like powder and lotion. She touches the green silk scarf tied in a smart knot at her throat. It's soft and silky.

"What about Uncle Moonie?" Roadie says.

"He'll do fine," Mrs. Patrick says.

Whenever the topic of Uncle Moonie comes up, Glory says Mrs. Patrick has the hots for him, which is a bad idea. *Moonie came back dead down there*, Glory says.

Roadie offers Mrs. Patrick another Sanka.

Every morning before school, Roadie drinks a cup of coffee and zooms out of the garage on the junior Harley motorbike he bought with his own money. He meets Jeremy Patrick midway to school where he waits revving his reconstructed dirt bike on the corner of the Interstate. They ride together toward Romeville Free Academy, not minding the weather, or even the jokes. Roadie makes everyone call him by his new nickname, which is way better than what they used to call him—Junior.

On the weekends, Roadie and Jeremy take turns giving Cee-Cee rides on the back of their bikes. Once she burned her leg on the exhaust pipe and Glory smeared it with butter.

Roadie likes it better when he gets to sleep at the Patricks' house and eat fried hot dogs and beans for dinner, then watch TV before getting tucked into clean sheets with a kiss.

But things are different now. Roadie has to stay home and keep an eye out.

Sleep tighty-tight, the monsters tell Baby Pauly, which keeps him up at night. *How is someone supposed to sleep like that?* Baby Pauly wonders. *Tight.*

"Don't look so glum," Mrs. Patrick says. "Your folks will patch things up. They always do."

"Is that a prediction?" Anthony shouts.

He keeps raising the volume on his soap opera to drown out the conversation in the kitchen. Right now all the characters are in a hospital corridor, whispering about love and death and betrayal at the top of their lungs.

Mrs. Patrick lets Cee-Cee and Baby Pauly off her lap, even though Cee-Cee tries not to let go.

"Don't you ever put on pants, Anthony Gerard?" Her voice rings like pleasant music, not like the way it sounds when Glory is scolding someone. "It's embarrassing to come over and find you half-naked all the time, Mister."

Anthony snorts.

"You two stay off them bikes 'til the storm passes, you hear?" Mrs. Patrick sits up straight again. "Has Frank tried to find her, Roadie?"

Anthony shouts an answer from the other room, "She probably ran off with some guy again!"

"Wasn't talking to you!" Mrs. Patrick rolls her eyes.

Roadie's voice is quiet. "Frank hasn't been home."

"Shame on him," She says, "I wish he'd stop giving Cee-Cee Benadryl like it's going out of style…No wonder she hallucinates angels and talks to God."

Anthony mutters, "Oh, Christ."

"Saying your prayers in there, Anthony?"

Roadie and Jeremy Patrick smile.

They bend their heads together, emitting a warm pink glow.

Baby Pauly and Cee-Cee can see the light around everyone; they watch for it. Roadie glows when he's with Jeremy Patrick. Glory glows green and red like a Christmas tree when Baby Pauly is having a tantrum. Frank glows like a piece of charcoal, flecks of dark orange in black, worse if he's been drinking.

Whispering but stern, Mrs. Patrick has them form a huddle. "You kids stay away from Mr. Bad News in there, you hear?"

Mrs. Patrick is right: Anthony never glows.

"I'll take that second Sanka, hon. Then, I got to get back to my laundry."

Sometimes Mrs. Patrick tells Roadie how he'll make some girl a wonderful husband one day. Today she slips him money, clucking her tongue. "A boy like you shouldn't have to be a mother before becoming a man."

Roadie shrugs.

"Order a pizza for dinner, and keep Cee-Cee away from that medicine." She smooths Cee-Cee's hair and feels her forehead, which for the moment is cool. "We always wanted a beautiful little girl, didn't we, Jer? A boy and a girl make a perfect family, Jeremy's dad always said, rest his soul."

It's Cee-Cee's favorite story.

But Mrs. Patrick's husband died in the middle of a snowstorm, shoveling. He keeled over right during the worst of it, and Mrs. Patrick had to hire someone from *Il Duce* Snow Management to come and dig him out.

"Life is unpredictable." She stares out the window. "And men have weak hearts."

Outside it's heading toward dusk, the time of day Cee-Cee and Baby Pauly dread most.

Following Cee-Cee down the basement stairs to the bathroom near the sump pump, Baby Pauly is on the lookout. Real monsters don't come out until nighttime, he's pretty sure, but it's good to stay prepared.

He pulls a long string hanging from the ceiling, clicking on a bare bulb.

On Saturdays, Anthony sometimes makes them play touch football on Frank's old wrestling mat in the far half of the basement. Roadie and Baby Pauly team up and play against Anthony and Cee-Cee. Anthony wants Cee-Cee on his team because she can catch a football better than anyone.

The saggy feet of Cee-Cee's tights gather sawdust from the stairs.

Cee-Cee and Baby Pauly stick close together, stepping further down into the pungent moldy place. She stops at the long punching bag hanging from the ceiling and gives it three good belts.

She leads the way to the little unfinished bathroom, a room with a door but no doorknob, a toilet but no seat.

"You're never afraid?" he asks. "Not even a little?"

"No," Cee-Cee says.

She looks for a washcloth under the sink. The basement ceilings are low and the rooms are dark, but she still leaves the light off.

Baby Pauly does a little sword fight with the broomstick, a pretend monster that steals children from their beds at night. He saves Cee-Cee twice from its clutches—her protector, knight of her round table.

She is his leader.

Cee-Cee finds a box of detergent and hops up on the counter to look at herself in the mirror. "St. Rose of Lima rubbed pepper and stones into her cheeks to be ugly so she could save herself for God."

"You're not pretty." Baby Pauly feels scared; he wants to go upstairs. He takes the detergent away from Cee-Cee. "Do you see my color?"

"Not again, Sollie!" She uses his secret name.

"Show me," he says. "Please."

Perched on the edge of the bathroom vanity, she stares at him through the dark until he feels the warm fog pushing through his skin. From his hands, he sees the happy light emerge, so transparent it's barely any color at all.

He beams at Cee-Cee. "Purple!"

She takes a stick of gum out of her pocket and rips it. They each chew a half-piece, looking at each other and smiling.

"Want to see a card trick?" she says, reaching for the little deck in her pocket.

They barely notice when the sump pump punches on with its loud *kerchunk–kerchunk*.

"Hey!" Anthony calls from the top of the stairs. "What are you two doing down there?"

"Quick, hide!" Baby Pauly whispers. "Monsters!"

They run up the other set of stairs at the far side of the basement.

There is only one room in the house with a lock on it: the upstairs bathroom.

All afternoon during commercial breaks, Baby Pauly sneaks to the upstairs bathroom to bring Cee-Cee food: a baloney sandwich, a piece of Nonna's lasagna, a glass of milk. Whatever passes under his nose to eat.

In the bathroom, Cee-Cee pulls out all the bath toys from under the sink and arranges them in order from biggest to smallest, then by color, then by favorite. Sitting on the counter with her feet in the sink, she braids her hair. She brushes her teeth, inspects her toes.

Later, she can hear the television through the air vent next to the toilet.

Anthony and Baby Pauly are watching *Lucy*, the one where she has bright orange hair and works at a bank like Glory. She never mentions Little Ricky. Baby Pauly and Cee-Cee think the black-and-white ones are better.

"Hey!" Anthony grabs Baby Pauly's shirt. "Where are you going?"

"GOTTA PEE!" Baby Pauly pulls away.

Upstairs, he leans up against the bathroom door.

By now Cee-Cee is having a full-on vision; the backs of her knees are numb, her hands go rigid, her head jerks a few times. Then she is sitting inside the feeling. It is not a bad feeling at all. She wants it to last, so she holds still, tries not to breathe. It feels a little like floating in water, only she's in dry air.

"What's happening?" he says. Through the door, Baby Pauly's voice is far away.

"Don't you hear it?"

"Hear what?" Baby Pauly says.

She sings a sad slow melody that is playing inside her heart and lets it slide under the door. *"I am the river of life."*

"I don't believe you."

"I wouldn't lie," she says. "The rest of the message is coming tonight."

Baby Pauly speaks into his hand. "What else?"

"Drink from me and you shall not thirst."

He is silent.

"Enter me and you shall not drown."

"What does it mean?"

"I don't know," Cee-Cee says. "Maybe it's about that missing girl. Maybe she's coming back."

"What about her?" He is alarmed. "Is she okay?"

"We have to wait and see."

Baby Pauly goes to his bedroom and writes with crayon on a piece of construction paper. He slips it under the bathroom door, across the tiles, and presses his face to the floor, so he can see Cee-Cee's feet through the crack.

She steps on the message, which is in some sort of code, triangles and colored circles. "What's it say?"

"It says, *No one ever gets found, and Glory's never coming back*," Baby Pauly whispers. "It says, *Stay in there, forever.*"

Baby Pauly is afraid of Cee-Cee's visions and messages. He has seen them delivered in the night by the one with the fierce wings crackling and sparking like popcorn kernels busting into light.

Enter me and you shall not drown. Cee-Cee gets in the tub.

For a moment, there is no sound, no light, no song.

Baby Pauly lays his head on the floor and rests, checking once in a while for signs of life, but there are none.

For the longest time, there is nothing.

IT'S DARK WHEN CEE-CEE wakes to the sound of Uncle Moonie pounding on the front door. "Open up! I brought burgers!"

Even through the bathroom vent upstairs, she can tell he's in a bad mood.

Sometimes Uncle Moonie tells stories about how to survive in the jungle by eating bugs. Or he gets up a game of poker, walking around instructing everyone how to make a good play and how many matchsticks to bet. When he takes Mrs. Patrick and Jeremy to the movies, he recounts entire plots and acts out the good parts. He can fix a carburetor by snapping it out and drying it off on his shirt. Even in a sulky mood, when he kicks out Frank's tan recliner and stares at the TV, it's better than having Grandma Bianco around with her oxygen tank and her flannel nightie.

Once when Norbert and Cee-Cee found a field mouse in the yard, Uncle Moonie told them they couldn't keep a rodent for a pet. He picked it up and looked it in the eye. "There are people in the world who eat mice for dinner."

Baby Pauly laughed, until he saw Moonie was serious.

"Watch," he said, filling a bucket of water with the hose and dropping the mouse in with a splash. "You don't even have to kill him."

They watched as the little mouse swam and swam in a circle.

"What's going to happen?" Norbert said. "He can't get out."

"He's going to die," Baby Pauly said.

Uncle Moonie nodded. "It's the best way to dispose of a mouse."

Cee-Cee begged Uncle Moonie to let her save it, but he just shook his head. "Lots of mice in the world."

But this was already Cee-Cee's mouse. It wasn't fair.

"You think this is bad," he told her. "You should see how farmers drown kittens. They hold them down in a bucket of water until they're dead. This way, the mouse is killing itself."

Ever since then, Cee-Cee has kept an eye out for cats.

Twice she's made Glory pull over so she can pick up a stray on the road and bring it over to Mrs. Patrick, who lives far away from all the farmers and never turns them away.

Everyone says Moonie's bad moods are from Vietnam where his leg got blown off. Anthony says Uncle Moonie went all the way to Albany to get a plastic replacement, which may or may not be true.

To Baby Pauly and Cee-Cee, his legs look fine. But Anthony says you have to see past the knee where he straps on the fake part. He says Uncle Moonie has a closet full of plastic legs, each with a different shoe, because the Viet Cong sliced off his leg while he was asleep. Frank says Uncle Moonie shot himself in the foot to get out of having to kill the gooks, and it got infected.

Glory says there are lots of bombs buried in people's backyards in Vietnam. You never know when one of them will go off and take your foot with it.

"We ate pizza for dinner," Roadie says.

Uncle Moonie grunts. "Are you going to let me in?"

Roadie steps aside, letting Moonie shuffle over to the refrigerator to deposit the burgers and get one of Frank's beers.

"Hi," Jeremy Patrick says.

At the kitchen table, Jeremy Patrick, Roadie, and Baby Pauly are cutting out pictures of motorcycles. After Moonie arrives, they go downstairs to the basement to finish pulling apart their motorbikes, so they can put them back together.

Moonie's boots slap unevenly from the kitchen linoleum to the carpeted TV room. He is probably wearing Army fatigues, which is all they ever see him wear. No one knows what he wears to work because his job is top secret—*Uncle Moonie is a spy*, Anthony likes to say.

People are always trying to get him to spill the beans about what he does for a living, but he won't talk about it. He says he's signed an agreement that bought his silence on what he does at Kodak. Once he even swore on an actual *Bible* that the President of the United States came to see his project. *Nixon himself!*

But wouldn't say why.

Glory didn't believe it. *Go on, Monaldo, you're full of it.*

Frank laughed. *Probably making tourist cameras. Big Kodak secret!*

In the TV room, Uncle Moonie drops into Frank's recliner. "What're you watching?"

Anthony turns up the volume. "Wrestling."

"Don't you have a girlfriend yet?" Moonie asks the same questions all the time. "You're old enough now, aren't you?"

Among the Biancos, the oldest son is always the favorite. That's how it is with Moonie and Frank. That's how it is with Anthony and Roadie.

Everyone defends the order of things, no matter what.

"Where is everybody?" Moonie asks.

"Glory's gone."

"Yeah," Moonie says. "Where to this time? That girlfriend of hers in Buffalo?"

"Who cares?"

Moonie cracks up as if Anthony is the funniest guy in the world. "Seriously, where is everyone?"

Anthony hates being questioned. "What the hell do I look like? Somebody's mother?"

After midnight, Roadie and Jeremy Patrick come up from the basement, sneak past the TV room and knock on the bathroom door next to Roadie's bedroom.

"You can't stay in there all night, Cee-Cee," Roadie says.

Baby Pauly guards the door. "She has to. We're waiting for a message." He has a pillow from his bed tucked under his armpit and a ripped rag of a blanket wrapped tight around his fist.

Roadie rolls his eyes. "You're going to sleep out here?"

"Have to." Baby Pauly slides down the bathroom door and settles in.

"Let them stay here," Jeremy Patrick says. "What's the difference?"

Giving up, Roadie follows Jeremy Patrick to his room.

In a few minutes, the house is quiet. Everyone is in his own bed, except for Pauly and Cee-Cee. You can hear Uncle Moonie snoring on the couch and branches scraping against the windows. A big open sky looms over the house, bringing together all the people in the world they know and love, including, somewhere, Frank and Glory.

From certain windows in the house, you can see the famous sign that sits on the Revere Copper Works, where Glory's father used to work. A big orange and green light flashes in and out as Paul Revere keeps taking the same midnight ride to warn that danger is coming.

Sharing a wall with the bathroom, Roadie's room has the best view. Cee-Cee waits until everyone has said his prayers to close her eyes.

Tucked in bed, Roadie waits. From his sleeping bag on the floor, Jeremy Patrick also waits.

"You think they're all asleep?" Jeremy Patrick whispers.

Jeremy stands up and pulls his pajama bottoms down. Roadie lifts his hips up off the mattress and takes off his pajama bottoms, too.

"Hurry, it's cold." Jeremy Patrick whispers. He stands next to Roadie's bed.

Roadie turns his face to Jeremy's body. "Are you ready?"

Jeremy Patrick answers quickly. "Ready."

Roadie touches him.

"That feels good."

Roadie touches himself.

Jeremy Patrick shivers as Roadie puts his mouth on him.

After a moment, Roadie pulls his mouth away and asks the next question: "Do you think…?"

"Shhh…don't talk…"

Then comes the feeling, like the flapping of a thousand migrating geese lifting from the spine through the center of the body, to the surface of the belly and down, down, down, to the tunnels and vessels. They flutter through Roadie and Jeremy Patrick.

There is a small flying away, and then silence.

Roadie sees the sky, blinks at the stars as if he might witness himself in a constellation overhead. It ends quietly, with a slow pleasant throbbing, a prayer.

Everything must be done properly: pajamas replaced, hands wiped, bedcovers straightened, sleeping bag zipped. *People know about you, Roadie*—Anthony's words echo in his ears.

He sits up. "Is someone there?"

A shadow stands in the doorway of his room. Roadie gives a little yelp.

"Gone," the shadow says.

The bathroom door is swung wide open, light illuminating everything.

It's Frank standing there, slurring. "Where is she?"

Roadie pulls at his pajama top. Jeremy hops behind him, stumbling and yanking his pant strings.

"Glory left," Roadie says. "That cop took her somewhere."

Frank is unsteady on his feet. "What cop?"

Uncle Moonie appears on the staircase in his old Army fatigues; now the three of them stand silently in the dim hallway—Roadie, Moonie, and Frank—as if this were a house of mirrors reflecting only one face.

Anthony drifts out of his room, a pale ghost. "What is it?"

"Nothing," says Uncle Moonie. "Go to bed."

Frank stumbles, keeping his gaze on Roadie. "You and your little friend? You two do everything together. You sleep together. You shit together?"

Uncle Moonie takes a step forward. "I said Jeremy could stay over."

"And who the fuck are you?"

Before Moonie can answer, Baby Pauly appears in the hallway. "SHE CAN'T BREATHE!"

"Shit." Frank points at Roadie. "Didn't I tell you to give her that medicine?"

Moonie leads the way to the little bathroom with the chipping tiles, the faucet with its drip-drip-dripping, and the echo of Baby Pauly's shriek bouncing off the fixtures.

Moonie pulls the shower curtain away from the tub.

"Jesus Christ," Anthony says.

Roadie elbows his way through to grab Baby Pauly and cover his mouth. "Shut up for a second."

They look in the bathtub.

Baby Pauly sees water rising up over the edge of the tub, spilling out in rivers of ice on the bathroom tiles. His sister's eyes bulge; she is blue, drowning. He sputters for breath, opening his mouth, but releasing no sound.

Uncle Moonie sees the faces of the Vietnamese children he watched get torched in every village for months on end, tiny limbs and almond-shaped eyes, bodies piled in a ditch no bigger than a tub and set on fire.

Frank sees only his daughter's downy limbs, inhales a sudden scent of lily and roses—such soft skin—then just like that, it stops: the pounding headache, the terrible itch to drink…gone.

Roadie sees a forest floor, dirt and mud. The trees sway noisily as Jeremy kneels by the little body. "Save her!" The wind swallows Jeremy's voice. He turns to Roadie. "We need to do *something*."

But Roadie can't move.

Anthony sees nothing at all: just his sister, a stupid girl, asleep in a bathtub. She looks exactly like she does when she's sleeping in her bed and he stands over her trying to understand what it is he's supposed to do. Pinch her flesh until it bruises? See what it would be like to rub up against her? Somewhere deep inside his mind a tiny bell goes off; a dull paralyzing sensation comes over him. His heart stops for a moment, his body coming alive at certain places.

Uncle Moonie pushes everyone out of the way and lifts Cee-Cee from the burning tub, as if she is the last surviving villager from his own private hell, the last person on earth he will ever save.

"Move out!" he orders.

They lurch toward the bathroom door.

Baby Pauly regains his breath. "Is she alive?"

"Of course," Jeremy holds his hand, bringing up the rear of Uncle Moonie's makeshift platoon. "She was sleeping."

Frank pulls out a bottle of pink syrup. "It'll help. Give her to me."

Moonie doesn't budge. "Go sleep it off."

The others wait to see if Frank and Moonie will end up in a fistfight, but instead Frank slinks toward the master bedroom, muttering to himself.

Anthony heads back to bed, disappointed. He'd have liked it if someone got punched in the face.

Carrying Cee-Cee down the hall, Uncle Moonie places her on top of her mattress. He stands awkwardly at her bedside.

"Were you sleeping in there?"

"Sort of," Cee-Cee says.

"What do you mean?"

"It's more like floating, no words—and happy."

"Really?" he says. "Happy?"

"Like riding-a-bike happy," she says. "Or eating-ice-cream happy. But better."

He thinks this over. "Huh."

Cee-Cee sits up. "It's easy to be happy, Uncle Moonie."

He sits tentatively on the edge of Cee-Cee's bed. "Go to sleep now. Your Mother will be back tomorrow."

Cee-Cee nods. "All you have to do is ask."

Moonie looks into his empty hands. "Please just go to sleep."

Cee-Cee kisses his cheek and lets him tuck her into the cool sheets.

After she's asleep, Moonie sits on the floor in the dark and cries.

By morning, the storm has passed without hitting.

Amanda feels unsettled by the strange warm front that has crossed over from the mountains through the Mohawk River Valley.

Today she's got limited resources. Brother Joe drives, and Sister Pius sits between them in the front, barely tall enough to see over the dash.

Amanda directs Brother Joe to drive to Pilgrim's Pond.

Normally she refuses to interfere in the lives of Our Lady's parishioners, but this time the child in question is the granddaughter of Marina Petramala, a devout woman and personal friend of hers. Everyone has heard reports of the girl's special gift, of the family's problems, the mother's disappearances.

The house is big and white with crooked peaks and broken shutters, somehow more imposing in the breaking daylight.

"You're stopping here?" Sister Pius says, leaning forward and looking at the house. "Are you sure, Mother?"

"Don't they usually slam the door in your face?" Brother Joe asks.

"I'll be right back," Amanda says.

Heading up the front path, she checks her watch. It's 7:35, a luxury to still be canvassing at this hour. Our Lady's schoolchildren are on Christmas break. Still, Amanda will have to be quick; at the Manse, the rest of the Sisters, who know nothing of these private morning missions, have been praying now for hours. They will begin to suspect that something is going on if she doesn't get back reasonably soon.

Ringing the front doorbell, Amanda prepares a speech for Marina's daughter, the girl's mother, whom she has only met once or twice. This time, Amanda plans to wedge her boot into the door and force a conversation about Catholic school. Perhaps she can offer a scholarship so the parents will at least consider the option. Amanda would like to see personally to the child's spiritual and educational needs.

She rings again, and at last a small boy answers the door. He stares up at her.

"Hello, there," Amanda says. "I'm a friend of your Nonna's."

"I saw you on TV," the boy says. "Nonna's not here."

Amanda crouches down to look him in the eye. "Where's your mother, honey?"

"I don't know."

She smiles and rubs his cheek. "What's your name?"

"Pauly Bianco."

"I'm here about your sister, Pauly."

The little boy touches the buttons on Amanda's coat as if considering the situation; then he takes her hand and leads her through the sleeping house, around piles of clothes, toys, boxes of pizza, over books and papers, and up the stairs. Arriving at a little bathroom at the end of the hall on the second floor, Amanda stands on the cracked bathroom tiles before an old claw-foot bathtub.

"There she is." The boy points into the tub where the little girl is sleeping with a blanket tangled around her legs.

"Why is she sleeping in there?" Amanda whispers.

"She can't sleep in her bed." Leaning against Amanda with a warm and reassuring weight, the little boy yawns and stretches. "They talk and wake her up at night."

"Who does?" Amanda studies the girl: long tangle of black

hair, dirty clothes, sleeping face, some kind of stuffed toy tight in her grip. She looks like any other neglected child, and yet a light feeling comes into Amanda's heart, buoying her up, a sense of hope perhaps.

"The angels," Pauly Bianco says.

Climbing into the tub, he sticks his thumb in his mouth and sits on the edge. He yawns and curls up next to his sister.

Amanda covers both children with the blanket.

She is tempted to pick them both up and carry them out of the house, but instead she kisses the little boy's cheek and passes a hand over the girl's head.

She must pay close attention to what she does and how she does it, or all will be lost. She's worked too hard to make mistakes now. Christ's Most Precious Wounds have many eyes, she knows—some more prying than others.

"I'll come back another time," she says.

The little boy waves the fingers of his sucking thumb at her and closes his eyes.

Pulling the door partway closed, Amanda makes her way back through the mess and lets herself out of the house.

CEE-CEE LISTENS TO SNOW drop off the roof.

A big warm sun has risen over Route 177, and suddenly everything is melting. It is a long time before anyone else in the house will be awake.

Anthony is the last one up. Some mornings his trouble starts before he even gets out of bed, but today he feels like he's got himself under control. He gets dressed and goes downstairs, looking for Glory.

Even before he realizes she's not back, it happens: his skin starts to shrink the way it does on bad days. He feels his flesh popping at various angles: joints and bones, elbows and feet. It's as if an invisible crank were being turned from the inside, making him smaller, tighter. Now he blinks, darting his eyes around the kitchen.

It's only nine o'clock, and already the pressure is too much.

"Stop it." Frank lights a cigarette at the breakfast table. "You're making me nervous."

Anthony is grateful for the smoke; it makes him feel like he's sitting at a bar, somebody else entirely, not a kid with shrinking skin.

Frank pours glasses of orange juice and bowls of cereal for Baby Pauly and Cee-Cee. "Eat up, you two."

Three of Anthony's toes jump up off the kitchen floor, then

settle back down. A tingle in his spine derails his thoughts; he twists, concentrates on speaking clearly.

"When's Glory coming back?" Baby Pauly says.

"Soon," Frank musses Pauly's hair. "Christmas gives that woman bad ideas."

"She usually calls by now to tell us where she is," Anthony says. "Unless she's leaving you again."

Frank picks a piece of tobacco off his tongue and breathes out some smoke, as if his lungs were on fire. "She'll be back today. Mark my words."

But Anthony is nervous, and whenever he gets nervous, Frank tries to give him advice. *Relax!* he'll say. *Make friends with some athletic kids at school. A cheerleader will fix this, or a girl on the track team.*

Anthony can't see how getting rejected by a popular girl is going to help him.

Now Frank puts an arm around Anthony's neck, wrestling him into a half-hearted choke hold, his version of a hug. It's an old routine from when Anthony was little, and he and his father were close.

"It's going to be okay." Frank sighs. "You need another outlet is all; find a girl; wet your dipstick. I'm telling you."

His father's reassuring touch and the smell of tobacco let Anthony relax. Maybe there is a way out. He just has to see the signs and know their meaning.

Roadie and Jeremy Patrick interrupt his thoughts. The two boys push each other up the basement stairs and knock into the walls, laughing.

"Act like men, not schoolgirls," Frank says when they appear.

Roadie stops short in the kitchen archway. "Why are you still here?"

"There's food in the fridge." Frank gets up. "Your mother will be home later."

Anthony closes his eyes, imagining his mother walking

through the door.

"I believe you," Cee-Cee says, looking up from her Lucky Charms.

"Atta girl!" Frank says, winking.

Anthony's stomach contracts, then hurts. He can't leave things up to Frank to fix; he has to be the one to figure out how to get Glory back.

From the door on his way out, Frank gives Anthony a nod. "Have a little trust, will you?"

Anthony is afraid of what will happen if his mother doesn't return. Something bad. He knows this for sure.

He watches Jeremy Patrick and Roadie pour coffee into matching mugs.

At least no one has to go to Nonna's. When they were little and Glory pulled a disappearing act, they sometimes ended up staying at Nonna's house for weeks. *God camp*, Frank used to call it. *You'll either come home batty or a believer.*

Nonna is a maniac for Jesus.

She knows everything there is to know about the saints: who was shot through with arrows, whose skin peeled back, whose bones pulled out, who got nailed to a tree, head chopped off, stoned, or impaled on a stake. She loves to rattle on and on: This one was raped; that one starved and murdered.

The thought of it makes Anthony want to pinch somebody, hard.

By lunchtime, the sun is shining brilliantly, melting snow off the roof, creating new slime and mildew. Anthony feels the stuff creeping up his legs: *mold.* Even when Glory scrubs the walls and sprays Lysol, he can still feel it growing on him. He scrubs his hands and lathers his legs. At the slightest hint, he takes off his jeans, walking around carefully in his underwear.

Glory disappearing for days is a bad sign. The weather getting warm is a bad sign. His shrinking skin is getting worse.

Things are going very wrong. He has to do something to fix it, to bring his mother back. He tenses his arms to stave off a twitch.

Then a little bell goes off in his head: they'll get out of the house for a while and get some air. They'll go deep into the woods where he will find an answer.

Anthony's shoulders ache. His ears burn. "Pauly, go get Cee-Cee's coat."

Baby Pauly looks up from playing and scrambles to the hall closet.

Anthony points at Roadie and Jeremy Patrick. "We're going for a walk in the woods."

"Why would we do that?" Roadie asks, looking up from the sink where he is washing dishes from breakfast. Jeremy waits at his side to dry with a hand-embroidered dish towel.

"An adventure," Anthony says. "Besides, it's warm out there."

Jeremy Patrick looks out the window and sees that the storm has passed; the sun is shining. "It looks muddy."

Roadie is nervous. "I'm staying here."

Anthony is suddenly calm. "Nope. Everyone's going…even you two ladies."

Dropping the bowl he is washing, Roadie lunges across the kitchen. Anthony grabs his neck, wrestling him to the ground. The contact feels good. He wants his brother to punch him hard; maybe that will fix things. But Roadie twists to get away.

Anthony mounts him and clenches his teeth. "Say 'Uncle!'"

Shoulders pinned, Roadie flails his hands, sending suds into the air. Anthony draws back, landing a solid punch on Roadie's nose with a dull popping sound. The release of knuckles into the soft cartilage instantly stops the noise in Anthony's head—a relief.

Baby Pauly returns dressed for the cold, carrying Cee-Cee's coat. Seeing the small smudge of blood under Roadie's nose, he stops short.

"Say it," Anthony demands.

Roadie presses his lips together.

Jeremy Patrick makes a low gurgling sound in his throat, wrings his hands.

Cee-Cee appears in the doorway.

Anthony pulls his arm back to punch Roadie again, but Baby Pauly rushes forward, hot tears springing from his eyes. "UNCLE, UNCLE, UNCLE, UNCLE."

Everyone stops what they're doing.

"Okay, okay," Anthony gets up. His head feels clear now, his body loose. "Shut up, Pauly. It was just a game."

Anthony looks down at Cee-Cee and reaches out to touch her arm very gently. "We're just horsing around."

No one seems able to move, except Cee-Cee. She goes to the phone and dials a number.

"Mary Margaret, please," she says.

There is a long pause.

"Hello. It's me."

Baby Pauly takes a step closer and looks into his sister's face.

"Yeah," Cee-Cee says into the receiver.

Roadie and Jeremy look at one another, then at Baby Pauly.

"Yeah…the missing girl. I can find her." Cee-Cee listens to the voice on the phone. "Right. Norbert, too…Okay, goodbye."

She hangs up the phone.

Roadie stands up, brushing himself off and pinching his bloody nose. Jeremy Patrick gets him a Kleenex.

Taking Cee-Cee's coat out of Baby Pauly's hands, Anthony kneels down. He pulls the little wooden pegs through the big green loops, and smiles. "Want to make snow angels with me?"

"No," Roadie answers. "She doesn't."

"Let's play cards instead," Cee-Cee says. She holds up a small deck of cards with mice dressed as kings and queens.

"I want to make a snow angel." Baby Pauly hops on one leg to the door.

Anthony stands up. "Time to go. There's a game we can play

outside; it's like cards."

Anthony is going to fix everything, especially himself.

Roadie puts his hand on Cee-Cee's cheek, barely touching the baby hair that grows there.

"No," Cee-Cee whispers.

"It'll be okay." Roadie tries to believe it himself. "I promise."

In the woods, everything is melting.

They walk single-file through the thicket of trees behind the house. Cee-Cee goes first, with Roadie steering her shoulders. Bringing up the rear are Jeremy Patrick, Baby Pauly, and Anthony. When they get further into the woods away from the house, Jeremy Patrick pulls ahead and starts breaking twigs to mark the path.

"Cut it out, boy scout," Anthony says. "This is far enough."

They are a few yards into the woods where a circling of trees has made a small clearing. In the woods behind the house, the snow is melting earnestly.

Overhead, a warm breeze blows.

Baby Pauly looks around at the half-thawed forest, eyeing the melting clumps of snow, a checkered pattern of brown and white as far as the eye can see. Little nervous rivers run between his muddy boots.

"We can't make snow angels in this!" he says. "What's the game? What game are we going to play?"

Jeremy Patrick unzips Baby Pauly's coat. "It's warm out here."

Baby Pauly starts rooting around in some bushes like a small animal. "I'll go find the snow!"

The sun is warm on their skin.

When Cee-Cee closes her eyes, she can suddenly see all the missing girls in the Mohawk Valley and beyond. It's part of the message: they are buried in wheat fields and stashed behind train tracks, or sprawled at the bottom of the canal. *Could have been you,* one dead girl says, smart-mouthed. *But instead it was me!* A live one tied up somewhere in a basement cocks her head: *But, guess what—you're next!*

Cee-Cee tries to focus, but a terrible headache rises from the back of her neck, as if someone has struck her there. She should take her medicine, but Mrs. Patrick took away the little pink bottles. In the thicket overhead, the branches are picked clean as bones, no longer swaying. Now she steps back until her heels butt up against the fat oak tree.

In the woods, everything is silent. Even the trees stand still.

Above her in the branches, Jesus appears with an entourage of adoring virgins who surround him, fawning and cooing. They watch what happens below, nodding at one another and holding hands. They are all the teenage saints who ever were, older than Cee-Cee, and happier because their fate is complete. They dance in the wind, mutilated and proud: Sassy St. Lucy with her eyes plucked out. Pretty St. Ursula with the arrows stuck through her skin. St. Agatha with her tiny budding breasts sliced off and served up on a plate. St. Hypatia lynched for being good at math. Maria Goretti who was stabbed eleven and three times rather than submit to rape, as tough an Italian girl as any. The little queen, St. Catherine, Bride of Baby Jesus, holding a book, a wheel, and a sword. There's Thecla, Julia, Dotty, Maura, and Philomena. There's Raisa, and Quiteria with her sisters. And all the others: God's favorite girls, miraculously joyful, the littlest gems. Spewing teeny-bopper adoration, they shine and point their eyes toward Jesus, who reigns above, a movie star in sunglasses.

Jesus focuses on Cee-Cee.

Everyone suffers, He says. *Even I suffer. I suffer for you.*

Cee-Cee bares her teeth. She does not remember how to smile.

Feeling a distant pain rip through her middle, she ascends to the trees to join the littlest saints in song. There is an awful calm and a crossing over. The whole time, Jesus keeps His kind, loving eyes pinned on the action; He will cry for Cee-Cee, but he has already saved the world as much as He can by hanging on that cross. Now the most He can do is offer a little comfort.

From far away Cee-Cee hears a voice: "KIDNAPPER!"

There is the sound of fighting, then the sound of nothing.

Almost done, Cecilia Marie! the pretty little martyred saints sing. *Almost a virgin like us!*

Below on the ground a girl is sprawled and broken. Cee-Cee sees that the saints are singing to the poor thing. She joins in, singing and floating above in the trees. The broken girl on the ground has turned herself into a tree, her little arms growing brittle as branches, her little legs rooting into the ground, wooden and strong. Her pulpy heart bangs itself senseless in the wooden cage of ribs. She could easily be chopped down, compressed into a piece of paper.

Cee-Cee sways with the hundred faithful virgins as they cling to the air and hum hallelujah. Cee-Cee hums too. She doesn't even worry about that poor girl lying in the snow, hair fanned out around her head like a black halo on the ground; she knows there'll be a resurrection; isn't there always?

One minute longer! they sing.

They all hold Cee-Cee's hand and sing together: *Now we are all the same: Virgins! Brides of Love.*

Below, there is shouting.

"I DON'T LIKE THIS GAME!" Baby Pauly comes running back to the circle of trees. "STOP!"

He looks up at his sister flying in the air; she waves at him and he waves back. He looks down at the girl, also his sister, lying in the mud; she doesn't move, and he cries. "YOU KILLED HER!"

From far away, Cee-Cee hears footsteps coming down the path toward them. The pain subsides. The hymn gets softer, until everything stops.

"THE MAILMAN IS COMING!" Baby Pauly shouts. "THE MAILMAN WILL SAVE US!"

Baby Pauly runs as fast as he can, tripping over branches and roots, picking himself up from mud puddles. He is trying to run to the house for help, but instead takes a wrong turn and heads further into the woods toward Pilgrim's Pond.

In the air, his floating sister buzzes above him, following him like a yellow light through the trees. She will keep him from getting lost. She will keep him safe. At the pond he stops to catch his breath. Ice drips from the branches where Cee-Cee hovers, beating down on him like the sun. But there is only so much a person can do without a body.

The pond expands and breathes.

Beneath Baby Pauly's feet is the sound of ice cracking.

IT TURNS OUT NOT to be the mailman at all.

Instead it is sweet, slow Norbert Sasso limping through the woods. All morning he's begged his mother to let him put on his new school clothes. In January he is going to a special place for people like him. He has cut through the woods to show Cee-Cee how he looks in his new school's uniform. Tears stream down his face as a cold wind picks up from Canada and sweeps across the fields and through the trees behind him.

The uniform—blue pants with a dark stripe and shiny shoes—does not disguise his slack mouth and oddly shaped eyes. It only makes him look more like himself.

Norbert stomps unsteadily, stumbling across the circle of boys.

Anthony sneaks up from behind him. "What do *you* want, Fat Norbert?"

"What's wrong with Cee-Cee?" Norbert wrestles him aside. "Why is she lying there?"

"A stranger hurt her, Smelly," Anthony says. "We chased

him off, but now we can't find him."

Norbert swings around, agile for his size despite his too-short leg. "Don't call me that!"

"The guy might still be out here somewhere," Anthony says. "You'd better go home to your Mommy. He's been kidnapping people like crazy, and he just might come after you."

When Norbert comes over to play, Glory always says, *Poor dumb bunny*. He stands around with his white socks and greasy hair while Glory scratches under his chin where his hair sprouts unevenly.

In the growing cold, Norbert examines his little friend; when the girl on the ground opens her eyes, it is Cee-Cee looking through them. She gazes at beautiful Norbert, who is stuffed like a sausage in the pretty blue fabric. His nose drips. Sweat runs down his face.

He bends to touch Cee-Cee's coat, covering her legs. Eyes burning against the chilly wind, he makes a noise with his mouth, the thick squeal of something gone wild.

"What did you do?" Norbert says to Anthony, crying.

"We saved her, Norbert," Anthony says. "What do you think we did?"

Pushing them away, Norbert continues to straighten out Cee-Cee's clothes and pull up her tights. He pushes her hair away from her face to try to make her seem as good as new.

"There was a stranger in a blue ski jacket, Norbert," Roadie's voice is shaking like he's about to cry. "We chased him away."

Jeremy Patrick wipes tears from his face, too.

"We fought him off and made him run away," Anthony says. "Why don't you go find him, peanut dick?"

Hefting Cee-Cee up off the ground, Norbert steadies himself with his elbow against a tree for balance. Prancing until he is loping forward in wide, uneven strides, he carries her toward the house, using his huge unwashed body to shield her from the wind. Jewels of sweat form on his forehead. A string of mucus hangs from his nostrils. His determined tongue wedges between his chapped lips.

"Don't worry," he says when they are on their way through the woods back towards Cee-Cee's house. "I know where you live."

Far away, Baby Pauly struggles against the weight of the ice cold water. *Enter me and you shall not drown.*

Cee-Cee knows he is sinking, but she cannot speak.

Norbert strains, panting and sucking air through his nose as he lumbers unevenly through the woods. He practices saying his own phone number out loud. Cee-Cee listens closely to the sound of his breathing (*rattle-huff, rattle-huff*), hanging on where his neck is thick and rubbery. They pass the pitted back yard and the dented garage. Cee-Cee's eyes are fastened on Norbert, pimply and sweaty and absolutely pure: his is the face of God.

At the house, Glory bursts out of the back door, home just in time. She runs into the cold to reach them.

"Where is everybody?" she shouts.

Norbert hands Cee-Cee over. "In the woods."

"What happened?" Glory cradles her daughter. "Did she faint?"

Norbert shakes his head. "I don't think it was the angels this time."

By evening, word has spread: the Romeville Snatcher was spotted in the woods behind the Bianco house. He hurt the little Bianco girl and made off with Baby Pauly, who is still missing. Women from the neighborhood lock their children at home and gather in Glory's kitchen with casseroles. Relatives no one has seen for years help Nonna cook food for the long night ahead.

In the meantime, with the sun going down, the melted slush has turned quickly to ice. By now a brand-new sprinkling of snow has covered up all the tracks in the woods.

"Please find my baby boy," Glory cries.

Frank's former colleagues from the Caxton Air Base form a posse, saddling their belts with flashlights and reflector tape.

"We'll catch him." They clap Frank on the back. "We'll string the sick bastard up once and for all."

The cops come in and stand around the kitchen, drinking hot coffee and talking to each other.

The head cop points a pencil at Roadie. "One more time, kid; take it from the top."

Roadie blinks, tightening his grip on the kitchen chair.

The cop prompts him. "You said you were playing in the snow and you lost track of the little girl. Then you saw her talking to a stranger?"

"She has these seizures, and it's like she's in a trance; sometimes she wanders off," Roadie says, "And there was this man in a blue ski jacket."

"Did he say anything?"

Roadie looks around. "No."

"No?"

"We couldn't hear what he said."

The cop reads from his notes: "But you say he came from the direction of the Interstate. And you didn't see him until he was hurting the girl? Then he sees you coming and picks her up and starts to walk away with her. Is that right?"

Anthony nods.

"Then what?"

Jeremy Patrick looks down at his lap.

Anthony clears his throat. "Our little brother ran after him, yelling for him to stop."

"And that's when he put your sister down?"

Roadie nods.

"You recovered the little girl, but you lost the little boy?" the cop checks his notes again.

Anthony clears his throat, his lip twitching slightly. "We don't know where Pauly went. He probably got scared when he saw the stranger. There was a lot going on."

Roadie grimaces. The cop nods, writing a note in his pad.

"Then one Mr. Norbert Sasso came and found the girl in the snow, so he picked her up and carried her home. Is that right?"

Roadie nods.

"You were running after the stranger when Mr. Sasso took the girl home, and you started searching for the little boy. Is that correct?"

"But we couldn't find Pauly," Anthony said. "So we came home and that's when Glory called the police."

All three of them—Roadie, Jeremy Patrick, and Anthony— are nodding, staring blankly at the cop.

Frank sits in the kitchen, wet-eyed but sober. He half wants to join the men in hunting jackets, his friends, who are searching the woods, and half needs to stay where he can hear the story again.

"The temperature's dropping," Uncle Moonie says. "We're running out of time."

The policemen who stand in the hallway drinking Nonna's coffee discuss their strategy with Moonie.

"It's really starting to snow hard out there," one of them says.

Vinnie hangs back by the door, checking his watch. Soon it will be too dark outside to find anything, let alone Glory's kid. He feels responsible; he's the one who drove their mother to the mall to get cash for the presents. She'd asked him to wait, it would just take a minute, but he shouldn't have, since he was late for picking up his partner. He dropped her at the bus station without asking where she was going.

"What about the little girl?" the head cop says to no one in particular. "We'd like to interview her."

Frank steps forward. "She's upstairs. She's got a fever."

"It'll only take a minute."

Lying in bed, Cee-Cee sees Baby Pauly floating quietly in the cold pond. *Drink from me and you shall not thirst.* Her stomach hurts, and she is bleeding a little between the legs, but no one knows it yet. No one has examined her. Glory put her to bed without even taking off her coat. She sent Nonna up to help as soon as she arrived with her army of Sisters for backup support.

Now Nonna pulls out a large black satchel, more doctor's bag than purse. Cee-Cee is so happy to see her that she opens her eyes wide and tries to smile.

Behind Nonna three women dressed in dark suits and sensible shoes are praying; they are the prettiest of Christ's Most Precious Wounds, Nonna's friends from the TV.

Small and squat in her gray wool dress, Nonna squints her eyes as if God Himself has sent her. "Who did this?"

Cee-Cee forms her lips into an O, silent and dry, but her voice is still missing. Her mouth only gulps at the air. She wants to tell Nonna about the hundred virgins and Jesus appearing like a rock star in the trees, but she can't make a sound.

Nonna snaps the covers back to give Cee-Cee the once-over. "Speak!"

Cee-Cee moans. Her legs are two wooden sticks in dirty tights.

"Jesus," Cee-Cee says.

The Sisters stutter for a moment, look at one another, then resume their prayers: "*Hail Holy Queen, Mother of Mercy; hail, our life, our sweetness and our hope…*"

Somewhere out there Baby Pauly is holding his breath.

"No," Nonna frowns. "Who gives you evil eye?"

By the time the cops come upstairs with Glory and Frank, Moonie and the boys, the chorus of Sisters is quiet, and Nonna is deep into a solo prayer.

"*In nome del cielo, Delle stelle e della luna, Mi levo questo malocchio, Per mia maggior fortuna!*"

She drips olive oil from her fingertips into a bowl of water, whispering in Italian as she makes the sign of the cross over the bowl, her own forehead, and her body. She drops more oil in the water, repeating the ritual several times.

No one moves.

Eyes closed tight, Nonna waits, and then waves a knotted hand over the bowl, crossing herself in a flurry of motion. Just when it looks like she's going to dive into the oil again, she shouts: "*Mal'occhio!*"

Glory steps forward, disrupting the nuns, to touch her mother's arm. "Let me see, Ma."

They gather around the bowl.

"The oil didn't separate," Glory says. "That means it's a curse—the evil eye."

Nonna gives the bowl to a large line-backer of a Sister. "Wash," she says. "No drop." She leans over Cee-Cee, shoving a thermometer under her tongue.

Propping herself up on an elbow, Cee-Cee looks around the room, two bright spots moving over each and every face. She sees a kind face under one of the short veils. Amanda smiles and steps forward.

"I'm so sorry, sweetheart," she whispers, taking Cee-Cee's hand.

In the hallway, Roadie asks the question everyone is wondering: "Is she going to be okay?"

No one knows the answer.

Nonna leans forward, snatching the thermometer. "Something to say?"

Cee-Cee's ribs are brittle branches bearing up under a rising white light from inside. Bones bowing, lungs swelling, heart filling, lip pressing against lip. Beloved enough to rival the moon, Cee-Cee smolders in her skin, understanding at last what the angel meant: She has become her namesake: spotless virgin.

To prove it, she must tell them the truth.

"What's wrong?" Glory asks her mother. "What's

happening?"

Flopping back on the pillow, sweaty hair sticking to her face, Cee-Cee answers at last.

"I know where Baby Pauly is."

IT TAKES LESS THAN five minutes for the women to bundle Cee-Cee in coats and blankets.

Uncle Moonie picks her up and sweeps her out the door.

Night has frozen into a new shape, barely recognizable from what it was in the daylight. Now the ground is frozen. Now the trees scrape and twist like old women with their heads uncovered. It is a cold grief that separates the new night from the warm afternoon; the trees bend to mourn and whisper.

Snow swirls in the wind, icing everything to a dangerous slick.

In the distance, a train makes its way past Utica, heading through Romeville to Albany with cargo for the capital. Carried at Uncle Moonie's shoulder, Cee-Cee squeezes her legs together tight under the blankets to staunch the pain there. Concentrating on his hunting cap, his broad shoulders, she tries to ignore the bitter churning of her stomach. She winces with each step back through the forest.

One leg plastic. She chants to distract herself. *One leg good.*

She can hear Roadie, Jeremy Patrick, and Anthony marching behind, ice crunching under their feet. Several men follow a few feet behind with an army of flashlights to light the way.

Glory and Frank are somewhere nearby.

The crowd murmurs and breathes as if to create heat. Cops whisper about the coming storm like weathermen, propelling

Uncle Moonie forward at a quicker pace.

Vinnie the cop speaks into his radio: "People don't just disappear."

Cee-Cee points her finger out toward the pond.

Cold squat structures hide in the dark: the knitting mills and canning factories, soap- and iron-works, Romeville-Turner Radiator Co., even the Air Depot where Cee-Cee was born. Somewhere out there, over all of the buildings, a neon sign shines, and Paul Revere rides through the town sounding his silent warning.

Slowing from the cold, Uncle Moonie shifts Cee-Cee in his arms. She can still hear the Sisters praying: *"O Clement, O Loving, O Sweet Virgin Mary. Pray for us, O Holy Mother of God…"*

At the canal near the Locomotive Works, they turn and head further west. In a clearing near a large rock, Cee-Cee tugs on Uncle Moonie's hat. Bending, he slides her gently to solid ground.

"Just point, honey," he says. "The pond may not be solid."

The grown-ups gather round, their individual flashlights forming one solid beam of intense heat on Cee-Cee's face. She inches slowly to the pond.

Be careful, they shout. Only their lights follow her now.

Baby Pauly's heartbeat is loud in her ears. Stepping closer, Cee-Cee clears the freshly fallen snow with her boot.

The light burns her skin. The cold bites her fingers.

The face of God is chapped and lathered with drool, each eye spinning like an independent orb, a blue world set free.

I am the river of life, the angel delivered God's message. *Drink from me and you shall not thirst.*

Behind the blaring light, Glory is sobbing.

Enter me and you shall not drown.

The crowd leans in, silent, except for Nonna's loud praying.

Cee-Cee stands firmly at the edge of the pond, as the new storm's snowflakes dance and drift, lit up by flashlights.

Leaning ever so slightly forward, Cee-Cee points beyond her feet where a red smear of jacket can be seen under the crystallized ice. "He's under there."

Snowflakes stick to her skin.

Nonna falls to her knees, crying out a prayer. Father Giuseppe offers a novena, and the three Sisters of Christ's Most Precious Wounds pray for the snow to stop dropping, for the soul of the little boy frozen under the ice.

Cee-Cee drinks in the crisp night.

She is a tiny torch, an ember for God. If the search party switched off all of the lanterns, leaving her in the dark, her words would shimmer: a prediction, a message, a miracle.

Her mouth is filled with light.

"He's alive," she says.

THE SECOND

MARY MARGARET WOULDN'T MIND sticking a fork in her stepfather's neck.

She eyes the perfect spot, a crease near his collar where the stubble grows like ugly speck-sized insects. For sure, this man, her mother's husband—a complete stranger before he moved in and adopted her—is the reason her mother's babies keep dying.

Half-brothers and sisters, Mary Margaret reminds herself.

It happens while she's asleep in her room: he sneaks into the nursery, pillow tucked under his arm, and smothers them dead. Crying buckets at their graveside is his ingenious plan to throw everyone off track—*almost* everyone.

Mary Margaret's mother keeps count of the dead babies in a small red notebook she stashes in her nightstand table. On afternoons when Mary Margaret is bored, she thumbs the pages: Little Rosalie was violet, a wildflower found in her crib, dead. Tiny Antonio was streaked and waxy, pale as the evening sky before dawn. Angelina was atmospheric blue, barely blue, wrapped in a cloud on her way up to Heaven. Baby Rocco was Mary Margaret's favorite, the first baby she remembers; he came along shortly after she'd made it safely out of diapers. He was rushed to the hospital in the middle of the night, mouth-to-mouth performed at every traffic light, kept alive for another six months until one day Mary Margaret found him dead in his crib—dead for real. Blue as a car seat.

So far she's seen more tragedy in her life than most adults.

She pushes the obvious and dangerous questions aside: *Why hasn't someone come in the night to kill her? Why has she been spared?*

In Ithaca, people got sick of seeing Mary Margaret's family rush into the hospital with bundle after bundle of trouble. Once an emergency room doctor told them to move closer to the hospital—*a different hospital,* he said. Leave it to Mary Margaret's stepfather to come up with Romeville, New York, a bumpkin place for prudes and tattle-tales, a rickety rail stop on the way to Albany, famous for some dumb sign of Paul Revere who never lived here. Everyone knows the Midnight Ride took place in Boston.

Mary Margaret stabs a piece of meat and says, "As soon as Cee-Cee Bianco gets to Our Lady, I'm having her sleep over with me."

Mary Margaret doesn't mind going out on a limb.

Her mother raises an eyebrow, leaning forward with a hand on her still distended belly. Mary Margaret's most recent half-brother is a quiet no-name baby, cooing and gurgling in a playpen at her mother's feet.

Her stepfather waves a fork. "Isn't that the kid from the newspaper?"

"Saved her brother from that pond, Russ," Mary Margaret's mother says. "Hardly any old *kid.*"

"Raised him from the dead!" Mary Margaret adds. "Now she lives down the street with her grandmother."

"Marina Petramala, Russ," Mary Margaret's mother says, but her stepfather only grunts. "You know, the one from the church. Think that little miracle girl will be going to Our Lady?"

"Sister Amanda says she's smart enough," Mary Margaret says. "The other Sisters say she's going to skip a bunch of grades and be in the sixth with me."

Her mother nods.

"Cee-Cee Bianco snuffs out evil," Mary Margaret lies. "She

told me. Snuffs it out the minute she sees it. Evil deeds and evil *people*."

Her stepfather keeps chewing his steak, not even looking up from his plate.

That's how stupid he is, Mary Margaret thinks.

CATHOLIC SCHOOL IS DELAYED for weeks while Cee-Cee burns with a fever in Nonna's spare bedroom. Even with her connection to God and her faithful troops of old women praying in Italian, Nonna can't stop Cee-Cee's temperature from spiking.

Father Giuseppe and the Sisters stop by with communion and holy water, waiting to hear a confession or explanation, but Cee-Cee cannot lift her head to see or open her mouth to speak.

Amanda, Sister Robert-Claude, and Brother Joe sit at Cee-Cee's bedside in rotation. Even cranky Sister Edward comes and prays once in a while, though she thinks the whole thing is a hoax. Sister Edward leans forward when the room empties out and whispers, "Are you faking, Little Miss? Because I think you're faking."

People come in shifts. Coffee is brewed, Bibles cracked. Voices blur together and wash away.

The night at Pilgrim's Pond comes back to Cee-Cee in a fevered dream: the white light, the sky, Baby Pauly yanked out of the ice like a frozen fish. She sees it over and over: how the police officers slap Baby Pauly's bloated body to the ground, how they poke and prod for signs of life. How for the longest time, he lies so still in the snow, blue and motionless. Cee-Cee prays until at last he sputters and chokes. *Enter me and you shall not drown.* To everyone's surprise, a cork of ice pops out of Pauly's mouth, expelled by a rush of water. And then just like that Pauly James Bianco is a little fountain for Jesus, spraying forth air, spraying forth life. He burps out the final dribble of water until there's nothing left for him to do *but* breathe in.

One loud inhale; one loud exhale: Alive.

Alleluia! the crowd shouts, amazed. *It's a miracle!*

Everyone rushes forward in a hopeful press. They lift Cee-Cee off the ground—*Get help! She's fainted!*—and for a while she hangs over their heads in and out of consciousness like an offering to the dark sky above. She strains to watch the cops below working their air into Baby Pauly's tiny blue lips and upturned nose; Vinnie the Cop huffs and puffs, refusing to give up.

Later, there's the sound of an ambulance, and somebody shakes Cee-Cee awake. Someone else carries her to a car. After voices and sirens, she is in a church, then with a doctor, then at her own house and ultimately where she has been for weeks, in bed at Nonna's. Only then do things quiet down into the endless fever that loops her back to that horrible night over and over.

Nonna and the Sisters pray and whisper, come and go.

When the room empties, something unusual: A beautiful lady stands near Cee-Cee, smiling. Cee-Cee wants to touch her long sparkling dress, her gold and white shawl.

The lady says: *You are the little flower of my heart, Cecilia Marie.*

Sunlight washes into the room from the window. Cee-Cee has to squint to see; she wants to touch the lady's hair, hold her hand.

All the world's children are like a garden, she says. *But you are a special bloom: "Heaven's Lily," just like your name means.*

Cee-Cee kicks off the blankets, wanting to get closer.

Do you know who I am? Above the lady's head a sign reads: *The Mother of All People.*

"Everybody's Mother?" Cee-Cee says.

The lady smiles: *Miracles are everywhere, little Cecilia. See them and believe.*

Bowing her head, the lady spills a great warm light onto the bedspread. Cee-Cee feels her temperature boost another degree, and yet somehow she is cool. When the lady is gone, she sleeps for days and opens her eyes feeling perfectly rested.

Nonna sits in the rocker, fingering a rosary, listening to the radio: "...*further investigation into possibly illegal activities...*"

"Watergate," Nonna mutters. "Crooks."

She sets aside her rosary beads and presents Cee-Cee with a steaming breakfast of toast, butter, jam, bacon, and oatmeal, as if she knew all along that today would be the day. "*Mangiare?*"

Miraculously hungry, Cee-Cee sits up and eats with Nonna rocking and watching. When she finishes, Cee-Cee asks for some paper.

Rummaging around in a drawer, Nonna pulls out a small notepad and pencil. Cee-Cee spells out the lady's message, and shows it to Nonna who nods gravely.

"Baby Pauly?" Cee-Cee asks.

Nonna shakes her head and presses her lips into a grim line.

"I hear his heart beat," Cee-Cee says. "I know he's alive."

To Nonna it's a matter of interpretation.

Once Cee-Cee is strong enough, Nonna cranks up the old Chevy. Every afternoon, she drives her to All Saints Rehabilitation Center.

"Dead is dead," Nonna says.

Cee-Cee is dressed for school, but all that has happened so far is paperwork: Nonna's guardianship, state papers declaring her authority to enroll Cee-Cee in the school, files and forms. There are aptitude tests, personality tests, standardized state tests. They spend the morning in Sister Amanda's office, Nonna talking while Cee-Cee rests on the leather sofa.

Without much fuss, Cee-Cee has been declared fit for the sixth grade.

Nonna pulls into the hospital parking lot at All Saints, rolling her window up and then down, and then up again slightly, hoping to achieve the perfect balance of sun without glare, air without chill. Rather than step foot inside the stale rectangular building, home to Romeville's paralyzed and vegetative, she studies the dirty winter snow at the edge of the parking lot. She grunts at the dramatic radio announcer: "*The truth must out...or a nation will fall!*"

Everyone claims to be innocent these days, Nonna knows, dedicated to finding the truth. There's the president of the United States, for one, Richard M. Nixon; there's also the joint Senate Hearing Committee and Archibald Cox, who keeps coming up with more questions. The future looks grim: reports and convictions, resignation after resignation.

"*There are rumors of deeper wrongdoing...*" the radio announcer says. And yet no one confesses.

People are weak, Nonna thinks. She doesn't bother with the sad, unmoving souls inside the hospital at All Saints, the paraplegics and brain-dead vets. She knows what it's like in there. Years ago, when All Saints was still the Old Soldiers' Home and Nonna's husband had a stroke, she sat by his side day after day until it finally occurred to him to die.

Sweet, stupid man. Nonna frowns.

As far as she is concerned, Baby Pauly has already gone to Jesus. What's left on earth is a shell, a husk, the trappings of a little boy who's already mercifully escaped this world. Nonna is not about to waste any more time on the dead when mostly it's the living you have to watch out for anyway.

"Waste-a you time," she tells Cee-Cee.

Nonna squints across the vinyl seat. Cee-Cee is slumped in a plaid Catholic school uniform, dazed and messy, white blouse rumpled, knee socks drooping. It seems to Nonna that the child is waiting for something to come along and save her.

Or maybe the girl is simply having an ordinary crisis of faith.

Nonna cuts the engine.

Plenty of people have temporarily succumbed to the darkness of the soul: Julian of Norwich, St. Paul, St. John of the Cross, St.

Theresa of Avila. Even Jesus had His agonizing moment in the garden at Gethsemane.

But here's what's also true: this little saint's hair never stays braided, her mouth is always full of gum, her clothes stain like everyone else's, and the room where she sleeps requires just as much dusting as any other room in the house.

Is that what it looks like to be chosen? Nonna wonders.

"*Policia…*" Nonna says, looking her granddaughter straight in the eye. "They say rape?"

"It happened all right," Cee-Cee confides. "Just not to me."

With a deep sigh Cee-Cee gets out of the car and crosses the parking lot. She is as confused as anyone, bereft. When she reaches the hospital's automatic doors, they zip open like magic and let her in.

ON THE FOURTH FLOOR of All Saints Rehabilitation Center, life is simple and unmitigated: a heartbeat.

Baby Pauly floats in a coma, distant and hapless, a loose canoe. He rolls away shallow and unfixed with no one manning the oars. His thoughts, if he has any at all, are a light wind with no direction.

What if there's only drifting now? Drifting and loss.

Sitting in an orange plastic chair behind a white curtain, Cee-Cee touches the pliant tubes and tangled wires attaching her brother to the machines and monitors. She studies the gadgets hanging on the wall behind his head, shiny equipment responsible for keeping him alive, his little body incapable of laughter, speech, or sighing. His fingers curl inward, wrapped around rolled wash cloths so they make the matching letters "C."

"It's terrible without you," Cee-Cee says.

Her words are met with a mechanical clank, a sigh of air pushed through a tube into a hole in Baby Pauly's throat. The pump puffs his lungs full, then lets them deflate. A line of light makes its way across a blank screen, signaling the repositioning of various levers and dials. Every few minutes, there is silence in which to consider the situation—an instant of peace—but every time it comes around Cee-Cee's mind goes blank.

Gurgle saliva, drip urine.

Then, with a whir and a wheeze, the cycle of life begins again.

This is how Cee-Cee's twin is resurrected: a series of beeps and blips, an electrical pulse tracking across a blue-black screen. No brain activity, no reflexes, just vacuum cleaner hoses to breathe for him and a yellow tube to remove his urine.

Everything before was a dream. Cee-Cee thinks. *This is what's real.*

Not a hair on her brother's head stirs.

She pulls out her deck of cards and shows him a thumb fan and a one-handed deck cut she's been working on all week. But he doesn't say a word about it.

Outside Room 404, Cee-Cee hears the nurses come and go on quiet shoes. They drink coffee, get married, have babies, celebrate promotions, and plan divorces. If she sits there long enough, Cee-Cee will overhear entire lives being lived. They smile on their way past to roll patients over, drip medicine into veins, rub lotion into doughy skin. If anyone there has heard about Cee-Cee's special talents, they don't let on. Instead they call her ordinary pet names, winking and smiling as they breeze on past. Do they notice how heartlessly the minutes turn to hours, and hours to days?

Closing the curtain around her brother's bed, Cee-Cee gets on her knees. At first, she cannot think of a prayer: *Hello?*

But what's the use? Who is listening now? No one comes with messages, or to show them visions. Maybe God is no longer with them: that Punisher, Prankster, Fool. Or maybe God has a depressed imagination: Jesus on the cross, the world gone wrong. Maybe suffering is all there is for everyone, even for Him: write what you know, no matter how crappy.

Or is suffering simply the thing that lets you know you're alive?

"It's different now," Cee-Cee says.

Pauly doesn't move a single muscle.

When a stout nurse bustles into the room to adjust some wires, lower the volume, Cee-Cee sits back in her chair and points to the problem. "Something's wrong with his hands."

The nurse inspects Baby Pauly from elbow to fingertips. "It's a little early for contractures, but we can splint him." She smiles at Cee-Cee. "Normal coma business, Ladybug. Nothing to worry about."

This nurse likes to remind Cee-Cee that Pauly doesn't know what's going on, which is the number one benefit to being in a coma. Sometimes people come out all right, she says, but mostly they don't.

"Just be glad he doesn't suffer!"

Getting ready to go, Cee-Cee smoothes Baby Pauly's hair where the aides have come by with scissors and groomed him crooked.

"I'll be back," she says.

The machines pump their sad goodbyes.

There's no one in the corridor on H-Wing. H is for hopeless. On her way to the exit, Cee-Cee hears the nurses laughing; onc shift ending, another beginning.

The elevator dings and delivers her down to the cramped little lobby with its few chairs and magazine racks. Today, a handful of visitors fill up the room, making it seem smaller than usual.

The attendant behind the desk seems mostly asleep.

It takes Cee-Cee a moment to realize that the man in the lobby chair is Frank; the woman reading a magazine is Glory. A cold feeling runs through her body; she turns to find Roadie and Anthony sitting on a faded yellow sofa, kicking their feet against a dirty brown carpet.

Seeing her brothers for the first time since she's been taken to Nonna's, Cee-Cee understands something new: Her memory is a broken glass. She can't recall the last time she saw any of these people, her family. Has it been weeks or months?

Glory hugs Cee-Cee fiercely, sobbing into her hair. Frank picks her up in his arms and twirls her around.

"How's my baby doing?" He puts her down. "You look good. You must feel better."

Roadie pats her shoulder. "Are you okay, Cee-Cee?"

From across the room, Anthony looks the other way. "Hi," he says.

Frank and Glory walk her past the doorman's desk to the door.

"We're going to get you back home as soon as we can," Frank says. "We're working on it every day."

"Pretty soon we'll be allowed to have you come for visits, the social worker says," Glory adds. "Wouldn't you like that, honey? To come home for visits?"

Cee-Cee nods.

Her family is familiar but uncomfortable, a small crowded room she's stood in all her life. She isn't so sure she belongs here anymore. The electric doors whiz open, casting her out alone into the pale gloom of the afternoon.

In the car, Nonna sits waiting for a report.

"He's shriveling."

She frowns and starts the car. "Not so nice now, you-a miracle."

THE OFFICER ARRIVES PUNCTUALLY and accepts a cup of coffee to be polite. At Nonna's kitchen table, Cee-Cee closes her notebook and looks up at him expectantly.

"Pick a card," she offers. "Any card."

"You don't have a deck," Vinnie says.

Cee-Cee shrugs.

They both know Cee-Cee can't answer his questions, but he comes every day after school anyway and sits in Nonna's kitchen hoping to make headway. Working against the clock, Vinnie watches the minutes tick closer to the time when Nonna stands up and escorts him out the door.

He sighs, noting Cee-Cee's strange eyes for the hundredth time: dark, spooky, calm, a strange color with flecks of gold.

Cee-Cee flashes them at him now, then goes back to her notes.

He watches her write steadily, chewing gum, flipping the page and writing again, as if he weren't there.

All and all, he thinks she seems calmer, more regularly bathed and rested.

On the other hand, the grandmother doesn't seem to make a move without first consulting the church, which could ultimately lead to problems. The Sisters from across the street are awfully involved in the decision-making, always buzzing in and out. If Vinnie's going to make something of this case, he may very well end up having to navigate nuns.

"Tell me how it happened again," Cee-Cee says.

"Today," he says, "you tell me."

It's a game they play. He knows she will not be the one to speak first. She knows he doesn't like to think about that night.

He starts the story the way he always does: "*Miracle at Pilgrim's Pond*, the newspaper said the next day." The headline seemed like a sick joke to Vinnie.

Sure, he'd been the one to dive into that icy pond and fish the kid out. He'd even sealed his own lips over the little boy's face, forcing in air to inflate his lungs like shriveled balloons. But he was extra careful to tell the reporter that someone *could* actually survive so many hours in freezing temperatures. It was a known fact. The drowning section in his officer's training manual had diagramed how hypothermia could keep people alive during long submergences by slowing the body's mechanisms down. He told this to the reporter, a perfectly good explanation.

"You never give up on a drowning victim," Vinnie says.

Cee-Cee nods.

Still, the front page had gotten it wrong: *Cop Declares Boy's Survival Impossible.*

It's hard to imagine what people got so worked up about. *Faith*, Vinnie guesses, a topic far outside his area of expertise.

"But you can't just ignore what people believe," he tells her. They think she resurrected her brother from the dead, brought him back to life.

"They think it was you," he says.

In no time, religious nuts started flocking out to where the old highway crossed Route 177 outside the Bianco home. For a while, Vinnie and his partner, Al, had to drive out there on daily patrols to keep the peace. Now it's been weeks since the kid emerged like a Popsicle, but holy rollers still make drive-by pilgrimages, gawkers still slow and lay on their horns.

Honk for a Miracle, the signs along the road say.

Vinnie thinks the whole thing is a terrible shame, a perfectly good kid like that.

"I don't see how a frozen kid all purple and bruised from a lack of oxygen is what convinces some people to get on their knees and pray," he says. "But, then again, what do I know about God?"

"Not much," Cee-Cee says.

"But I was there," he tells her.

He'd seen the aftermath for himself when the emergency workers peeled the blankets away. No one could believe the boy was still alive, if that's what you could call it. Bloated as a dead fish, but still breathing.

In the emergency room, Vinnie had thought he'd seen Cee-Cee rocking in the corner, moving her lips—praying maybe. But he quickly realized she couldn't have been there. The crowd at the pond had spirited her away immediately.

A nurse passing by touched Vinnie's wet uniform. *You'll catch your death.*

He hadn't noticed the cold rivulets running down his back until the moment of her touch—a perfect stranger. That's how it was with Vinnie: it took a female hand to bring him back to reality, teeth chattering and skin goose-bumped.

That was when he overheard one emergency technician tell another it was probably the cold that had damaged the kid, shut down his kidneys, though the ice had slowed his breathing and kept him alive. *Should be burying the little guy,* the attending doctor had said, *not putting him on a ventilator.*

Later, he'd read the official police report, which filled in the gaps—how after the ambulance took the boy away, the grandmother and the priest carried the little girl, limp and fevered, to an undisclosed location. She was bleeding, it turned out; they did a full examination, which was supervised by a doctor from the Diocese. Still, the police chief confirmed there'd been a sexual assault of some kind. Guys at the precinct said an escaped convict from Dannemora Prison was responsible, a kidnapping like all the others, but this one gone awry.

At home that night, after a hot shower and a can of soup, Vinnie turned on the news.

Divine hysteria, a priest said in an interview. They were sending for a Monsignor from Albany to interview the girl. A spokesperson for the Catholic Church chimed in: *We've seen cases of stigmata before.*

Sitting under an electric blanket in front of the TV, Vinnie had to laugh out loud at the amazing shit people came up with. *Like hell*, he'd said to his empty apartment. Who'd ever heard of stigmata down there?

"Someone hurt you," he tells Cee-Cee now.

In the grandmother's kitchen, Vinnie always feels like she half-knows what he's thinking.

"I can't tell you what happened," Cee-Cee says. "Because I don't remember."

"No?" Vinnie says. "Nothing?"

She stares at him.

"Does what happened to you that day have anything to do with the disappearance of the Iaccamo girl?" It's a stupid question, but Vinnie is running out of ideas.

For a minute it surprises them both to have a new conversation on the table.

Cee-Cee's eyes sparkle. "She's been missing since Christmas."

"That's right." Desperate enough, he risks another question. "Can you help me find her?"

"She's alive."

"I think so too."

Cee-Cee looks through him for a moment. "Ask her brother at the high school."

Most of the school-aged Iaccamo kids go to Catholic school now, so it doesn't make sense. The older ones all dropped out of public school after tenth grade anyway. Not a single graduate among them. In fact, the last Iaccamo through the public school system was the missing girl. Vinnie knows because he's done his homework.

"Is that all?" Vinnie's voice is almost a whisper.

"Yes." Cee-Cee looks back at her page and starts to write, then stops. "Also: pray."

LATER, SITTING IN HIS patrol car in the grandmother's driveway, Vinnie imagines the girl is still with him. Her presence is part of what can help him figure a connection if there's one to be figured. Problem is people are unreliable when it comes to reporting crimes. Memories are fleeting; details melt away. Eileena Iaccamo is—what? Gone, dead, a runaway, a kidnap victim, a corpse in a snow bank? And the perpetrator in the blue ski jacket? What about him? Is he a pillar of the community? A fiend? A ghost? A convict on the run? There's nothing more frustrating than a mystery in the middle of an investigation, Vinnie knows, unless of course it's two mysteries in the middle of two investigations.

It's another grey afternoon with drizzles and drips of icy rain, indicating that February has arrived.

Sometimes Cee-Cee peers through a second story window, parting the curtains to watch him sitting there in the driveway mulling things over. Occasionally, she offers a flicker of inky fingers, the smallest possible acknowledgment that they have somehow joined forces. Vinnie returns the exact greeting, barely lifting his fingers off the steering wheel.

He switches on the radio and scans the channels for something interesting. NASA gives him hope, proving that all it really takes to right the course is a little elbow grease and determination, a little creativity. A mission can start in total disaster, something completely unexpected goes wrong, prompting predictions of pieces of equipment hurtling to earth at nightmare velocity.

All it takes is a bunch of guys to make a few minor adjustments in zero gravity conditions—teamwork and ingenuity—and before you know it, a failed operation is corrected, the dream restored.

Vinnie scours the radio, checks his watch: twenty-five minutes until his shift. Then—*at last*—his brain kicks in.

No lightening bolt, no dramatic shift in temperature or energy, just Vinnie realizing what Cee-Cee meant about the brother at the high school. Just like that: clarity. This is the kind of clear thinking that will save everything: his reputation, his sanity, his career. The guys at the precinct will stop making jokes about his losing perpetrators, about how they need to put an APB out on his ass and his elbow. This may even be the exact epiphany that puts an end to all these little girls who keep going missing.

His nascent plan seeds and takes root.

All he has to do is approach at the right time, ask the right questions; it couldn't be simpler.

Then, suddenly, another seed drops and plants—this one about Cee-Cee Bianco and the stranger who raped her. It is simpler still, a mere three words: *Follow the coat.*

He snaps his fingers, takes out his notepads, scribbles each idea down in its proper page: one for Iaccamo, one for Bianco.

Getting out of the car and ringing the grandmother's bell, Vinnie waits for Cee-Cee to answer the door.

"I wonder if you could come with me," he says. "It's about the missing girl."

Standing behind her, the grandmother looks stern and shakes her head.

"Both of you," he pleads. "It'll only take a minute. I think we have a lead."

THE SCHOOL IS ABANDONED, except for a few cars in the corner by the concession stand where parents sell hot dogs during football games. Painted in bright red letters is the team's name: *Romeville Saints.*

Nonna and Cee-Cee sit in the back seat, a cage separating them from their driver.

"She isn't here," Cee-Cee says confidently. "The missing girl."

"But the brother is," Vinnie spots his guy peddling marijuana to a hippie in a banged-up Volkswagen bus. "Just like you said. Remember?"

He is suddenly unsure about the plan. Wasn't this Cee-Cee's idea in the first place?

"Wait here," he says. "I'll be right back."

Circling around behind the bleachers on foot, he manages to sneak up on the drug deal, so only the hippie can see Vinnie in his uniform. The hippie changes his mind and peels away.

The kid has freckles and a sad, ruddy face with those telltale cow-eyes. You can spot a Iaccamo from miles away; no one else in town looks quite so dumb. This particular Iaccamo has been selling marijuana at the high school for at least a year.

Vinnie holds him by the scruff of his coat in the direction of the squad car, but Cee-Cee makes no sign. She doesn't nod or shake her head. She only stares at him. For a minute Vinnie is stumped, but he keeps his stride.

"Where's your sister?" he says to the guy.

"Gone, man."

"Awfully young to go traveling," Vinnie says.

"She's visiting relatives."

"Which relatives?"

"Aw, come on."

Vinnie shakes the kid; then looks back at his squad car and sees the girl peering though the window at him. Again, her face is blank.

Vinnie eases off. "I don't think I heard what you said."

"I don't know!" The kid surrenders in Vinnie's grip. "She's thirteen. And crazy. Ask anyone."

Vinnie relaxes a little. "What's your first name, Iaccamo?"

"Liam."

"Help me find your sister, Liam, so I don't have to arrest you."

For the first time since Vinnie flashed his badge, the kid looks scared. "No one knows where she went."

"I *am* going to find her, Liam—dead or alive—and you're going to help me. Tell me about the day she disappeared."

"What about it?" Liam says.

"Did your folks notice she was gone?"

"Seven kids is a lot to keep track of; one of my older sisters figured it out."

"Did she have a fight with anybody?"

"We fight all the time at my house."

"Not one thing out of the ordinary happened the day she disappeared?"

Liam shrugs. "I don't pay that much attention to girls."

Vinnie's shift starts soon; he has to get Cee-Cee and her grandmother home before picking up his partner, Al, at the station. "I don't want to see you up here again, do you hear me?"

Liam flashes a grin when he realizes he's being released.

"Don't go far, Liam, because we're watching you."

Somehow he means himself and Cee-Cee, but it's the first time he's said so out loud. Before Vinnie can finish the sentence, Liam is wading through the yellow stalks of tall grass behind the school, already out of earshot. They catch a glimpse of his red hunting jacket.

Then with a flash through the wheat, he is gone.

At Our Lady, Cee-Cee trudges to her afternoon tutoring session.

The Sisters take turns catching her up on lessons from fourth and fifth grade, so she can join her new classmates at their level. All the Sisters pride themselves on their different specialties. Sister Alouicious diagrams sentences like a pro. Sister Lawrence carries a cartful of maps to augment every geography lesson. Sister Sebastian is a whiz at world history, putting on paper crowns and shouting, "Off with their heads!" Sister Eugene teachers the basics of Home Economics: sewing, cooking, stocking a pantry. Sister Robert-Claude demands that Cee-Cee read a book every week and write a report to prove it. Sister John of the Cross grades each report, quiz, and test with colored markers and stickers shaped like stars and angels.

Crossing from the school to the Sisters' living quarters, Cee-Cee reads signs on the doors telling all who enter not to let Sister James's cats out. If she sees Mr. Jingles, Calliope, or Whiskers, Cee-Cee stops to say hello. Sometimes she brings one of them to the refectory for company, where a Sister is always waiting at the end of a very long wooden table.

The room smells of lemons and damp dishcloths.

Today it is sixth-grade math, long division, which means several hours with Sister Edward.

"Let that dirty thing go!" Edward says when Cee-Cee

appears with ink-black Calliope in her arms. "Out, I said!"

Cee-Cee puts the pretty cat down and herds it back into the hallway.

"Sit," Sister Edward demands.

The others are more fun and always first ask how she's feeling and if she's learned any new card tricks she'd like to show. They braid her hair and fix her snacks: peanut butter in celery sticks or cheese with apples. Before even cracking a book, they say a prayer for wisdom and enlightenment.

Cee-Cee takes her seat across from Sister Edward, depositing a wad of gum discreetly beneath the seat of her chair. She knows that gum gets under Sister Edward's skin, though not quite as much as the new dishwasher that's been installed under the linoleum counter near the cross-shaped clock does. The dishwasher really crosses a line with its shiny knobs and extra rinse cycle.

"When I was a novice," she tells Cee-Cee. "All anybody ever needed was water, potatoes, and prayer."

Cee-Cee is not sure whether she's expected to answer.

"It's even worse than Sister Eugene's cooking classes," Sister Edward says. "I want to shout *Alka Selzer!* after every meal."

Sister Edward says mean things about Cee-Cee too.

Hypergraphia! She likes to tell the other teachers. *That's what's wrong with our little Miracle Girl.*

None of the others seem to take Sister Edward seriously. Mostly they turn and walk away shaking their heads, which doesn't stop her mouth.

The child is mentally ill!

Once during a physical fitness test in the gym, Cee-Cee overheard Brother Ignacio blow his whistle to cut her off.

Well, I don't know about that, Sister, he said, *but she sure does excel at jumping jacks.*

When the Monsignor had visited from Albany to recommend that Father Giuseppe take Cee-Cee on as a spiritual project, everyone agreed immediately that she should be placed in Sister Edward's Gifted and Talented sixth grade class.

A gift for you! the Mother General had told Sister Edward, presenting Cee-Cee one day after school.

Cee-Cee smiled up at her.

The girl has obvious promise, Father Giuseppe added. *We thought you'd be pleased.*

Sister Edward spoke openly: *You don't honestly believe in that voodoo, do you? What happened that night was a total fluke!*

All girls are miracles, the Mother General had said, placing an arm around Cee-Cee's shoulder. *That's Our Lady's philosophy.*

Best of all, Cee-Cee loves Sister Amanda, who everyone at the school calls Mother General, but she is never Cee-Cee's tutor. Instead, she spends long hours in Nonna's kitchen sipping tea and describing her plans for changing Our Lady. Sometimes she asks Nonna to host young women, who sleep on mats on the floor in the living room, and say "yes, ma'am," to everything Nonna utters.

"They are graduates of the program," Sister Amanda announces proudly, but no one knows what program she means. "They only need to stay a few nights."

The young women always come in pairs, and call themselves Miranda, no matter what.

"You're both named Miranda?" Cee-Cee says.

Invariably, they nod in unison.

Mostly they are teenagers, though they seem wiser and never smoke cigarettes, as far as Cee-Cee can tell. During the day, they disappear across the street, running errands for the Sisters. At night, they return exhausted, but still as polite as ever. They flop down on their mats, say a long, involved prayer aloud in perfect unison, and fall asleep without blankets or pillows.

To Cee-Cee, they are mysterious and exciting.

"We're Mother Stephen's Orphans," one of them usually ends up confiding when Cee-Cee asks who they are and where they've come from.

"You mean Sister Amanda?" Cee-Cee asks.

"We call her Mother. We're on a mission for peace."

Nonna feeds them breakfast and never asks questions. She doesn't wonder who their mothers are, or if they go to church, or whether they are going to take vows to join the order of Precious Wounds. From their long hair and loose clothing, Cee-Cee figures they are hippies or protestors.

"We're from Canada," they usually say.

Now in the refectory alone, Sister Edward leans in a little closer to Cee-Cee.

"You have a sluggish mind, smudged skin, and the appearance of someone who is severely malnourished. Your braids never stay plaited and your hair ends up hanging down like a dark cloak."

Personally Cee-Cee doesn't think she looks *that* bad. Lately she's even starting to feel a little better.

"Perhaps you are *slightly* more promising than the other dullards," Sister Edward adds, but only because Cee-Cee has so far mastered all her math quizzes—"and a very studious note-taker it appears—but God-given, Miss Bianco, you are not!"

"Of course not." Cee-Cee shrugs. "No more or less than anyone."

Sister Edward doesn't like her response.

"What do you know about Chinese checkers, Sister?" Cee-Cee asks. "I mean, how is it different from regular checkers?"

"I know nothing of children's games."

"Guess not."

"Are you always so grumpy, Miss Bianco?" Sister Edward stares into the girl's eyes. "Don't you *ever* smile?"

"Not much, Sister." Cee-Cee flashes her teeth. "You?"

Sister Edward does not like Cee-Cee's tone. "I thought perhaps the Son of God might arrive personally and advise you to lighten up."

"Nope," Cee-Cee says. "No one comes around for me

anymore."

Sister Edward thinks about sending her straight to detention, but something about the serious look in the girl's strange eyes stops her.

"Why?" Cee-Cee says. "Does Jesus visit *you*?"

"*Every* day!" Sister Edward says. "And I don't need a fancy visitation with angels and saints and secret messages to know what I know!"

In truth Sister Edward's prayers have gone unanswered for years.

"Consider yourself lucky," Cee-Cee says. "Take it from me, it's not fun."

The conversation strikes Sister Edward as absurd, audacious—rude even. But she lets her mind simmer until she can think of a response.

"You are merely lost and ill-mothered, young lady. You are nothing special, and I would venture to say, hardly chosen."

In Sister Edward's experience, when you pick away at even the ugliest scab, you find something ordinary underneath, pus and dirt. Cee-Cee, she decides, is nothing more than a pompous child in need of structure and focus.

It's no wonder.

An insidious shift away from spiritual devotion has been the trend for the past several years since young Amanda was installed as Mother General. The act itself was an insult to all the devout older Sisters of Christ's Most Precious Wounds, waiting their turn to be in charge, including Sister Edward herself, who is soon to be forty.

If it weren't sacrilege, Sister Edward would blame the Second Vatican Council for taking away what she loved most about her vocation: daily Masses in Latin, a cloistered world without distractions, a sacred time for study and prayer. It was the only place a woman could really get a break from the world and study God's mysteries in peace and quiet, but now all that's gone.

Now Catholic Sisters are sent out into a filthy world to work like dogs, provide charity, feed the poor, drive vans of loud, underprivileged children here and there. Now, service is valued above silence and discretion is obsolete. Even Sisters who choose to indulge in *particular friendships* refuse to hide their special bonds. Just last week in the chapel, Sister Edward happened upon Sister Robert-Claude kissing Sister Eugene full on the mouth. Of course they shot apart like rabbits when Edward stood up from dusting under the pews.

Do we no longer save our passion for Christ, Sisters?

Sister Eugene scurried off, ashamed, startled, or both.

But Sister Robert-Claude merely smirked at Edward: *You waited quite a long time before announcing yourself, Sister. Hope you enjoyed it.*

Mannish and swaggering, Sister Robert-Claude has always had a fresh mouth. Nonetheless, Sister Edward was not intimidated.

Chastity, Sister, she told the old diesel. *Lest you forget your vows.*

If this were all, Sister Edward would suffer without complaint and go about her business. But she knows for a fact that the young Mother General is a danger to the church, with associations to the Utica Seven, arrested last year for underground bomb-making and God knows what else.

"The Mother General," she tells Cee-Cee, "is a supporter of priests and sisters gallivanting in so-called service to the peace movement."

"Am I excused?" Cee-Cee asks, hopeful. "Are we done yet, Sister?"

"One more thing," Sister Edward says. "What do you think of her? I mean, personally. What's your opinion?"

"Sister Amanda?" Cee-Cee shrugs. "I think she's good at cards."

"Indeed." Sister Edward says. "I suspect that she is capable of just about anything. You know she's friends with that horrible priest accused of plotting to kidnap Henry Kissinger? Flannigan? Oh yes, she knows all the unsavory elements of the Catholic Church."

Sister Edward watches Cee-Cee's face for a sign that she understands. She is trying to decide whether she can confide in the girl.

She has no one else.

"I'll tell you a secret." Sister Edward's breath smells like coffee. "The Federal Bureau of Investigation is interested in your beloved Sister Amanda's activities."

Sister Edward has seen with her own eye the avalanche of envelopes addressed to "Amanda" from known political zealots. She has steamed open the seal and read one or two, noting that they sign off with their first names, dropping all religious titles: Father, Brother, Sister, Mother.

Sister Edward gives Cee-Cee a meaningful look. "The FBI is under the impression that she is heavily involved with the radical underground. And do you know what they call that, Little Miss?"

"No, Sister," Cee-Cee says.

"They call that *abetting terrorists*."

Sister Edward is on a roll now: "The federal agents suspect that somewhere at Our Lady there's a secret room or tunnel, perhaps even a stockade of weapons. And they believe that the Mother General is somehow participating in the conspiracies of those depraved hooligans."

"Did they ever find anything, Sister?" Cee-Cee asks. "Tunnels or weapons?"

Sister Edward sighs. "Not yet."

In fact they have found exactly nothing. Not a single thing: no secret bunkers, no bombs or materials to make bombs, no shred of evidence that the Mother General committed crimes on or off Our Lady's campus. They couldn't even unearth a single letter from a single criminal or even a measly radical peacenik.

The cagey woman must have burned all her letters somewhere in one of Our Lady's fireplaces.

"Mark my words," Sister Edward says. "She's up to something."

Sister Edward still occasionally gets a call from her own special bureau investigator. Most recently he'd wanted information about Mother General's Peace Circle, when it meets and where. She told him what she knew: how it was voluntary, mostly involving the sisters and brothers from Our Lady, occasionally a young candidate to the Sisterhood from Canada. They meet several times a month in the back offices.

Have you ever attended? the agent asked Sister Edward over the phone. *What exactly do they do in there?*

The answer came as a surprise as much to the agent as to Sister Edward. *They pray for peace.*

Come again, Sister, he said. *There's static on the line.*

Sister Edward cleared her throat. *What they do in the Peace Circle is pray.*

LATER CEE-CEE DOES HER homework in Father Giuseppe's inner office with Sister Edward supervising. Really, though, Sister Edward hardly pays attention. She is caught up in the week's accounting—red wine for Mass, tiny orthopedic shoes for Sister Pius, a miscalculation in last week's collection for the poor. She shows the ledger to Cee-Cee, who points out the error.

Sister Edward is so impressed with the girl's eagle eye that she almost doesn't hear the police officer knock.

He is tall and dark with kind eyes. "May I interrupt you for a moment?"

He pushes the door open with a large hand and gently steps inside.

"I'm afraid Father Giuseppe is in Albany all week."

The policeman nods, putting away his badge. "Maybe that's

good."

Sister Edward maintains a calm expression. "How may I help you, Officer?"

He looks at Cee-Cee and smiles. "Well, look who it is!"

"Step out into the hallway, Miss Bianco," Sister Edward instructs. "Finish those math problems, and I will be out in a minute to check your work."

The police officer motions for Sister Edward to take her seat behind the enormous mahogany desk. "I'd like to ask you a few questions about the good Father, if you don't mind."

"What kind of questions?"

"Sit down, Sister," the officer says. "Relax."

In her heart, Sister Edward knows that Father Giuseppe, an irritating man to be sure, is in no way involved in treasonous activities or conspiracies brought upon Our Lady by the Mother General and her radical, bomb-making friends. Sister Edward is certain he hasn't fallen for any of her activist nonsense.

Perhaps Father Giuseppe has bad breath; perhaps he is stubborn. But he is no criminal, political or otherwise.

Sister Edward sits. "I think you're quite mistaken about Father's involvement."

"Involvement in what, Sister?"

For a moment, Sister Edward waivers. Her lip trembles, a tiny movement. "Involvement in anything," she says, recovering.

It is odd that Father Giuseppe indulges the Mother General, managing to ignore her suspicious behaviors. As a pastor, he plays favorites among the flock. Nonetheless, Sister Edward is not about to abandon him now. She has placed her trust in Father Giuseppe, as she has in Jesus, and the Church.

She prepares to defend him when the officer says, "I've received a tip that your priest owns a blue winter jacket. Is that true?"

Sister Edward inhales more air than her lungs can hold. He's not here to ask about radical plots and bombs. She sifts through her memory, hoping to ascertain the significance of the article of clothing in question. "A blue down vest, you say?"

"A ski jacket, actually. Does Father own a blue down vest?"

At last Sister Edward alights on her current student's situation. Cee-Cee Bianco: an assault, a drowning, a blue ski jacket.

"Heavens, no!"

"No, he doesn't own a down vest?"

"No. I mean, I don't know. But you couldn't possibly think...?"

"Think what?" The police officer trains his marvelously mysterious eyes on Sister Edward's face, as if only she exists. He smiles warmly. "Is that a coat closet behind you, Sister?"

Sister Edward doesn't turn around, but keeps her gaze steady on him, stung. She does not interest him as much as the coat does.

"I don't believe it is, Officer."

The handsome man gets up. Walking close to her chair, he pauses at the closet door, hand on the knob. Sister Edward doesn't stir.

"Will you join me over here, please, Sister?"

She gets up quietly, pushes in her chair, and calmly walks to the closet. "I really don't see the point."

"NASA," the officer says under his breath. Or perhaps Edward has misheard.

When he swings the door open, they both freeze a moment, standing and looking at the contents. Three casual winter coats hang on wire hangers—all of them navy blue, one of them puffy and filled with down.

"Oh!" Sister Edward's hands flutter like pale butterflies to the officer's wrist.

If someone were to be standing in the doorway, hidden by the barely closed door, snooping around, say, instead of working on math problems, it might appear that a Catholic woman of faith were taking a police officer's pulse, seeking a suppler heartbeat under the stiff, starched uniform.

IN THE DARK BEFORE the sun rises, Cee-Cee gets up and dresses in her Sunday best for the Monsignor's visit.

Nonna is already at the breakfast table, perfectly groomed in a gray wool dress, deep in prayer. She sits as tall as her shrinking form allows and begins her litany using the school roster tucked inside her kitchen Bible: *"La Suora Eduardo."* She pauses and opens one eye, waiting for Cee-Cee to sit down and join her.

"I don't see why I can't just wear my school uniform," Cee-Cee whispers. It's the same question every time.

"Sisters Robert-Claude and Eugene," Nonna says, switching to English for Cee-Cee, but keeping her head bowed. "Sisters Alouicious, John of the Cross, and Sebastian. Sisters James and Lawrence. Sister Pius—the dwarf. Brother Ignacio of the Gym, and Brother Joe, the Janitor." She takes a breath, pausing for effect: "And bless Amanda, my friend, the Mother General, and, last but not least, Father Giuseppe."

When she has made all the rounds, praying for everyone who is sick in the parish, all her old friends, the Italian *gumbas*, plus the dead and the dying, they cross themselves and sit for a moment in silence.

"I need a new notebook," Cee-Cee says.

Nonna lifts her eyebrows. *"Si?"*

"It's not that; nothing's happened. I just want to write about this part too."

"L'abbandono?" Nonna asks.

"Yes, the abandonment." Cee-Cee yawns. "And do you think I could have an allowance? I'd like to buy a yo-yo."

Nonna frowns. "You sleep here, home."

"It's what people do in junior high, Nonna. They sleep at each other's houses. I want to stay over at Mary Margaret's."

Sighing deeply, Nonna gets up to prepare the toast and tea. Making the sign of the cross again, she cracks open a new jar of jam.

As it is, the Monsignor from Albany is Nonna's main consultant concerning Cee-Cee's situation. But like all Nonna's advisers, when he arrives and listens to her concerns, he mostly urges patience.

"No demands on the girl," he says.

"No," Nonna confirms. "No?"

His eyes drift lazily over to Cee-Cee, then back to his coffee cup, pinkie ring flashing bright gold.

"Let her be the one to bring things up. That means no talking about the past, no having spiritual expectations, no bringing up pious topics, no reading aloud about the saints or Christ's Passion, and no forcing conversation or prayer."

"What's left?" Nonna wants to know.

The Monsignor smiles. "I understand it seems strict, but we must let these things happen in God's time, not ours, Marina."

In the driveway, a chauffer sits at the wheel of a very long shiny car that has brought the Monsignor to Nonna and Cee-Cee. Now at Nonna's kitchen table, he waves his hand and snaps at the archbishop and his two assistants, then continues tasting Nonna's Italian cookies.

The archbishop leans forward and removes Cee-Cee's gum with his fingers. He looks inside her mouth and ears. One of his assistants passes a flashlight over Cee-Cee's eyes.

"Nothing," the archbishop says, giving back the gum.

They all write something down in different files on different clipboards.

The Monsignor looks at Cee-Cee. "You have had a quiet time lately, yes?"

"Yes, your eminence," she says because Nonna has told her how to respond.

"You have had no divine visitations?" He wears a crazy satin outfit made up of purple robes.

"No, your eminence," she says.

"Holy apparitions do not last forever, my child," he says. "Few are ever repeated. This can be disappointing?"

"Kind of a relief, your eminence," she says. "To tell the truth."

He personally runs through the checklist today, taking the paperwork out of the archbishop's hands. He has Nonna coughing out answers as usual: Yes, Cee-Cee has felt fine lately. No, God hasn't said anything important to her. No, she hasn't heard the virgins singing. No, God's Holy Angel has not reappeared. No, she hasn't written down anything important this week. Yes, she eats regularly and sometimes sleeps through the night. No, there hasn't been blood, other unusual signs, or stigmata.

After the interview, Nonna hands over a week's worth of Cee-Cee's worn underwear, and the two assistants get busy zipping them into separate plastic baggies.

"Is that really necessary?" Cee-Cee asks.

The Archbishop tucks them away in a briefcase without answering.

Next, they rip away pages from Cee-Cee's notebook and put them in a manila envelope marked "Private and Confidential."

"Hey!" she says. "I want those back!"

They pat Cee-Cee's head, amused at her antics.

"You think I'm kidding?"

Next visit, she will have to create a dummy notebook, one that doesn't matter. From now on she plans to hide her writing under the mattress.

"We must encourage humility and acceptance," the Monsignor tells Nonna. "It's not easy for a child who is...special."

Cee-Cee rolls her eyes.

The Monsignor's committee in Albany will be on the lookout, he tells Nonna for the hundredth time.

They will know about a second divine intervention before

anyone else does. If and when such an event occurs, he will alert the proper authorities.

"By which I mean the Vatican," he says—as if Nonna has never heard of *The Congregation for the Cause of Saints*.

The conversation causes Nonna to glance obsessively in the rearview mirror on their drives to All Saints, as if she is searching for holy undercover investigators. How else will they know if another miracle occurs? How else will they know if Cee-Cee performs all three miracles needed to justify an official investigation?

"We will observe, assess, and evaluate," the Monsignor says. "In certain special cases, perhaps exceptions may be made concerning the subject still being alive, concerning the necessity of documenting three miracles."

"*Si?*" Nonna asks.

"It hasn't happened yet," the Monsignor answers carefully. "But let us say, for example, if there were extenuating circumstances. Let's say the child's brother were to waken without medical justification from the coma…"

Nonna shakes her head sharply, indicating that there's no chance.

"Well," the Monsignor says. "We needn't worry about that now."

Sister Amanda tells Nonna not to hold out hope for the Monsignor anyway. She says His Reverence hardly has the budget to follow up on every miracle.

Nonna takes this under advisement.

At the end of the visit, Cee-Cee gathers her books and walks across the street to meet Brother Joe, who walks her to her tutoring sessions with various Sisters, depending on a carefully scheduled calendar of who's available when. Some mornings Brother Joe and Cee-Cee take a stroll around the garden. Others they stand before the statue of Fatima tucked behind a huge yew bush near the Manse, barely visible from the road. They chew gum, and play cards, or just sit around and think about things. The eyes of the alabaster statue stare back kindly as if they too were tending sheep somewhere in Portugal.

"What happened to the children of Fatima?" Cee-Cee asks. "I mean after they saw Our Lady."

"Two died right away of the Spanish flu," says Brother Joe folding his arms. "The remaining visionary became a Carmelite nun, Sister Lucia. They say she's the keeper of the Secrets of Fatima."

"What secrets?" Cee-Cee touches the tallest statue of the Fatima children—about her height.

"Nobody knows."

"I didn't get secrets," Cee-Cee tells Brother Joe.

"Secrets are hard." His voice is deep and warm. "Maybe you've been spared."

They stare at the statue a moment longer. Brother Joe tells Cee-Cee that the statues of Our Lady were moved to the back of most churches once Vatican II removed The Hail Mary from Mass.

"Why would they do that?" Cee-Cee asks.

Brother Joe says, "Some men don't like women very much. I guess they worry she will steal the show."

"She would never do that. She only ever leads people to her son."

He holds her hand as they walk.

"Pretty soon you'll be in class with the other students," Brother Joe says. "Are you ready for that?"

"I don't know," Cee-Cee says. "Are they ready for me?"

Brother Joe chuckles.

Cee-Cee imagines how strange the two of them must look from behind: a large black mountain of a man beside a little white reed of a girl.

"Who are Mother Stephen's Orphans?" Cee-Cee asks. "The older girls who come in pairs and stay at Nonna's sometimes?"

Brother Joe rubs a hand over his face. "You must never speak of them to anyone. Do you understand?"

"Okay," Cee-Cee says. "Just wondering."

"It's better not to."

On the way back to the classrooms, Cee-Cee stoops to look at an anthill in a crack in the grass.

"Ants can't think on their own," she says, inspecting the insects. "But a colony is like one gigantic brain, only smarter."

Brother Joe has a look at the ants, then ties his shoe before standing and fluffing his enormous hair, an Afro the size of a small fourth grader.

Nothing in all the rest of the day is quite as good as Brother Joe.

After weeks of tutoring, Cee-Cee is finally ready.

She stands before Sister Edward's Earth Science sixth grade class prepared to give her first public presentation.

"The Ecosystem," she says.

Sister Amanda slips into the back of the room next to Father Giuseppe and smiles at Cee-Cee. A few of the other of Christ's Most Precious Wounds wander in to offer support. The presence of so many adults makes everyone nervous.

One of the Iaccamo kids bounces a rubber-band ball under his desk. His name is either Cork Quinn or Quinn Cork, but no one can ever remember which. He is chiefly known for his bright orange hair and his missing sister. He claims to have seen her twice since her disappearance, but you never get to ask where or how because he spends half his time in the office with Sister Amanda.

Eileena Brice Iaccamo still haunts the town.

Kids say she kills farm animals and eats them raw, a rumor Cee-Cee writes in her notebook for later investigation.

Now Sister Edward bangs a ruler on the desk to call the class to attention.

Sitting up front, the popular girls quiet down on cue. Sister Amanda calls them *damp little flowers in their dewy pots of faith.* They believe whole-heartedly that any girl could turn famous at any minute: like poor battered St. Christina, or confused St.

Dymphna or athletic St. Joan. They love Rose of Lima best, that saintly glamour-puss for Jesus. From Sister Amanda's office, Cee-Cee has seen them on their way between classes, peering into the doorway to catch sight of her.

Cee-Cee's head is always bent over a notebook, her hands are always shuffling a small deck of cards, marked with blue ink, her hair is always tangled. She looks like a runt. Still, the girls at Our Lady Junior High take their miracles seriously; they wave shyly at Cee-Cee through the window on their way home from school.

Today, they get their first good look at the new presentable Cee-Cee in the flesh. She is scrubbed clean, skin perfectly porcelain, hair held back loosely with a tie, but brushed to shine. The color of her eyes seems to prompt the most excitement; a fleet of notes go sailing back and forth in the front row.

Golden, the notes say.

Sensing a new wave of energy, the classroom grows restless.

Paper ruffles, pencils tap. Mouth-breathers flip in their seats until Mary Margaret, the school's shining star of bad girls, can't stand it any more.

"Shush up!" she says. "Let her speak."

Cee-Cee sputters and starts over. "The Ecosystem."

Sandy Sorrentino blows a spit bubble. "You said that already, *EcoSpasm*."

"I'll knock you, Scabby," Mary Margaret warns, then whips back around.

"Continue, please," says Sister Edward.

"In our precious water supply—ponds, rivers, and streams," Cee-Cee says, "there's a universe of unexplored beauty that gets destroyed every day with toxic dumping."

Sandy pops an eye open. "Walk on water if you're so great."

Father Giuseppe squeezes Sandy's shoulder, causing a few of the slower students to giggle from the back rows. Someone else slings a rubber band, a bright yellow butterfly of elastic that

Mary Margaret catches midair.

Sister Edward taps the desk again. "Who wants to go to the principal's office?"

Sandy droops his lids to half-mast.

"With a microscope and a drop of water," Cee-Cee says, "you can see many important life-sustaining organisms."

"*Orgasms.*" A whisper, a wind, a ventriloquist's trick.

Sister Edward's sigh is tragic. She is too tired to make a real effort and inspects her gold band instead; everyone knows it is a wedding ring from Jesus.

The Sisters and Brothers, guests at the back of the room, shift and nod, encouraging Cee-Cee to finish. All in a row, the pretty girls, Black-Eyed Susans, bow their heads, listening intently. *Miracle Girl,* they call Cee-Cee behind her back.

Cee-Cee clutches a jar of pond water, pointing out the finer details of a homemade poster showing disruptions in the food chain. This is the water that saved Baby Pauly, the water that kept him alive. She wants to mention that this is the reason for her choice of topics, but she cannot bring herself to say his name in public.

When her presentation is over, everyone applauds.

Mary Margaret whistles through her fingers and shouts. "Bravo! Bravo!"

"Spazospasm!" Sandy shouts, equally impressed.

Father Giuseppe and Amanda file out of the room with the other adults, leaving Sister Edward to do her thing.

Cee-Cee pitches forward into an awkward bow.

Marking a red B+ in her book, Sister Edward looks up just in time to notice that Cee-Cee has doubled over, an unexpected moan escaping her lips. Then without warning, she hands her jar to the Sister and drops to the floor like a stone.

Later, the school kids at Our Lady Queen of Sorrows will say something magical happened at the end of Cee-Cee's presentation. But there is a difference between a miracle and a collapse. Cee-Cee knows this for a fact even if they do not.

After class, Mary Margaret catches up in the hall. "Awesome report! The Big Wigs were impressed."

Cee-Cee seems to be on her own today without the Sisters as escorts or the Brothers shooing people out of her path when she needs to use the girls' room. It's made her feel self-conscious.

"Driving me crazy," Cee-Cee says. "I didn't think they'd ever let me into the classroom."

Words flow from Mary Margaret's lips. "It was hard getting to you. I have morning detention after vespers, a total drag, so I could sometimes see them putting you through the ringer if I peeked in the window. They got all sorts of weird stuff in that conference room. Ever notice? Maps and blueprints, photographs. People say Sister Amanda makes bombs in a secret room behind the chapel and sells them to the peaceniks to fund some sort of mission."

"That's what Sister Edward says," Cee-Cee says. "That she's up to something."

Mary Margaret's eyes light up. "Maybe it's true."

Faster than Cee-Cee can open her mouth, Mary Margaret fires more questions. "Do you miss your family? Do you always faint like that? Do you want to sit together in the cafeteria? Don't listen to Sister Edward; I mean she's creepy, but she's basically harmless. Don't get on Sister Robert-Claude's bad side; it isn't pretty."

Except for Mary Margaret, Cee-Cee already feels a little doomed.

The Junior High itself is a Catholic mish-mash of local kids funneled together from separate grade schools. Around every corner, on every wall, the paint is chipping, the floors are scuffed, and the windows need cleaning. God hangs judiciously here and there with outstretched arms on wooden crosses. Our Lady's campus is cramped with its steepled church and dreary administrative offices in The Manse. Father Giuseppe lives with Brother Joe and Brother Ignacio at the Rectory. For the Sisters of Christ's Most Precious Wounds, there's an entire separate living space.

Unlike at home, here Cee-Cee can do no wrong.

If she refuses to pray, the Sisters praise her for being humble.

If she doodles in her notebook, they say she's artistic and all want to see what she's writing.

If she mopes, they think she's deep in meditation.

The most anyone ever disciplines her is when Sister Amanda kneels by her desk and holds out her hand for Cee-Cee's gum or urges her to join in with the others at recess and music class.

It's important be a part of things, Sister Amanda says. *It'll help you feel better.*

But Cee-Cee's focus is gone; she can barely even see Sister Amanda's pretty face. Her classmates float in and out of her peripheral vision, which is syrupy and slow. A strange block of light blurs her view. It's as if a hole has been drilled into the back of her head and things keep falling out of it.

Whole days go by in a jumble of headaches. The words get stuck in her throat.

Secrets creep down the hallway toward her ears, but Cee-Cee cannot decode what they mean:

"The Mother General's cell was raided again."

"When?"

"At Vespers…Brother Joe suspects an inside job. Someone's leaking information."

"Judas Iscariot! We'd better tighten the ship."

"Keep it under your habit, Sister. We've got a school to run."

Luckily, Brother Joe still makes time for her. He is one of the bright spots in her day, amazing to look at with his sleek forehead and wide smile.

He keeps an eye on her.

"Lonely?" he asks.

Cee-Cee watches his nose crinkle when he lights up a cigarette.

Sometimes after school, they sit together in his office chewing gum or playing gin rummy. He shows off his calendar with a different European automobile for every month.

"Aren't they beauts?" he says, flipping past February and landing on March.

Cee-Cee looks through his stack of *Car and Driver Magazine*, asking about the poster with the big black fist. Sometimes he puts a bright African Kenta cloth over her shoulders like a cape.

"Someone's got to bring a holy message into this world," he says. "Might as well be you."

Cee-Cee pretends he cheers her up. "The messages have dried up."

He pats her arm. "Must be part of the plan."

Sometimes he leaves an orange in her locker as a surprise.

The only other people who speak to Cee-Cee are popular blue-eyed Maureen and Mary Ellen McNulty. Once in a while they stop her in the school cafeteria to get a closer look.

They are identical in almost every way except coloring.

"So you're the new girl?" says the blonder sister.

When they raise their hands in class, it's like seeing double.

"Ever played three-card monte?" Cee-Cee says.

The twins look down their noses at her.

"I have a twin," Cee-Cee says. "But he's a boy and a year older than me."

"We know," they answer in unison before walking away.

But that's all.

Now, in the hallway, Mary Margaret grabs Cee-Cee's pond water. "Watch this!" She runs with her twin braids swinging. "Scabby Sorrentino, wait up!"

Seeing her rush him with water sloshing unevenly from the open jar, Sandy Sorrentino ducks, but not fast enough to avoid the wave of pond scum splashed down his front. Sandy sputters and groans, soaked all the way down to his Catholic-school loafers.

He grins. "You slut!"

Sandy has no neck, which makes him even shorter than the girls. The rest of him is pretty bad too: a pockmarked face, Ringo Starr haircut, and small white hands.

Mary Margaret wrings out his school-issued necktie. "Lay off, Scab. Cee-Cee's my best friend, see?"

Cee-Cee inspects the jar, now empty except for a green smear of algae around the rim. "Best?"

"Of course." Mary Margaret leads her to the gymnasium. "How come you fainted?"

"I don't know," Cee-Cee says. "It just happens."

"Sister Pius says you're like Saint What's-His-Name, the one who was so holy he used to faint and levitate all the time. She's a dwarf, you know. Hey, should I take you to the nurse's office?"

Cee-Cee would like it if Mary Margaret never stopped talking.

Mary Margaret flips her braids. "I don't know what your old public school was like, but they get bent out of shape around here about everything: gum, cigarettes, cursing. And forget about boys; they don't allow kissing of any kind in this prison. I got caught once and you'd think I'd murdered someone."

Cee-Cee fingers Mary Margaret's colorful neckerchief around her own throat; all the girls trade them to spice up their drab uniforms.

"Scabby's the worst! He deserves to drown."

Cee-Cee is caught up short on the image. Luckily, Sister Edward appears from nowhere before she can find anything to say.

"Who's responsible for this mess?"

Cee-Cee glances around at the bland yellow hallways, a desert about to give way to an oasis, to Mary Margaret herself, who shimmers alive with heat and light. She is a summer rain after years of crawling through sand.

"Everybody's got something," Mary Margaret whispers. "With me, it's the dead brothers and sisters, lots of them."

The second bell rings.

"This mess?" Sister demands. "I'm waiting."

"My fault!" Mary Margaret says. "I slipped and spilled some of Cee-Cee's pond."

Brother Joe arrives in his robes and rubber boots to mop up the mess. He smiles at Cee-Cee and winks, humming.

"We will see you after school, Miss Cortina." The punishment for most school infractions is ten light lashes with a belt and ten Hail Mary's. It's the only rule Father Giuseppe insists be enforced at the school.

"Right-o, Sister!"

Mary Margaret says it isn't bad. Sister Amanda stands in the office making sure Brother Ignacio goes easy with the belt. Afterward, you have to go see Father Giuseppe in his office and say confession, but then Sister Amanda comes in and holds you close while they have their millionth fight about the belt as a form of reprimand.

Sister knows how to turn up the guilt: *Should not every precious child be protected from bodily harm, Father G.?*

Pulling out her schedule, Cee-Cee locates her next class.

Mary Margaret salutes, disappearing into the locker room, her sharp face back in the doorway a moment later. "We still have a sacred mission to find You-Know-Who, right?"

Cee-Cee nods.

"When are you sleeping over? This weekend? Want to?"

More than anything, she wants to say, but Nonna stands in the way. "I'm working on it…not easy."

The third bell rings.

Mary Margaret flashes a pointy-toothed grin. "We'll see about that!" She disappears a final time.

AFTER SCHOOL IN THE girl's locker room, Mary Margaret shows Cee-Cee the pale spider scratches from Brother Ignacio's belt. For a brief shining moment, Cee-Cee understands Mary Margaret's secret wish that she press a small white finger into each of her wounds and heal them. A tiny miracle just for her in the name of best friends forever. If only it worked that way.

Cee-Cee says, "I don't see anything."

Mary Margaret pulls her shirt up higher. "Right here."

"Does it hurt?" Cee-Cee marvels at the steep price of devotion.

Mary Margaret grins. "Worth it!"

ROADIE STANDS OUTSIDE IN the cold waiting for his sister.

Some mornings he skips school entirely and makes his way through the wheat fields to the Catholic junior high. The nuns who teach there are methodical, throwing open the back doors at ten every day to let the children loose for morning recess. At least there's something reliable: the opportunity to see his sister, talk with her, make sure she's okay.

The Sisters shout encouragement, hustling along after the children. "Get the blood flowing, people! It's good for the heart!"

Roadie prefers to look away from their strange holiness, weird shoes, veils with dresses cut to the knees, which are fat or knobby. During recess the Sisters stretch, eat fruit, take orderly laps around the blacktop, while the children play ball or skip rope. The nicer ones smile and point to Cee-Cee; others shoo him away, frowning.

Roadie is careful not to show up too often.

Today three sturdy Sisters stand under the eaves, rolling cigarettes. They don't seem to notice any of the cutups on the playground stealing hats and tugging scarves, smart alecks who deserve a good thrashing. The imposing women don't glance up at Roadie but stay in a tight huddle, whispering and breathing smoke. Roadie dodges past them, heading for Cee-Cee, who is much smaller than the other sixth graders.

Usually the girls are jumping rope, which Cee-Cee likes

because she's the best at it. But today, a group of girls surround her laughing and talking. One of them braids her hair; another holds her hand.

Maybe Cee-Cee hasn't been entirely ruined.

Seeing him at the jungle gym, she peels away from her friends, not even checking over her shoulder to see what the Sisters are up to.

Roadie pats her shoulder, awkwardly attempts a hug.

"Weird that it's so cold out," he says. "Should be warmer for the end of March."

Cee-Cee puts her hands in her coat. "I guess."

"Things all right?" It's the only thing he ever manages to ask.

"Yeah."

"It's okay at Nonna's?"

"It's nice." Cee-Cee says. "She lets me practice on her."

"Nonna?"

"She's always amazed when I pick out her card."

Roadie smiles.

"She doesn't know it's just a trick," Cee-Cee says.

They stand in the cool morning breeze, not knowing what else to say.

"Pauly moved his thumb last week." It's the best Roadie can do, all he has. "The nurses asked him to—and he did it."

"I heard."

Roadie wishes he could say he's sorry, but he doesn't know where to start. "Glory thinks it's a sign that he'll come back."

She stares at the ground.

Roadie backpedals. "The doctors say it's probably a twitch, though."

Cee-Cee shrugs. "I better get back."

"Can you tell me again before you go," Roadie looks past the school, past Nonna's house, to the horizon beyond. "What the lady said?"

"She said you are loved."

"She said me—my name specifically?"

"Yeah, she said you and the others like you—you're God's special ones." Cee-Cee scuffs her shoes on the pavement. "'Cause it's harder for you."

"Are you sure?"

"She loves everyone, Roadie." The bell rings, and Cee-Cee's classmates line up at the door. "That's the thing people don't get. We're all special in some way."

Roadie takes a couple of blank notebooks out of his book bag and gives them to his sister. "I can get more for you next week."

"Thanks," she says, taking them in her arms.

"Oh," he says, pulling packs of Wrigley's gum out of his pocket. "These too."

She smiles and takes the gum. "Double the flavor."

"Yeah," he says sadly. "Double the fun."

Helpless, then, he watches her walk away.

LATER, LEANING AGAINST THE concession stand at Romeville Free Academy, Roadie shivers in the cold. He worries that the frozen months are here to stay, that the longest winter of his life will never give way to spring. He watches the morning sun glint off all the parked cars in the high school lot: windshields, hoods, tire rims. He knows which vehicles belong to the teachers and which to the upper classmen. He knows who takes off at lunch and doesn't come back. When someone leaves the headlights on, Roadie reports it to the office secretary, who makes an announcement over the loud speaker. It's like paying something back. Roadie hopes it counts.

Mostly he watches. Standing outside the school, he waits, watches, and waits some more. Jeremy Patrick stopped coming to school on his motorbike weeks ago. Now he takes the school bus, or gets rides with his mother, or hitches with his new friends.

Roadie knows because he has become an observer.

No more surprises.

If done right, watching will save the world, and he will never again be caught by surprise in the woods. He will never again freeze and let terrible things happen. He is determined to be alert, to face down every single moment of the rest of his life, hoping that one day his redemption will come. He will repent and be forgiven. He will return to his old self, or better yet, a new improved future self.

For now, he gets what he deserves. Jeremy refuses to look at him when they pass in the hall.

Roadie counts up the facts, organizes the details, tries to predict the moods and actions of others. He draws conclusions, anticipating the potential outcome of every situation. It's exhausting to live this way. A constant stabbing behind his left eye is a pain designed to remind him of his cowardice. But when he is redeemed, it will all be worth it.

And why shouldn't he be redeemed?

Shouldn't there be a moment of salvation for him? After all, wasn't he ruined, in an unimaginable instant of destruction and surprise? The smallest fraction of that day, a mere speck in a lifetime, is exactly how quickly the terrible thing happened, the thing in the woods he cannot name. He can still hear the ticking in his head—the moments he was unable to save his sister.

His parents know he's to blame. He wasn't a watcher then like he is now. When Glory looks at him, he knows she thinks: *You were supposed to look out for them.* When Frank speaks to him, he can feel the disappointment. *It's your fault for not paying attention.*

The first time he cornered Jeremy Patrick at school was after Christmas break. Jeremy was at the drinking fountain by the school auditorium.

Please don't tell anyone about the woods; people won't understand.
Jeremy laughed in his face. *Why would I ever talk about you?*

It's like that guy from CCD class, Bonhoeffer, the one who tried to kill Hitler, Roadie said, trying to make Jeremy remember a time when they meant everything to each other. *The Sister said he was made a saint to let people know that you can't just let horrible things happen without trying to stop them. But we didn't try! Don't you see? We didn't do anything.*

When Roadie tried to stop Jeremy from leaving, Jeremy shoved him into the wall.

Leave me alone! He walked away. *I don't know you.*

It wouldn't have mattered if Roadie had kept talking forever. His friendship with Jeremy Patrick was over the moment they stepped into those woods. Roadie knew it then. And standing in front of the high school on the coldest day in March, he knows it anew.

Another thing he knows: The number of steps you take into the forest is the same number of steps you have to take out.

AT THE SECOND BELL, a handful of burnouts scurry to class, leaving Roadie alone to bounce on the balls of his feet and turn his back against the wind.

He gets up every morning to catch the bus, as if nothing bad ever happened. Anthony goes to a special school in East Verona with Norbert Sasso on a stubby van that picks him up in the driveway. Cee-Cee is with the Sisters across from Nonna's, and the doctors say Baby Pauly's brain is damaged, so even if he comes out of that coma, he'll probably never go to school again.

Jumping up and down in the cold, Roadie catches a glimpse of the familiar red hunting jacket through the tall grass. The guy he's been waiting for. In even strides, the guy glides across the parking lot, offering up the same wry smile he always does.

"Where the hell have you been?" Roadie says. "It's freezing out here."

"Mary Jane's worth it, Franco Bianco," the kid says. "Probably the only girl for you."

"Fuck you, Iaccamo."

"Aw, c'mon!" Roadie's pot dealer is in a cheerful mood today. "You think I don't know about you? You don't think it's the same for me, man?"

Roadie finds the uninvited familiarity irritating. He gives they guy money for three fat joints, watching him count and pocket the cash.

"Okay! Fire it up, man!"

The dealer is five years older than Roadie—an unbridgeable gap—but he's not bad-looking if you squint and the light's just right—the only reason Roadie hangs around to smoke with him.

"You don't even know my first name, do you, Bianco?"

Roadie looks at the orange-haired Neanderthal. Could he be the messenger of Roadie's redemption, the one who delivers his salvation?

"It's Liam! I think you should know that, Bianco."

Roadie turns away from the wind to shield his joint. "Does it matter?"

But Liam doesn't hear; he's too busy swallowing smoke into his lungs and making pronouncements in a strangled voice. "Mary Jane will fuck your brain."

Roadie takes another hit, considers going inside for fifth period.

"You want to see something?" Liam asks.

"Nah, I have math in a few minutes." Roadie is just a piece of dust in a gigantic universe, which doles out either shit or favors, depending on who you are, and what you've done. But every little thing counts toward something. "Um…thanks anyway, Liam."

"C'mon," Liam says, grabbing Roadie's hand.

Running through the tall grass after the red-haired dealer, Roadie gets a cramp. After skipping gym for weeks, he is out of shape—desperate, stupid. Stopping to catch his breath, he wonders what the hell he's doing.

"Stop! Wait!"

Liam lopes back around, graceful as a boxer. "What's wrong?"

"I've got to go back," Roadie says. "You can't help me."

Liam sends a cackle up over the field. "Hell no! You're going to help *me*, Franco Bianco!"

"Seriously," Roadie says. "This is stupid."

"It's not stupid." Liam folds his arms across his chest, looking straight up at the sky. "My sister needs help, and you're the person I'm asking."

Roadie swallows. "I'm not good with sisters."

"It's not about you, idiot." Liam grabs Roadie's shoulders. "Just bring my sister some food next week. That's all I'm asking. Fruit and bread, something from your refrigerator. I've got a cop on my ass."

Roadie is wary.

"Just a couple of days. Until I can figure something else out."

"Figure what out?"

Liam pinches a handful of weeds, flirting. "It's a long story."

Roadie drops into the tall grass. "Okay."

Liam sits. "You can't tell anyone. I'm trusting you."

"Who am I going to tell?"

Liam touches Roadie's sleeve. "My sister Eileena is your age. You know her, right?"

"Everyone knows her. Your family is on the news as much as mine."

Liam nods. "Everyone thinks she's dead—except me and my little brother. And I guess one of the nuns at my little brother's school, and this cop."

"What cop?"

"Never mind." Liam frowns. "Just leave food outside the last rail car in the old train cemetery."

"She's alive?" Roadie says. "You've talked to her?"

"Food's always gone. I leave her notes."

Roadie shakes his head; he knows what it's like to be so

desperate that you get stupid about things.

"Bianco, just make sure nothing bad happens, okay? How hard is that?"

"Harder than you think," Roadie says.

Roadie feels the wind rippling through the field and hears the hushed sounds of each stalk of grass brushing up against its brother. The quiet rustling, like whispering, fills him with a boundless sorrow. The worst he's ever felt. Dropping his head in his hands, he shakes some tears out of his eyes.

"Aw, Christ, Bianco," Liam says gently.

There are no words for Roadie's sadness, no sound, no reason; there's only the rush of the grass telling secrets. Soon, in the distance, they will hear the school bell ring away another day. Liam throws an arm over Roadie. They sit like this for a long time waiting for Roadie's grief to come to an end.

PARKED ILLEGALLY IN THE crosswalk at Our Lady at the end of the school day on Friday, Glory watches Cee-Cee weave between the big yellow school buses.

During these few months away from home, her daughter has become a complete stranger. Now close up, Cee-Cee leans into the half-open passenger window.

"Hi, Glory."

A tall girl with matching braids salutes Glory from the sidewalk.

"Hi, baby." Glory smiles. "Who's this?"

Cee-Cee opens the passenger door, gesturing for the girl to get in the back, where the vinyl seats are warm from the afternoon sun. "This is my best friend."

The girl drapes herself over the seat and offers Glory a gap-toothed grin. "You're prettier than I expected!"

Glory is on probation; she wears a simple outfit, hair pulled back, barely any makeup at all.

"Am I supposed to know you?"

The girl holds out her hand. "Mary Margaret Cortina."

Glory drops her head slightly, grabbing the steering wheel. "Is this necessary?"

"She's coming with us to see Baby Pauly today," Cee-Cee says. "And then I'm staying over at Mary Margaret's house."

Glory should be thrilled that her oddball daughter has any friends at all. Even this girl, whose mother is the topic of all kinds of gossip. Marion Patrick says there's a cemetery on the hill behind the girl's house filled with dead babies. And that's just since they moved to town.

"And we're having a sleepover."

"Sleepover," Glory says. "Does Nonna know?"

"We need to study together," Mary Margaret lies. "Big project for school."

"Nonna said it was okay."

Mary Margaret grins. "Finally."

Glory is still catching up. "But what about *our* family dinner? I'm picking up fish fries. Your brothers will be disappointed if you don't come."

Cee-Cee doesn't blink. "They'll get over it."

When did she become so hard? Glory wonders.

"What will I tell the social worker?"

Cee-Cee shrugs.

"My mom's making tuna noodle casserole; Norbie Sasso is coming too. Then we'll get to work. Tell the social worker we've got a big school project on our hands."

Glory addresses the interloper from the rear view mirror. "Listen, honey, this is all I get right now, a couple of hours a week, a drive to the hospital. It's not much, but it's something. So…"

Mary Margaret nods. "You won't even know I'm here. I don't have to eat ice cream with you after either. I'll just watch, silently."

Glory looks at Cee-Cee, who stares out the windshield.

"Mostly Glory smokes cigarettes, so you can have hers."

Glory takes a deep breath to keep from losing her cool. "You'll be happy to know, smarty, that I quit yesterday."

Mary Margaret gives Glory a friendly punch on the arm. "Hey, me too! I quit all the time."

A dwarf cinched in an orange-neon safety vest herds a group of students across the street; they disappear into the waiting mouths of fat yellow vehicles. Glory rubs her eyes.

"Are we going?" Cee-Cee says.

Sighing, Glory weaves the car through the maze of buses and turns silently onto Main Street. She needs to stop blaming everyone else for what's happened. Most of all, she needs to stop blaming Cee-Cee.

She's just a kid, Glory reminds herself.

Anthony tells her it's good that Cee-Cee lives with Nonna. *Good for us.*

She's afraid to ask him why.

The state mandated that Anthony attend sessions with a tiny Asian social worker. She seems to be making progress with him. He is helpful lately, hopeful, almost calm. There are whole days during which he doesn't twitch, not even once.

Frank is more doubtful. *How about the constant washing?*

The social worker assures Glory and Frank that a little soap and water is nothing to fear. *He suffers from a simple adjustment disorder. Common in adolescence, and perhaps his normal response to tragedy.*

Normal? Shrinks make Frank angry. *You should see our water bill.*

His hands are raw, Glory adds. *The skin is peeling.*

Loss is tricky, says the social worker. *Lotion does wonders for chapping.*

At All Saints Rehabilitation Center, Mary Margaret is the last to enter Baby Pauly's room. She touches one of the clanking machines. "Holy Cannoli!"

Glory heads over to the bed.

Baby Pauly's hands are stretched out and tied to aluminum paddles. His kidneys are working great, the doctors say, common in someone so young. Now if only his brain and lungs would kick in.

"Hello, little handsome!" Glory sings "How are you today?"

Mary Margaret hangs back. "Does she always talk like that?"

"The nurses say people in comas can hear," Cee-Cee explains. "She doesn't want him to miss anything."

Glory continues in her cheerful voice, "A beautiful, sunshiny Friday. The frogs are jumping. The grass is growing; you can hear it if you listen."

Mary Margaret rubs her fingers along the bed railing. "Is he going to wake up?"

"Of course he is." Glory rubs Pauly's waxy skin. "Aren't you, Baby? Everybody's waiting!"

Mary Margaret nudges Cee-Cee with her elbow. "Wake him up."

Glory takes a closer look at the neat weave of Mary Margaret's braids, the explosion of freckles across her nose, the faintly ironic smile. She doesn't like her one bit, she decides. But there Cee-Cee is, holding the girl's hand, happier than she's ever been.

Mary Margaret looks around. "Just call Jesus. He'll fix things up!"

"It doesn't work like that," Cee-Cee says.

Glory smiles, pleased that the annoying girl doesn't get it anymore than she does.

ANTHONY IS GLAD WHEN Glory gets home and announces that the family dinner is canceled. It gives him some time to breathe.

If only Glory would stop going nuts because her plans fell through, everything would be perfect. *Status quo.* He overhears her pleading with the social worker to change dinner supervision from Friday to Sunday, so Cee-Cee can sleep over at a friend's house, and Glory can still have her precious dinner.

You know how girls are about their friends? Glory says, trying not to sound desperate. *How can I say no? But as a family, we also need our together time.*

The call doesn't seem to go very well. Glory takes a pill and goes straight to her bedroom to lie down.

Anthony knocks on her door. "You okay?"

She says something he can't hear, which is okay with him.

On the outside Anthony is now a regular boy, calm, cautious, almost confident. He's learned what to say and how to say it; he knows what to do to keep the social workers and teachers off his back and get by without raising eyebrows. On the inside, somewhere remote, Anthony's old self, twitching and flinching, raging like a bull—a tiny, tiny bull—is too diminished to cause anyone harm.

Too small for even Frank and Glory to notice.

If he manages to keep the internal roaring to a whisper, Anthony sleeps like a baby. Otherwise, the chant keeps him up: *Pauly—my fault, Cee-Cee—my fault, Roadie—gay.* Even a pillow over his head doesn't help.

To keep his good self big, and his bad self little, Anthony must avoid contamination. He must wear the same-colored clothes, sit only in wooden chairs, eat food cut into small portions. He avoids the school lunchroom, stands at the back of the auditorium for assembly, but allows church because of the wooden pews.

Cars are tricky.

At home, Anthony prefers to eat on his own bed, though he can sit at the dinner table for forty-five minutes, as long as no meat is served. Red meat is the worst; also anyone who eats red meat.

On Fridays at the family dinner, all bets are off. Even the slightest problem can set him off: a grain of salt on the tablecloth, a wrong-colored napkin. He has to clamp himself down, then close his eyes; he has to wait for his sister to leave.

Today he's gotten a pass. He is free.

He only has to deal with Roadie, who in no way counts. And when Frank and Moonie get home, they'll let him do what he wants. He can probably take his dinner plate and eat in his room. He can go a whole night without anyone touching him.

His social workers and teachers are the only exception to the "No Touch" rule; they get too angry when he slaps them away. Now he suffers their patting his head with a smile. When they give him a hug, which some do regularly, he puts his arms around them in a wide circle and mimics affection. At school he has to respect their rules. He does what he's told because he must.

At home he strips off his contaminated uniform and takes a hot shower. He puts on matching clean clothes, a blue shirt and blue jeans, including blue sneakers that have never been worn outside the house.

Some days it takes five showers to get clean.

There are other rules too: no singing, no soft fruit, no animal skin, no perfume, no garbage, no chewing gum, no inhaling near other people who are exhaling, especially meat eaters. No talking on the bus to Norbert Sasso with his constant baloney sandwiches.

There is salvation in some air, but there's no way to know for sure. Anthony's lungs get tight and his skin pops when the air is bad.

Sleep is the only way to get truly clean. That's why it's okay to touch Baby Pauly's hand—he is permanently asleep, clean forever. Which is how Anthony knows he is the one keeping his brother alive.

Later, in the jump seat of Uncle Moonie's truck, Anthony studies the back of his father's head. He also notices how Moonie is starting to go bald. He listens to Roadie's slow steady breathing in the dark by his side.

If Anthony could forever remain in motion, untouched, always going somewhere but never arriving, his life might work out okay.

Out the car window, downtown Romeville whizzes by.

Anthony has to play along, pretend he's okay. He would have tried to avoid Frank and his "night out with the guys," but he has a new rule to avoid complaining and resisting. People touch you a lot less, he's noticed, if you keep your thoughts to yourself and go with the flow.

Uncle Moonie drives, whistling an airy tune—almost undetectable.

Ms. Ling-Ling, his social worker, says everything is actually under Anthony's control; that's the biggest secret. She says all Anthony has to do is to tap into "The Giant Good" by thinking the right thoughts. All he needs to do is plug into joy and goodness and peace. Closing his eyes, he tries to think of all that is good in the world.

Something specific: Frank taking him to the zoo when he was little.

Something else: Nonna praying in church for everyone's soul.

He runs into trouble when he thinks about any of the others: Glory, Roadie, Baby Pauly.

Moonie drives toward All Saints, arm resting out the window. "Anyone up for ice cream later? Hard to believe how warm it is for April."

It's a mild night, warmer weather than they've had, a hint of rain in the air. There are already crickets chirping, as if warm summer were only a minute away, instead of months.

Ice cream is good. If Roadie orders for him, Anthony won't

have to get out of the car.

Frank rolls down the window. "I hate this shit."

Moonie counters. "Nothing we can do, Frank."

Anthony feels a twitching between his legs: Not good. Frank's ideas are always dangerous. Everything might still be okay, though, if he can find something good to think about, something extra good. But first Frank needs to shut up.

"Turn off those damn machines," Frank says.

Roadie clears his throat. "You can't do that; he'll die."

Frank turns around in his seat.

Anthony can see the white parts of his father's eyes shining in the dark, clearer since he started going to AA with Uncle Moonie. But the view makes Anthony's small self grow a little bit bigger. He closes his eyes, imagines Frank hauling off and hitting his brother square in the face.

Not good.

Anthony's social worker says it only works if there are more good thoughts than bad.

"I didn't ask for your opinion, did I?" Frank tells Roadie. "Anyway, he *is* dead."

Sweat beads up on Anthony's forehead. He tries not to picture Roadie disappearing into the nobody Frank thinks he is. He tries not to think about where they are going, All Saints, where bodies are naked and twisted under thin sheets. Anthony imagines his own naked body with nurses coming in and out to bathe him with a sponge. He cannot tell: good or bad?

Bad, he decides.

The other thing his social worker says is to think before speaking. She says, *Try to remember that other people are human beings too.* Just thinking the words *human being* helps him ignore the image of Frank's fist popping into Roadie's mouth.

Resigned, Frank faces forward again.

Moonie continues driving. Roadie continues breathing. They turn into the parking lot, a puzzling jumble of yellow lines, arrows pointing every which way.

Anthony tries not to think about Frank shutting down Baby Pauly's machines.

"No use talking about it," Frank says, but it's too late.

The idea is out there now.

Anthony squeezes his eyes shut and thinks the best thought he knows, the one he keeps in reserve in case of an emergency: *Sister Saint Cecilia.*

MARY MARGARET USHERS CEE-CEE into her house.

"We're home!"

Slamming the door behind them, Mary Margaret slows her pace to coo at a big fat happy baby who is sitting in a contraption on the kitchen table.

A wan woman in white slacks, Mary Margaret's mother appears from the other room. She has a blonde pageboy with blue eye shadow caked up to her eyebrows, but somehow she seems deflated, a day-old balloon still recovering from this most recent baby.

"You must be Mary Margaret's new friend?"

"Best friend," Cee-Cee says.

Humming a lullaby, Mary Margaret's mother sits to feed her baby a bottle while she admires a stack of clothes at her elbow.

"After num-nums, we'll play dress up," she says.

Mary Margaret frowns. "Hello, Tiger-Wiger. Were you a good boy today?"

"He doesn't have an official name yet," Mrs. Cortina tells Cee-Cee. "We're waiting."

"Superstitious," Mary Margaret says.

The little house has dark wooden panels, a crucifix above the sink, and orange curtains everywhere.

"He's such a good baby when he's not screaming," Mrs. Cortina says. "Aren't you, Brother Boy?"

"Ignore her," Mary Margaret says.

Once they are in the den, a small orange corner of a big open room across from the kitchen, Mary Margaret makes a beeline for the TV and turns on the local news.

Mrs. Cortina comes to the doorway, holding the baby out in the air. He is wearing a striped blue hat and overalls. "Turn that off, please; you have a guest. Besides, it's depressing!"

Cee-Cee and Mary Margaret consider Mrs. Cortina with a single gaze.

"Look at Dumpling Wumpling." She bounces the baby. "He's a train conductor!"

Mary Margaret switches the station to a flash of glum teenagers exiting a church. *Still to come,* the voice-over announces, *Orphans from Canada at Peace Rally! And the weather!*

Mrs. Cortina comes back a few minutes later holding Tiger out like a toy. "Look! Now Pea-Pod's a football player!"

Cee-Cee smiles at the tiny mesh jersey stuffed with baby chub, player number zero-zero. Satisfied, Mrs. Cortina leaves the room.

"Where does she get all those costumes?"

Mary Margaret shrugs. "She's like that with a new baby until she gets sick of it."

The local news gives way to national news. The somber theme song and Walter Cronkite get lost in the shuffle when Mrs. Cortina drifts back into the room carrying a plate of crackers and cheese. This time the baby is dressed as a sailor.

"Wash those filthy hands," Mrs. Cortina tells Cee-Cee. "You're covered in ink."

When Cee-Cee returns from the bathroom, the news is blaring away with a clip of the president sweating it out in front of the cameras.

Mrs. Cortina gasps. "I hate the news!"

Then, with a cloud of unknowing, Mary Margaret's mother ambles out of the room.

"She's kind of weird," Mary Margaret says.

"It's okay," Cee-Cee says. "The crackers are good."

Mary Margaret stuffs her mouth with cheese. "Do you think you can find them, Cee-Cee?"

Cee-Cee adjusts her plaid jumper and Mary Margaret's neckerchief.

"*Them* who?"

"Eileena Brice Iaccamo and her." Mary Margaret points to the television screen as it displays a haunting colored stencil of a young woman with reddish cheeks and mousy hair. Underneath another girl's name flashes. Missing person in California.

They stare at the bluish screen.

"There's always another one," Mary Margaret whispers.

Cee-Cee takes a sip of cola, thinking it over.

"I bet if you close your eyes," Mary Margaret says, "you can find every girl who's ever gone missing in the history of the world."

The thought makes Cee-Cee tired.

Cooking dinner, Mrs. Cortina jokes around in a fake Irish accent. "I am Sister Holy Mackerel! Pleased to meet you!"

Mary Margaret cracks up, as her mother shakes Cee-Cee's hand.

"So you're the little holy terror everyone's talking about, are you?" Sister Holy Mackerel asks. "Perform a miracle or it's thirty lashes of the belt!"

Glory is never fun like this. Cee-Cee laughs and claps when Mary Margaret's mother finishes clowning around.

She even takes a bow.

Cee-Cee shows them all her card tricks and Mrs. Cortina is best at guessing how Cee-Cee counts the piles and figures out which card is which.

"You could be a magician," Cee-Cee says.

"You don't even know how true that is!" Mrs. Cortina says,

enjoying Cee-Cee's compliment.

By the time Norbert arrives, doling out bear hugs, the casserole is ready.

"Tuna noodle with peas!" he whispers.

"I don't know how you stand living at your grandmother's, Cee-Cee," Mrs. Cortina says. "It can't be any fun."

"Nonna's okay. She's just old."

"*Old world* is more like it." Mrs. Cortina bobs little Tiger on her knee, patting him hard between the shoulders to get out a burp. His head wobbles as she holds him by the armpits. "Ladies and gentleman, I have an announcement: I am going out on ambulance crew tonight. So this party ends in half an hour."

Mary Margaret pours a ketchup puddle.

Norbert makes a siren with his throat. "Emergency. Medical. Technician."

"That's right!" Mrs. Cortina smiles. "My crew provides medical services to people in need. We're all trained volunteers."

Mrs. Cortina isn't nearly as pretty as Glory. She wears white shoes with big rubber Tootsie-roll soles. Her face is made up like a porcelain doll with eyebrows plucked into harsh, uneven lines. Cee-Cee can almost see each individual granule of powder on her face. She reminds her of the women at All Saints Rehabilitation Hospital.

"Are you a nurse?" Cee-Cee asks.

"Heck no," she laughs. "I'm in it for the fires, the heart attacks and the drownings."

Norbert pats Cee-Cee's arm, looking slightly distressed. "Uh-oh."

"Nothing personal, honey." Mrs. Cortina takes her plate to the sink. "I just like helping out in an emergency. It really gets my heart pumping."

She opens a black medical bag stuffed with equipment: several clear plastic respirators with blue tubing. Cee-Cee has seen equipment just like it in Baby Pauly's room.

Mrs. Cortina smiles. "These help people breathe."

"Like a little boy?" Cee-Cee asks.

Snapping the bag closed, she looks at Cee-Cee. "No, sweetheart, someone younger."

"A baby!" Norbert says.

Mrs. Cortina tilts her head, smiling sadly. "Norbert, can you please tell me for the last time why that darn chicken crossed the road?"

Norbert busts into wild laughter.

Mary Margaret rolls her eyes. "Can't we get another joke around here?"

"Norbert?"

Mouth full of noodles, he answers: "Because he didn't have thumbs to hitchhike!"

Mrs. Cortina fills the room with high-pitched laughter, then starts firing out instructions: "Clean up these dishes, chocolate cake for dessert; I'll drop Norbert home on my way to the ambulance."

"You two, stay out of trouble!" Mrs. Cortina says. "Get to bed before your stepfather comes home from bowling. If he's early, stay out of his way!"

Norbert keeps chewing and smiling.

"You know how he is, Mary Margaret." Mrs. Cortina pulls a baby-blue knit vest over her white uniform. "No need to rile him up with people he can't understand."

"What about Tiger?"

Everyone turns and looks at the baby lying on his back, smearing spit onto his feet. "Just put him to bed and give him milk if he cries."

Norbert stops chewing.

Mary Margaret watches her mother. "But what if…"

"Don't be silly, Mary Margaret Josephine!" Mrs. Cortina gets her coat. "That bad business is behind us now."

By 8:45, Mary Margaret and Cee-Cee zip two sleeping bags together on the floor and sit cross-legged on pillows, chewing gum.

"Let's go out on the roof," Cee-Cee says, looking out the window. "It's so warm out."

"Okay," Mary Margaret says.

Cee-Cee gets up and cranks open the window. "The garage roof's right there."

Mary Margaret steps out first. "It's getting chilly again."

When they sit on the asphalt tiles, Cee-Cee throws an arm over her. "You can see everything from up here."

Cee-Cee thinks about Baby Pauly, whose feet are turning in.

Mary Margaret thinks about Eileena Brice Iaccamo.

"Girls can go missing a long time and still be alive," Mary Margaret says. "Do you think you can still find her?"

Cee-Cee thinks about filling Mary Margaret in about the Mirandas, but decides better of it. She has promised Nonna, Sister Amanda, and Brother Joe to keep quiet about them. Besides what would she say? She doesn't know who they are or how they are related to Romeville's missing girls. That everything's connected is only a feeling.

"I don't know." Cee-Cee spits her gum up and out into the dark yard as far as she can.

Mary Margaret spits hers too but it lands in a plop a few inches from her bare feet, which makes them laugh. She lights up one of her mother's cigarettes and smokes it halfway. "Let's go back in."

In their sleeping bags, Mary Margaret rolls on her back, not letting go of Cee-Cee's hand.

"Missing girls give me a stomach ache."

"Maybe that's just what it feels like before a miracle," Mary Margaret mutters, drifting off to sleep.

For a long time, Cee-Cee is restless. She hears Mary Margaret's stepfather come home first, and then her mother. She hears the house go completely silent. She thinks about Mary Margaret's baby brother down in the nursery. He smells sweet like powder and carrots and looks so peaceful when you put him in his crib. That's the thing about babies; they are so impossible with their soft skulls. How does anyone ever grow up?

Down the hall, the very same thought ramps up Mrs. Cortina's anxiety. She can't bear that her baby boy might someday suffer at the whims of a cruel world. Cee-Cee tries to think about something else, but as soon as Mary Margaret starts to snore, she slips out of the sleeping bag and heads for Tiger's nursery.

She stops in the doorway, watching at first.

In the orange glow of the giraffe nightlight, Mrs. Cortina stands over the crib. Cee-Cee can hear her mixed-up thoughts: *I am the only one who loves him enough.*

Cee-Cee steps forward and reaches for the plastic tube in her hand.

Mrs. Cortina tightens her grip. Her voice comes out slightly strangled: "Are you for real, Cee-Cee?"

She may not be able to help her own brother now, but Cee-Cee can save Tiger Cortina with a single lie. "I'll get the angels to make sure he's okay."

Mrs. Cortina looks at Cee-Cee hard. "Do you double swear?"

"Triple swear," Cee-Cee says. "On my grandmother's life."

Cee-Cee loosens Mrs. Cortina's fingers and wedges out the tiny respirator, also removing the pillow from under her arm.

There may not be flaming angels or virgins singing this time, but Cee-Cee can still believe that something good has happened here, maybe something holy. At least Cee-Cee can pretend the way ordinary people do.

She will learn to pray and hope for the best just like everyone else.

As the Sisters say at school assembly: *Each child is a child of God.*

Abandoned, perhaps—but not without hope.

ACROSS TOWN THE NEXT morning, Nonna strips the sheets off all the beds in her house. She empties the garbage pails, and dusts her holy statues: St. Cecilia with her harp, St. Therese with her roses, and St. Faustina looking stern and slightly stunned by God's mercy.

At five a.m., the sunlight is scant, and the town is still asleep.

Dressed for Mass, Nonna threads her way along the hallway, stopping to pick up lint off the carpet and wipe down the handrails.

She pauses outside Cee-Cee's room and says a prayer.

Somewhere in the street a horn honks.

Nonna thinks of Cee-Cee sleeping under somebody else's roof. She will need to get used to this view: Cee-Cee grown up and walking away.

They all go eventually, she thinks.

Nonna passes a famous portrait of the Blessed Virgin Mary. *Mother of My God,* a phrase that has always brought great comfort. Nonna's own life has been a tribute to motherhood and all the accompanying heartaches and mistakes. Children never turn out as you hope, but there are always surprises. Who could have imagined Nonna having someone to love so late in life in Cee-Cee?

Then, she stops what she is doing and feels something significant is happening. It happens the way she always hoped it would: a warm presence pressing at her back, the Jesus-of-her-mind arriving in glory.

Making her way through the house, she listens to the voice: *Lie down, woman, and find peace; I have chosen you.*

Though her blouse and skirt are perfectly pressed, her shoes laced up and tied tight, Nonna lies down on her bed. She has already made up its smooth edges and hospital corners, but she stretches out on the covers just the same.

In the distance, another horn sounds, long and insistent.

It's not for her any more; she closes her eyes.

When Cee-Cee gets home from Mary Margaret's house, the shades are drawn in Nonna's bedroom. The bureau is lined with old perfume bottles, spare rosaries, yellowing photographs of people now long dead. There's a picture of Frank and Glory with a baby in their arms, Anthony. There are several of Nonna herself, looking resolute on her wedding day. Except for a shawl and some yarn, the rocking chair where she likes to crochet is empty. Cee-Cee rocks in it for a moment before getting up and going to the bed where Nonna lies fully dressed. It's not quite noon.

"Why are you in bed?" Cee-Cee says. "Are you sick?"

She doesn't stir.

"I'm home, Nonna." Cee-Cee presses a hand on her grandmother's cold arm. No motion, no warmth. "Aw, don't be mad."

Opening her eyes and looking at the ceiling for a moment, Nonna props herself up on an elbow and looks at Cee-Cee suspiciously.

Cee-Cee pulls out the yo-yo Mary Margaret gave her and shows Nonna her first trick: Walk the Dog. "Not bad, right?"

Nonna shrugs.

"It's really no big deal to sleep over at someone else's house," Cee-Cee say. "Kids do it all the time."

"She wants to kill the baby—*la madre?*" Nonna asks; sometimes she prays for Mrs. Cortina.

"Not anymore."

"*Miracolo?*"

Cee-Cee shrugs. "It's hard to tell, but I'm pretty sure that baby will get a name."

"Promise me," Nonna says, repeating the instructions she offers Cee-Cee at least once a month. "Something happens, you go. But only to the Mother General."

"I'm not going to become a nun, Nonna," Cee-Cee says.

"Go. Promise." Nonna thinks it over some more. "Only Amanda."

"Let's make lunch," Cee-Cee says, palming her yo-yo. "Aren't you hungry?"

Nonna frowns at Cee-Cee's messy hair and points to a brush on the bureau. Cee-Cee gets it and sits at the edge of the bed so Nonna can undo her braids and remake them over neatly.

"I had a nice dream," she says.

In Nonna's dream, lights streamed along the highway, and she was floating above, held up safely by something immense and warm and happy. She understood everything: the suffering, the world, her life, the meaning of all things.

Jesus was there, and all the angels and saints.

"Was I in your dream?" Cee-Cee asks.

"You were my dream," Nonna says.

AFTER A LUNCH OF sausage and peppers, Nonna feels the great warm light coming toward her again. She has always been obedient, riding out life's ups and downs without complaining. How strange it seems now that the world should go on without her. It will grind right along with all the same conflict and love, terror and beauty. Now standing in the transom, Nonna sees all this and feels happy at the chance to let it all go: the overflowing toilets, the crying children, the broken hearts.

She's not afraid of dying. She's saved herself through prayer.

Nonna clears the dishes and wipes down the counter. She kisses the top of Cee-Cee's head and makes her way upstairs.

Cee-Cee sits and waits, building a tower of cards.

When the sun starts its ordinary, spectacular descent, she gets up slowly, careful not to knock down her creation.

She puts on her coat, and walks out into the late April afternoon.

Hearing the lonely sound of her own footsteps on the pavement, Cee-Cee realizes for the first time since coming out of the woods that she is still alive.

THE THIRD

It's half-past five, which means the girl isn't coming.

Amanda has learned that not every girl can be reached; not everyone saved. In her line of work, you have to be patient.

In a separate pew of Our Lady Queen of Sorrows' chapel, Cee-Cee is also kneeling and thinking, but Amanda does not know she's there.

They are praying, but not together.

Amanda sits at the front of the church, Cee-Cee at the back. Cee-Cee watches Amanda straighten the missals on the little wooden shelf, waiting for the right moment to announce herself. Finally, Amanda makes the sign of the cross and gets up, genuflecting at the altar. Out of the corner of her eye, she catches sight of Cee-Cee's small shadow coming up the aisle.

"Sister Pius, is that you?"

"No. It's me."

"Oh, Cee-Cee!" Amanda's heart lifts. "On a Saturday? To what do I owe this pleasure?"

Cee-Cee points down the hall outside the chapel at a closed door leading to the recreation room. "My father's in there in a meeting. I have to tell him something."

"Unsupervised?" Amanda seems alarmed. "Does your grandmother know? Shall we go find her?"

"No, Sister," Cee-Cee says. "Nonna can't help now."

Amanda walks briskly toward the girl. "What do you mean?"

"She's gone," Cee-Cee sobs.

In the center aisle of the empty chapel, Amanda drops on one knee and wraps her arms around Cee-Cee as if to absorb her sorrow.

She cries for both their losses: Cee-Cee for losing her grandmother; Amanda for feeling like an orphan all over again. When their tears dry up, Amanda wipes Cee-Cee's face.

"I'll see to this," she says. "You're safe with me."

From the phone outside the rectory, Amanda calls an ambulance and arranges to meet the police across the street. Commandeering the first person she comes across, Amanda barks an order.

"Bring Cee-Cee to the sacristy, Sister Edward," she says. "Don't let anyone near her until I get back."

Sister Edward hurries Cee-Cee back into the chapel. "What happened, Miss Bianco? What is this about?"

"Nonna died in her sleep," Cee-Cee says.

"I see." Sister Edward checks her watch. "Condolences are in order then."

"She went with Jesus. It's what she wanted."

Sister Edward clears her throat and looks at Cee-Cee's inky hands, her messy hair. "Why is it, I wonder, God gives you so much information and leaves the rest of us in the dark? You must be much, much better than the rest of us are."

"God doesn't care about better, Sister."

"You pretend to *know* what God cares about, do you?"

"Only what I'm told."

Sister Edward nods impatiently. "And so you are…back in communication…"

"It's different now."

"And the…visitations…?"

"No," Cee-Cee says. "Nothing. It's kind of a relief."

Staring straight ahead at the altar and the large looming cross, Sister Edward sighs. "Shall we say a prayer for your grandmother's soul?"

They kneel together in the closest pew and bow their heads.

Sister Edward goes first: "If I were a piece of cloth, Dear Lord and God, my Precious Savior, I would not be worthy to clothe even your poorest, most humble creature on earth, and yet hear now these prayers for your obedient servant Marina Petramala as a measure of my love and humility…"

Looking up from clasped fists, Sister Edward and Cee-Cee are startled to see someone floating toward them from the center aisle. It is a girl so thin and insubstantial that Cee-Cee almost doesn't see her.

For a brief moment Sister Edward thinks she is the one having the divine vision. *A messenger from God, an angel?* With all her heart Sister Edward hopes not. She suspects she does not have what it takes to endure the impossible tests of faith and suffering reserved for God's visionaries.

"Hello?" Sister Edward says reluctantly. "Who's there?"

The girl steps out of the shadows, revealing that she is not a divine phantom at all, but a dirty, matted thing. "I came to join up."

Recognizing the red hair, Cee-Cee gets to her feet.

"Join up?" Sister Edward raises her voice menacingly. "This is a private school, child! You must properly apply. There is no joining!"

Cee-Cee takes a step closer. "It's you! You *are* alive: I knew it!"

"I'm looking for Mother General's Peace Army for Orphaned Girls," Eileena says. "I want to be a soldier. I want to save and be saved."

"But everyone's looking for you. Don't you want to go home?"

"Home?" she looks at Cee-Cee as if she has slapped her face. "No." Tentative as a trapped animal, she holds steady, taking out a small piece of paper and reads from it. "*A nation of girls will rise* *up in peace…*I want that. I want to go to Canada."

Edward lunges forward to grab her, shouting like a madwoman. "Kneel, child! You've been duped by the devil."

But Eileena slips Sister Edward's grip and runs out the side door, setting off an ear-splitting alarm.

To Cee-Cee, the high-pitched noise sounds like music. She has seen what could have been, desperate and covered in dirt: her own destiny, the destiny of many narrowly escaped.

She has seen the future that could have been hers.

Across the street in Nonna's bedroom, Amanda studies the crucifixion: Jesus' serene face and contorted body. It is a comfort to share her suffering with a God who suffers too. Before the ambulance and coroner arrive, she kneels by the bed and prays for her friend, Marina, who rests in peace on the bed. For the salvation of this pure soul, Amanda offers up her own life, her burns, scars, sacrifices, losses and all.

In the back of her mind, she can't help also running through Dan Flannigan's most recent letter. How careless he's become in his writing, referring to her mission as "a crusade"—just the kind of thing that could ruin her. He knows his correspondence is screened. He knows now more than ever that she cannot afford the exposure. She's gone so far as to start burning his letters one by one in Our Lady's furnace in the basement after the others are asleep.

In his letter last week, he wrote:

> *What the government doesn't know is that our radical roots—yours and mine—are based not in violence, but in love, not in destruction but in salvation. Jesus was the true pacifist; you and I strive to live as He did. That is to say, by any means necessary. That is why our work will never be understood by common minds. That is why I so admire your crusade.*

Amanda sighs and shakes her head.

By any means necessary? Maybe. But flouting the law is hardly Amanda's purpose.

If she were going to write back to Dan she would remind him what it means to live *through* Christ rather than *as* Christ. As Paul wrote, "He is our peace." Christ is "…the way, the truth, and the light," according to John. We are, none of us, Messiahs, nor should we fill ourselves with ego. It has come to light that here is a man with good intentions, but a man who has gone too far; he believes in himself perhaps too much.

But what's the use at this point in arguing theological differences? She will pray for Dan, but she will not write back—not now, not ever.

There's no time for such leisurely activities these days anyway. Amanda has a full schedule.

In a few hours, she will host two of her most recent graduates; the young women will arrive from Canada by train. Brother Joe will pick them up and bring them to Our Lady so they can explore the possibility of a postulancy with the Sisters of Christ's Most Precious Wounds. But more than that, they will help Amanda with her mission. Spring seems to bring more girls in trouble than she can handle. These older girls—the Mirandas—are always eager to be of service for a time, though none of them ever want to join the order. Of course Amanda can hardly blame them. Would she choose her dusty Sisters today if she had the choice of other, more modernized communities?

The Mirandas pass through on occasion, mostly to pay Amanda a visit, and offer some small service, a gesture of gratitude for having saved them from a life of violence. It is simple obligation that brings them, Amanda knows, though these particular Mirandas are also on their way to the Women's Peace Rally in Seneca Falls, a few hours west of Romeville.

Amanda closes her eyes and pats her dead friend's hand. "Peace, Marina. Until we meet again."

She gets up and opens the door, allowing the others in the room to do their various jobs getting her body to the undertaker and readying her for the final rest.

Vinnie walks Amanda back across the street, asking questions. She answers distractedly: the old woman died in her sleep, the State will remand Cee-Cee to a foster home if she doesn't act quickly. She has promised Marina to guard the child with her life, and she has to move fast, lest the father realize he could make a valid argument for taking Cee-Cee back home.

Amanda and Officer Golluscio meet Sister Edward, who is standing in the hallway outside the chapel with Cee-Cee at her side.

What Sister Edward notices most about her handsome officer is that he is all business today, no smiles. For a moment, Sister Edward wonders if he is playing it cool. Maybe he has come back to haul the Mother General to jail; maybe he has figured out that she is building some sort of radical army. Unless she has fooled him too, the way she's managed with Father Giuseppe.

The thought alarms Sister Edward.

She tries to signal Vinnie silently with her urgent message about the Mother General. She must let him know that the woman is in deep with terrorists and bombs, revolutionaries.

"Do you have something in your eye, Sister?" Amanda asks.

Sister Edward bows her head. "No, Mother."

"Officer Golluscio is going to help us inform Mr. Bianco of current events."

The name sends a strange tingle over Sister Edward's scalp.

At last he speaks: "I'm sorry, Cee-Cee. I'd like a word alone with you for a minute."

Amanda steps in and places her hand on the child's shoulder. "I think we've had enough interrogations."

Surprised, the officer looks up from his notepad. "Cee-Cee is the only witness. It's important we make sure nothing is amiss."

"It's been established that her grandmother died peacefully while taking a nap." Amanda is immovable when she wants to be, a mountain. "No more interviews...period."

Cee-Cee perks up, as if she has only just now entered the room.

Such an odd child, Sister Edward thinks.

Vinnie scratches his chin with a pencil. "There's a whole committee on miracles devoted to this case, Ma'am. The question appears to go beyond criminal matters. I don't think the Church will be put off easily."

"Cee-Cee is a child, Officer Golluscio, not a case. There will be no more meetings with committees, whether criminal or liturgical. As long as she is in my care, she will be protected."

Sister Edward is amazed at how reasonable the woman can sound.

Amanda looks at Sister Edward. "Thank you for your service, Sister. Please tell Sisters Eugene, James, Sebastian, Robert-Claude, and Pius to come see me now."

Heading for the door, Sister Edward glances at Vinnie one last time, trying to signal to him that something urgent has happened, or perhaps that something will happen if he doesn't stop it.

Emergency! Sister Edward thinks, pointing her thoughts in his direction as hard as she can.

YAWNING, FRANK ONLY HALF-LISTENS to the AA speaker.

In the meeting, he checks his watch, counting the minutes in the moldy church basement where he sits with about twenty other guys in a circle of folding chairs.

Losers.

It's going to be a long hour. A truck driver on Frank's left lights up a cigarette, prompting a rash of pocket reaching, cellophane crinkling, and lighter snapping that breaks the mood. In minutes almost everyone in the room is smoking.

Everyone but Moonie and Frank.

Frank reads a sign above the doorway, *Queen of Sorrows.* No kidding. With all these nuns and his mother-in-law's crazy religious passion, no wonder Cee-Cee is so confused.

Life is a kick in the teeth, Frank thinks. No games of toss in the backyard with Baby Pauly; no high school football, driving lessons, first dates.

Vegetable.

People regularly come out of unconscious states, the lady doctor at All Saints Rehabilitation has told them. Frank can see by the look on Glory's face that she's banking on a miracle. Cee-Cee needs it too; he can feel it whenever he sees her hunched shoulders and lost sparkle.

The room is quiet, except for the fidgeting of these poor sons of bitches, each ugly somber face a reflection of Frank's pathetic journey toward sobriety.

He hates them almost as much as he hates himself.

By the time his clearance came through for the job at Kodak with Moonie, Frank had sweated out the last of the DTs. His hands were steady enough for him to make it through his first day. Turns out that Moonie's big work secret is to develop several small prototypes for a reflecting telescope that can be used in space. About a dozen guys work every day polishing orbital mirrors to get just the right fraction of wavelength of red light to capture even the faintest objects. It's tedious work, but if all goes as planned, theirs will be the model NASA uses to create the first zero-gravity observatory lab in outer space.

The hope is to get there before anyone else does.

Frank looks at Moonie sitting across the circle of alcoholics with his arms crossed, feet still, a peaceful expression on his face. He and Moonie have established a kind of easy rhythm now: AA meetings on their days off, driving together to work and back, occasionally stopping to eat supper at an Interstate diner.

Mostly Moonie listens to Frank bitch about Glory.

Still, the dinners somehow manage to be cheerful, as if life were indeed lurching forward. Booze takes away more than it gives, and Frank is grateful for a clear mind and the company of his brother again.

"Just like the old days, huh?"

"Sure." Moonie always orders the meatloaf. "Except nothing's like anything anymore."

They're in a whole new game now. After work on Fridays, they pick up the boys and go straight to All Saints Rehabilitation Center. They stand around looking at what's left of Frank's youngest son.

At the diner, they rarely talk about work; it's confidential, anyway, even between them. Occasionally Moonie breaks code and tells Frank how the mirrors are being incorrectly ground.

"Wrong shape," he says, "too flat at the edges."

Frank can barely believe his ears. "But that means…"

"It doesn't matter." Moonie says. "Budget's run out. We'll get reassigned to the next project."

"That's it?"

Moonie shrugs.

Now Frank looks out the window, searching the empty playground, but there's no one there. It's Saturday, he reminds himself.

He's trapped.

He raises his hand to speak, but before he gets his chance, there's a loud ruckus in the hall behind him. Without warning, the gigantic wooden door swings open, bursting with several nuns in drab knee-length skirts and black veils, led by a very attractive nun he recognizes from somewhere. A few guys on probation shrink in their seats, but Frank stands up.

"This is an anonymous meeting!" one twelve-stepper complains; the others peer at the floor, their shame automatic.

The pretty nun's cheeks are ruddy. As Frank is about to smile at her, he sees his daughter, small and encircled.

"Cee-Cee…?"

The Sisters block Frank's way.

"I'm very sorry to have to tell you that your mother-in-law passed away this afternoon."

Moonie stands up. "She what?"

"Marina Petramala, the girl's grandmother," the lead nun repeats. "She's dead."

In unison, all the Sisters cross themselves. The alcoholics follow suit.

Frank knows his mother-in-law's death is both bad and good for his situation. He must act quickly. Lunging between two sturdy nuns, he lifts his daughter straight off the ground, hugging her tight against his chest.

The pretty nun gets tough. "Put the child down."

"She's my daughter. She needs to come home now."

Moonie places a hand on his brother's shoulder. "The state has to say it's okay, Frank. You can't just take her back."

"No, *we* decided!" Frank shouts. "It was *our* idea to send her to Glory's mother…that was *our* decision. Now that she's… passed, we get our kid back."

"They would have taken Cee-Cee away anyway," Moonie says. "That was the arrangement."

The cop who ruined his life appears and steps forward ominously.

"I'm the Mother General, here, Mr. Bianco, a close friend of your mother-in-law's; I believe we've met," the nun in charge says. "I'd like to offer to have Cee-Cee stay here with us for a while until things get straightened out legally. I'm sure you will agree that given the circumstances it would be better than having her placed in a foster home. Father Giuseppe will call and make arrangements."

She nods at Cee-Cee, who wiggles free from her father's embrace and steps back inside the circle of Wounds. Frank feels a terrible pain surge through him. Is he having a heart attack? The absence of his daughter, his old life, feels stronger in this instant than in all the weeks she's been gone.

"Kneel and pray," Cee-Cee says to him.

"What?"

Behind him, the circle of men get down on their knees, crossing themselves and praying for mercy in one swift motion.

"Mr. Bianco, we're going to leave now." The nun turns to the kneeling addicts. "Please excuse the interruption, gentlemen. Carry on with your important work of recovering. We include you in our prayers always."

The flock of nuns moves back toward the door, carrying off his child.

"She's not one of you!" Frank shouts.

This causes several of them to bow their heads.

"Father Giuseppe will call the girl's mother and explain

what has happened."

Frank is hardening into a block of cement, pain subsiding. Watching the tender white backs of his daughter's knees as she is led away, he has to stop himself from crying out.

"The officer will accompany you across the street, Mr. Bianco." The last nun prods him toward the door. "I believe the ambulance and coroner have some matters to discuss with you."

Moonie presses on Frank's shoulder, leading him out of the room. The cop trails behind.

"Why is it always you?" Frank asks the cop.

Vinnie doesn't take the bait, just continues to follow them out.

A hard idea starts to form inside Frank, a pit in the middle of soft fruit. He will find a way to work around Glory. He will save them all from this and further humiliation.

He is the father. His son must be spared.

DINNER AT CHRIST'S MOST Precious Wounds is a sparse Lenten meal.

Cee-Cee stares at the clear soup and stale bread. She is not hungry, but she manages a couple of spoons and a nibble.

After the Sisters take turns reading from *The Imitation of Christ*, Amanda stands and clears her throat.

"Miss Bianco is a member of Sister Edward's Gifted and Talented sixth grade class and a fine student at Our Lady," she says. "She is also a grandchild of the late Marina Petramala, whom some of you knew was a personal friend of mine. She will be staying here with us until further notice."

Cee-Cee looks up from her string game, a piece of colored yarn that she weaves into different shapes. She shows the Sisters a perfect inverted Cat's Cradle, holding it up for all to see. ("Purrfect," Mary Margaret would say.)

The Sisters clap politely, nodding and whispering to one another.

This is followed by a lively discussion about Nixon. Sister James suggests writing a play to explore the political climate.

"The children can perform it at the Easter pageant!" she says.

Sister Robert-Claude smirks. "We'll call it *Nixon Crucifixion*."

Some of the Sisters chuckle into their hands.

"What will we protest when all the U.S. troops are home from Vietnam?" Sister Eugene asks.

Their Mother General is nonplussed. "As long as there is poverty and starvation, there will be wars for us to protest, I fear."

A light bulb goes off for Sister James. "Einstein said enforcing vegetarianism would be the best way to promote peace!"

For comment, everyone turns and looks to Sister Eugene, the resident cook.

"Well, I did happen to see a lovely recipe for vegetable cassoulet in *Women's Day*," she says.

Sister Edward gives Cee-Cee a meaningful look.

After the discussion, the Sisters all head to the chapel for evening prayers, and Sister Pius leads Cee-Cee down a long hallway to a spare room.

In it are one desk, one window, and one bed.

"This is your cell…bedroom; we all have one. It's where we sleep," explains the Littlest Wound. "You must be exhausted!"

Cee-Cee studies Sister Pius' oddly shaped face and bright green eyes as she motors around, pointing out the tiny sink in the corner of the room and the window latch.

"I'm on one side of you, and the Mother General is on the other," she says. "So if you need anything, just call out. The walls are thin."

From nowhere Sister Pius produces a cotton nightdress, slightly too big for Cee-Cee, but good enough. "I'll send Sister John of the Cross to pick up your things."

"My notebooks."

"You really do like to write!" Sister Pius says. "I've never been good at it myself."

Cee-Cee wishes she had her notebooks now. "They help me figure things out."

"Yes!" Sister Pius smiles. "I think that's exactly what God does for me. Maybe writing is your way of praying."

Lifting her arms, Cee-Cee lets Sister Pius undress her and help her into the night dress.

When she is all settled in the little bed, Sister Pius perches near the headboard. "Any questions?"

"Can I visit Baby Pauly?"

Sister Pius pats Cee-Cee's hand. "Brother Joe is Our Lady's finest chauffeur. You'll surely come to love his sporty bright-colored car as much as he does."

"Nonna let me visit every day."

"I think that can be arranged."

"Can I sleep with one of the cats?"

Sister Pius seems uncertain. "We can ask Sister James, but I don't see why not."

"Can it be Calliope?" Cee-Cee chooses the cat that is ink-black, the color of her own hair.

When all is said and done, tears push against the back of Cee-Cee's eyelids. "I'm alone."

Sister Pius embraces her. "It is an essential truth that all of us are alone, and yet not alone. Not alone because we are children of God. And God is always with us."

Cee-Cee cries for herself anyway.

Too tired to care about the stiff sheets and hard pillow, the smell of lemon Pledge in the room, Cee-Cee lets her eyes close.

Sister Pius sings a lullaby.

A little later, Amanda pokes her head in the door. "Everything okay?"

Sister Pius whispers: "A little weepy."

Cee-Cee struggles to wake up to see Sister Amanda's pretty face. "*Rise up...you nation of girls...*"

"Yes, yes, but sleep now." Amanda kisses Cee-Cee's forehead. "Time enough tomorrow to change the world."

WHEN SISTER AMANDA LOOKS up from her papers where she is working under a single desk lamp in the office, she smiles as if she's been expecting Glory all along.

"Mrs. Bianco, I'm sorry about your loss."

Glory holds up a hanger, flapping a little dress in Amanda's direction. "For Cee-Cee to wear tomorrow?"

They stand face to face.

Glory can see the woman is sizing her up.

Everyone does these days; everyone looks at Glory with disdain.

A couple of times when there were still crowds clamoring for Cee-Cee to perform another miracle, Glory stomped out onto the porch in her bathrobe and slippers and yelled at them. What she saw, though, was something amazing right on her front lawn: faith growing, like a yellow-headed dandelion. Mothers held up their deformed babies, daughters carried their sick parents, women beat their breasts and knelt in the snow, praying to the Queen of Heaven, asking Cee-Cee to heal the world, stop the war, give the Indians back their land. A gaggle of women even help up signs that said *Martyrdom is anti-woman. Pass the ERA.*

Glory wanted to ask them what they knew that she didn't.

What have I missed? She ended up staring into the crowd of worshippers and protesters, all of them believers in something. *What am I missing?*

Other days, she was so frustrated with the noise and trash on her lawn that she wanted nothing more than to throw rocks at them. What right did they have? This was her life! Her house! But the thought of child-welfare workers in disguise restrained her rash impulses. She stayed at home, made dinner for her remaining children, and tried not to fly off the handle. When she backed out of the driveway, she ignored her urge to run people down.

Little boys fell into ponds all the time, didn't they? Strangers appeared out of nowhere to harm little girls.

She'd used the money to buy a bus ticket to Saratoga Springs for no reason at all, other than she had once been there in the summer to see the horses race. She checked into a motel. Frank and his drinking had been driving her nuts. The kids at home without school for a week would wear on her last nerve.

She remembered what it was like running away to Marion Patrick's when she'd wanted to marry Frank and her parents got in the way. How bewildered she'd felt coming home and finding her mother still droning on at the kitchen table about priests and nuns, her father hobbling around with the same small bag of garbage in his hand. To her surprise, neither her departure nor her return had caused an electrical surge, a spark in the circuitry.

The house itself had not burned down.

Not so mighty now, your heart? her mother had said.

A year later, when they were good and ready, they gave their permission for Glory to marry Frank.

Otherwise, it was as if she'd never left.

Now it was the same with her own family. Glory never got the perfect response from them either, whatever that was. In truth, she didn't even know. And yet, she has become something of a repetitive wind-up version of herself, stuck in her own desire to escape and return, escape and return. How is it that being gone always amounts to no more than never having left? How has she gotten so caught up in the click and hum of her own heartbreaking redundancy? A successful, life, she knows would never have come to this.

Could this tragedy have happened to any mother? It didn't even matter, did it? It had happened to her while she was somewhere else.

"I wasn't very close to my mother," Glory says suddenly. She is embarrassed to hear it come out sounding confessional rather than defiant. "But I loved her."

"Of course you did," Sister Amanda says kindly. "No one here questions that."

The gentle tone cracks Glory open a little. Sister Amanda pushes a box of tissues forward on her desk.

What is a person without a mother? Glory wants to ask.

Sister Amanda tilts her head. "What I admired about your

mother most was how fiercely protective she was of her family, especially Cee-Cee."

"There's such a thing as *too much* protection," Glory says. "She suffocated me when I was a girl."

"There's also such a thing as *not enough* protection. Balance is tricky." Sister Amanda strains to be kind. "I guess that's the thing we strive for."

Glory looks into her opponent's eyes. "How old are you?"

Sister Amanda barely reacts to the sudden shift in the conversation. "In my thirties."

"I had a house full of children when you were barely getting started," Glory says.

"We have a lot in common, Mrs. Bianco." Sister Amanda clasps her hands in front of her chest. "I've had 100 school children under my roof for quite some time."

You think it's the same? Glory wants to say.

"What was your own mother like?" Glory asks. "Did she suffocate you?"

"I'm afraid I grew up in an orphanage," Sister Amanda answers.

Then you don't really know! Glory wants to shout. *You have no right to judge!*

Instead a wave of sorrow wells up. Glory has to surrender her child to this over-stuffed orphan, and her own mother is gone forever, making her an orphan, too.

"It must be a shock," Sister Amanda says. "And a terrible sorrow."

Glory pulls herself together. "My daughter *will* come home where she belongs. I'll see to it."

Sister Amanda smiles. "I'll be sure she wears the dress tomorrow."

"The state shrink told me that Cee-Cee is making the whole thing up," Glory says, "that she wants to have a perfect family, like the Holy Family: a virginal mother, an all-powerful father, a brother who sacrifices everything to save her."

It's a manifestation of her most deeply held wish, he had said, an unpleasant little man with a beard. To Glory it seemed like a crock.

"I suppose everyone is entitled to a theory," Amanda says.

Glory stops at the door. "You think it's true about Cee-Cee, don't you?"

"Cee-Cee is a very bright little girl."

"But you actually believe God talks to her through angels and visions and messages."

"God speaks to all of us, Mrs. Bianco." Sister Amanda clasps her hands in front of her chest. "Some are just better at listening."

FIRST THING IN THE morning when Cee-Cee opens her eyes, she sees her black wool dress hanging off the doorknob. She moves Calliope off her chest and stands up. Slipping the dress on, she finds a note in the pocket in Glory's handwriting. *Home soon!* It says. A promise, or threat.

At breakfast, Cee-Cee eats a dry slice of toast.

"Sick children should be in bed!" Sister Edward scolds.

Frowning, Sister Eugene intervenes. "Leave the girl alone, Sister Edward. She's adjusting to our way of life."

Sister Robert-Claude barely looks up from her plate. "As I recall, Edward, you cried for three weeks when you were first here."

Cee-Cee feels sorry for Sister Edward, who doesn't know how to make friends. When she feels better, she's going to show her how to wow people with a card trick or two; that always helps break the ice.

Sister Edward defends herself: "Tell me you don't wonder why this child, of all children in the world, is given visions of angels and Our Lady! Why is she the one?"

Sister Alouicious, who rarely speaks at all, answers with a

quote: "St. Paul wrote 'the poor things of this world hath God chosen, things that are nothing.'"

"At least she's Catholic," Sister Robert-Claude offers.

Cee-Cee corrects her: "God doesn't care if we're Catholic or not, as long as we pray."

"Sacrilege!" Sister Edward's jaw drops. "Do you have any idea what you've said?"

Cee-Cee shrugs. "Only what I'm told."

"You are a confused child," Sister Edward says. "Therefore your message is confused, and therefore this whole charade is unreliable. *That which is received is received in the manner of the receiver.*"

Several Sisters look around the table with raised eyebrows.

"A simple error from an erroneous mind," Sister Edward continues. "Plenty of lost souls have made false predictions."

Sister Robert-Claude says, "Oh, poppy-cock! All saints start out and end up human! As flawed as you or me."

"Are we comparing her to a saint now?" Edward shakes a finger at Cee-Cee. "I think this Little Miss should have her head examined! Along with the rest of you!"

After a long pause, Sister Eugene says, "Joan of Arc was stark raving mad, Sister Edward…but no one disputes that she saw what she saw."

The other Sisters nod firmly.

End of conversation.

After the plates are cleared, and more prayers are said, Christ's Most Precious Wounds walk Cee-Cee silently through the building to the courtyard. As they near the church, a few of the Sisters start to fuss with Cee-Cee's hair and dress. They smooth her braids, re-tie her ribbons, pinch her cheeks for color.

Fixing Cee-Cee's collar, Sister Eugene asks the question on everybody's mind. "Perhaps you want to sit with us during your grandmother's Mass?"

"I don't think so," Cee-Cee says. "Glory will want me to sit with the family."

"Okay, then stand here and wait for the hearse." Sister John of the Cross deposits Cee-Cee on the top step. "But if you change your mind, I'll leave an open seat for you next to me."

Outside, under the old church archway, Cee-Cee watches the Precious Wounds make their way through the church. They pass Nonna's ancient Italian lady friends dressed in black, who clatter and sigh, complaining that no one speaks Italian any more. They liked it better when masses were in Latin. "*Regazza dei miracoli,*" they whisper when they spot Cee-Cee standing in the doorway. "*Regazza dei miracoli.*"

Cee-Cee scans the crowd for blue jackets, a nervous tick that will last a lifetime. She counts seven in all.

The hearse drives up, then Glory's station wagon, followed by Grandma Bianco's Cadillac and Uncle Moonie's truck. These vehicles release the remaining members of Cee-Cee's family: Grandma Bianco with her oxygen tank; Frank and Moonie dressed in dark suits; Glory with a little black hat that has a net to cover her eyebrows; Anthony and Roadie wearing clip-on ties.

Frank seems not to notice Cee-Cee standing there, or maybe he's still mad at her for going with the Sisters and not putting up a fight. Uncle Moonie pats Cee-Cee's head.

Roadie drifts over. "Hi."

"Remember the missing girl, Roadie?" It's the first time she's used his name since the woods. "Eileena Brice Iaccamo? Remember?"

"Yeah." He seems relieved to talk about something normal. "Her brother thinks she lives in a rusty freight car at the old dead train cemetery."

"I saw her yesterday here in the chapel. She's alive!"

"People tell ghost stories, Cee-Cee. It's probably not what you think."

Glory teeters up the stone steps in high heels, shooing

Roadie away. "Take Grandma Bianco to a seat up front, then come back and help get Nonna out of that hearse." She sniffles, taking Cee-Cee's hand. "You look nice in that dress, baby."

They stand outside the church, waiting for the big gray car to cough up Nonna's body. The driver and one of *Il Duce*'s brothers from the funeral home help Frank, Moonie, Anthony, and Roadie roll Nonna's casket out of the back and wheel it through the church doorway, heading for the center aisle.

Glory marches behind them, pulling Cee-Cee by the wrist.

The church is almost cheerful with its streaming sunlight from the stained glass windows. The votive candles flicker as the wall sconces cast off thick shadows. Jesus plays out His passion flatly from one colored-glass pane to the next, rolling out the most compelling story ever told like a dime-store comic book. Sweat falls off Jesus' lovely face in little ballooning drips as He carries a huge wooden cross all the way to Calvary. St. Veronica wipes His face and walks away with a cartoon image of His visage on her handkerchief. There's nothing in His expression at all that shows pain, Cee-Cee notices; He doesn't seem to feel a thing when He is strung up on the cross, wounds prodded with rags soaked in vinegar. When He rises from the dead, there's a yellow dinner plate stuck to His head to represent the light of the world.

Two elfin altar boys appear at the back of the church from behind the cast-iron Virgin. They slowly make their way through the dark church carrying tall brass candleholders with long lit tapers that glow far above their heads. One of them trips on his red robe, hitting his chin on a stiff white collar. Behind him, a shrunken visiting priest displays an open *Bible* at his chest, as if to ward off evil.

The Sisters of Christ's Most Precious Wounds bow and cross themselves as Father Giuseppe passes up the aisle looking tired in a festive purple robe. He clanks the smoky machinery of incense from one side of the aisle to the other. Carrying the

Eucharist in chalices behind him is the one and only McNulty family: Mr. and Mrs. McNulty in front, followed by the popular blonde twins from Our Lady. Mary Ellen and Maureen trail behind like faint carbon copies of their much prettier mother.

Nonna's Italian-witch friends beat their breasts in unison, praying in a foreign tongue.

The pallbearers take the aisle—Frank, Moonie, Roadie, Anthony, and two men from the funeral home—each with a hand on Nonna's casket. They wheel her straight up to the altar where Jesus looks on from the cross.

Glory and Cee-Cee follow behind.

An old woman leans out of a pew and presses her rosary beads to the back of Cee-Cee's head, bringing them up to her lips. Cee-Cee doesn't know what to do, so she nods at the people who meet her eyes. No one knows for sure whether Cee-Cee performed a miracle out at that pond, or whether she's just another Bianco in trouble.

It will be a long, long time before Cee-Cee gets to show Nonna a new card trick, or anything at all, for that matter. The sad thought flies away as soon as it lands in her mind. Feeling a little faint, she tries to concentrate on the people in the pew; she tries to stay on her feet.

Almost unrecognizable in regular clothes, Vinnie kneels at the end of a pew and crosses himself. Mary Margaret whistles and waves at Cee-Cee from a seat between Mary Margaret's strange giddy mother and big Norbert Sasso who bounces with joy when Cee-Cee passes.

He reaches out to hold Cee-Cee's hand, and she squeezes his fingers. His long happy tongue unfurls.

Mary Margaret gives Cee-Cee two thumbs-up and a sympathetic grimace.

"Keep moving." Glory tugs Cee-Cee's arm. "This isn't social hour."

Somewhere in the middle of the church, among the poor

farmers, the Iaccamos huddle together; Cee-Cee finds the face of the Italian man she saw in her vision, a man who growled at Eileena. Next to him is his silent suffering Irish wife.

Try it again, touch me or my sisters, Eileena told him, pointing a shotgun in his face, *and I'll blow you to kingdom come.*

Next are the humble railway workers in frayed coats and the shopkeeps. They smell like sweat and work. They clasp their hands in prayer, breathing out their petitions, hoping they will live long full lives and die in their sleep like Nonna. They bury their heads in their hands to hide the faces Cee-Cee has known all her life.

The military men and their wives and children sit up front, closest to God, with the owners of banks and department stores and the freight-exporting families. The women wear colorful spring coats with matching hats; their shiny earrings catch the light.

Have mercy, Cee-Cee prays. *And please don't let me faint.*

Glory moves up the aisle at a fast clip, squeezing Cee-Cee's arm just tight enough to stop the circulation. Distant relatives wait in the first pews, anchored by Grandma Bianco with her green oxygen tank and wads of Kleenex. Frank and Moonie flank her on either side.

In front, Roadie and Anthony sit in their own pew. Glory seats Cee-Cee with them at the end near the aisle, transferring Cee-Cee's wrist to Roadie and taking her place in the second row next to Frank.

Roadie's skin is sweaty. He smiles at Cee-Cee and doesn't let go of her hand. She sees him for a moment in a circle of trees. In the church, Anthony's bluish skin shimmers darkly. Cee-Cee can barely see the shadowy smudge of his eyes, nose, and mouth. She sticks her tongue out at him. He twitches slightly, facing squarely forward, waiting for the priest to invoke the first prayer.

Cee-Cee sees Anthony in the same circle of trees.

Snapping his head oddly, he slices his eyes over at Cee-Cee, and sticks his tongue out at her. She feels the lights instantly flicker. It's as if someone somewhere is pulling a plug.

Everything sizzles and burns.

A dull buzzing drowns out Father Giuseppe's droning.

For a moment Cee-Cee worries that somewhere a girl group is singing in the sky to Jesus, but it's only the static in her ears, the sound of someone abandoning herself.

When the congregation stands, Roadie pulls Cee-Cee up with him. Wobbling, she flashes on the image a third time, a circle of trees, a circle of brothers.

In this church, her family surrounds her, those who gave her life. They know who she is and where she came from. Despite everything, they care about her most in the world. Will they always love her best? Does that mean she's tied to them? Her thoughts start to swim together: Mother, father, sister. Brother, brother, brother.

Why can't they see who she is? Why can't she just be a weird girl with good connections? A person like her could come in handy for a family like theirs.

Anthony and Roadie pray. They are Cee-Cee's brothers, and yet not her brothers. She reaches inside for an answer to the puzzle.

Is she their sister? She is, but she's not.

Somewhere—very, very far away—someone is lying on a forest floor.

In the church, Cee-Cee's body remembers what her mind cannot grasp. Her bladder twinges as if it might empty. Her breath expands as if her ribs could crack. Her eyes go blind, blood roaring in her ears.

If she were not temporarily deaf, she would hear Roadie whisper, "Sorry, sorry, sorry, Cee-Cee. I'm so sorry."

Does an apology make any difference? Does it change who they are to each other and who they will become?

Cee-Cee can only hear the sound of her own blood rushing

around her head, an echo of Father Giuseppe inviting the congregation to stand. Her knees will not hold her up. Her eyes begin to roll back. Roadie grabs her under the arms as she starts to slip down to the stone floor.

Like magic, two stealthy Sisters appear at the end of the pew to catch Cee-Cee before she hits the ground. They prop her limply up and deftly pry open Roadie's hands.

"She's having a febrile seizure," Sister Eugene says. "We'll take her home."

For a moment, Roadie thinks they mean home for real.

"I'm sorry," he tells them. "Please forgive me."

Sister Robert-Claude presses a hand so firmly on Roadie's shoulder and looks so deeply into his eyes that for a moment he believes he is forgiven.

"Bow down and pray," says Father Giuseppe.

The church echoes with the sound of people scuffling and bowing.

Mary Margaret and Vinnie watch the Sisters whisking Cee-Cee back down the aisle, past the holy water dispensers, out the gigantic church doors, and into the weak April morning.

THE SISTERS CARRY CEE-CEE all the way to the tiny cell, once a broom closet, sandwiched between Sister Amanda's room and Sister Pius' room. It is already piled with Cee-Cee's things from Nonna's house. A few of Sister James's cats pad around her pillow, jump on the window sill.

"I won't let anyone hurt you," Cee-Cee tells the cats, but it comes out jumbled from the fever, nonsensical.

Nonna is dead, Cee-Cee reminds herself, a hard fact that sinks in and makes her feel terrible.

There is a neat stack of folded clothes, two pairs of shoes, a tower of notebooks, several packages of fresh blue pens, her jacks, jar of marbles, a rubber-ball on a paddle, two yo-yos, and some gum. Cee-Cee moves toward the desk to touch her things, wanting to show Sister Pius how to do Lord of the Flies with a yo-yo, but instead they steer her toward bed.

They strip off her dress and wrap her in cold wet sheets and towels.

They argue over ice cubes. "Too much! She'll catch pneumonia!"

"Fevers can make a child go deaf; I've seen it happen."

"We're teachers, not nurses."

"Someone scare up some aspirin!"

When the Mother General arrives at last, the Sisters abruptly leave their tasks, scattering out the door.

"I'm sorry, Cee-Cee," Sister Amanda says. "This must be awful for you."

"They're going to bury Nonna," Cee-Cee says.

"We can visit the cemetery as soon as you feel better."

"She was here yesterday," Cee-Cee says.

"I know," Amanda hugs her. "It's difficult to understand."

"No, I mean the missing girl. Eileena Brice Iaccamo," Cee-Cee says. "I saw her in the chapel. She was here. She was looking for you."

"She was here?" Sister Amanda says. "You saw her?"

"She wants to join your army."

"Army—is that what I have?" Amanda laughs. "We've been trying to reach her for weeks. Sister Pius has been sending messages every day, leaving them everywhere. I'm sorry I missed her."

"She ran away from home and can't go back," Cee-Cee says. "She's been living down by the railroad tracks."

"How do you know that?"

"I can hear her heartbeat." Cee-Cee strokes one of the nearby cats. "I hear all their heartbeats."

Mother clears her throat. "All?"

"Missing kids from everywhere," Cee-Cee says. "Even the

ones you keep here under Our Lady."

Amanda does not move her eyes away from Cee-Cee's face. "Those children are passing through, Cee-Cee. Do you understand? None of them are here to stay."

"Where are they going?"

"They are on their way to a place that's better than their home, a place that's safe," she says. "But we must never mention them to anybody; that's what makes this possible. Brother Joe takes them to safety."

"To Canada."

"Yes." Amanda measures her words. "Do you want to go to Canada, Cee-Cee? Do you want a new start? The girls I send to Canada are free and never ever harmed by anyone, ever again."

"I have to wait for Baby Pauly."

"Okay, but the girls must be a secret," she says. "It's very important."

Cee-Cee feels her exhaustion double, her sadness overflow. When she closes her eyes, she sees a few desperate girls crammed into close quarters, waiting to be freed.

"Perhaps you'd like to meet them?" Amanda says.

AFTER DRESSING CEE-CEE IN sweaters and warm tights, Amanda leads her to Father Giuseppe's office.

In the back of his coat closet, behind three jackets on hangers, Amanda pries free a large loose plywood board. Snapping the plank out of place, she puts it aside and switches on her flashlight. They use a rickety ladder in the crawl space to go down into the darkness underneath Our Lady.

Amanda heads down first, then she shines the light as Cee-Cee feels for each rung with her feet.

Once under the building, they follow a dirt floor through a long tunnel, which opens out into a small brick room.

Cee-Cee stands at the entrance holding Amanda's flashlight.

Six insistent heartbeats echo in her ears; beyond those come dozens and dozens of faint palpitations, the ghosts of girls who have passed this way previously.

Amanda pulls the string on a light bulb attached to the low ceiling; Cee-Cee looks around the musty room at the mossy brick walls. The air is dank.

"We are inside the church's foundation," Amanda says. "Deep underground below Father Giuseppe's office in the Manse."

Cee-Cee shivers. "Wow! It's creepy down here."

In the center of a big room with dirt floors, three cots are lined up together, each with two small drowsy girls lying head-to-foot.

Sister Pius watches over them from a wicker chair, reading her book with a flashlight. "Is anything wrong, Mother?"

"Everything's fine."

When Cee-Cee edges nearer to inspect the six little ones, they pop their eyes open, anxious as fidgety owls. One stands straight up on the bed and points at Cee-Cee; she is about nine years old and speaks with a southern accent. "Who are you?"

Wrapping a blanket around the girl's shoulders, Amanda presses her back down in the bed. "Shh. Go back to sleep."

Another pops up on her elbows. "Are you Eileena Brice Iaccamo?"

Amanda whispers. "No, darlings. This is Cecilia Marie Bianco, a friend of mine. Say hello, then rest again and stay quiet. You have a long journey tomorrow, and when you get there you'll be free and cared for and happy."

Sister Pius gives the last girl a sip of something from a plastic cup. "Drink this and sleep. It will warm you up."

"Where do they come from?" Cee-Cee asks.

"From everywhere," Amanda says. "Someone from their family took pity and brought them here. Someone who wanted to help them."

"I'm from Georgia," one of the little owls says.

Another pipes up: "Pennsylvania."

"Syracuse, New York," says a third.

"Shh!" Sister Pius tells them. "You mustn't talk. Mother General just came to check on you."

The girls put their heads back on their pillows. All but one closes her eyes and dozes off. It's the girl from Georgia. She smiles and shows Cee-Cee a bruise on her neck the size of a grapefruit.

"I'm going to Canada," she whispers. "I'm going to be on a mission for peace."

Cee-Cee thinks of the grown-up Mirandas who have slept on Nonna's living room floor. She can taste the girls' excitement in her own throat, the fear.

THE FIRST GIRL HAD shown up at Our Lady's doorstep shortly after Amanda was installed as Mother General: a bedraggled and desperate child named Enid who had been sleeping in the garage like an animal since her mother's death. After her father used an oil rag to strangle the newborn child he'd made her bear, she started planning her escape. Two years passed before Enid was able to get free, thanks to a neighbor who drove her to Our Lady.

Sister, please! The girl clasped Amanda's garments. *Don't make me go back!*

Wild-eyed, Enid needed more than Our Lady could provide: a safe home, a new identity.

During a religious conference months earlier, Amanda had heard a Canadian order of religious women discussing their petition to form a new community called the Sisters of Peace. They tossed around the idea of turning an old orphanage into a peace camp for girls. They'd described it as a safe place for rebuilding crushed souls, renewing faith, healing wounds—a kind of life-school for anti-violence education and pacifist training, girls only, a place where feminism and salvation would meet.

Perhaps it was divine intervention.

The night of Enid's arrival, Amanda bathed and fed the girl, tucked her into a cot in the safe room under the Manse. The previous Mother General, Augustus, had revealed the secret room to Amanda on her deathbed. *Tell no one*, the dying Mother Augustus advised. *A secret room comes in handy around here.*

As little Enid dozed off with the help of some sedating Benadryl, Amanda made a single phone call to Canada.

When the girl's father came banging on Our Lady's door looking for his daughter, Amanda knew she'd made the right choice. Hidden in the little room under Father Giuseppe's office, the girl trembled and whimpered in her arms.

Sister Eugene woke Father Giuseppe, who knew nothing about the situation, which turned out to serve them well. Suppressing his irritation at being awakened in the middle of the night, he refused to let the man in.

I assure you that no one is here but members of our religious community, Father said. *We'll pray for your daughter's safety.*

Before dawn Brother Joe drove Enid to the train station. He placed her on the train with instructions to get off at the Northeast Line's last stop, where the Sisters of Peace would be waiting to take her across the border to Canada.

In the hallways of the school, the Sisters who had helped passed knowing glances but spoke not a single word.

As it turned out, Sister Amanda's knack for turning doomed daughters into anonymous orphans grew steadily over the years until it evolved into a full-fledged operation with several headquarters and participating orders. The whole enterprise seemed miraculously fueled by the enthusiasm of industrious communities of Catholic Sisters positioned at key geographic locations up and down the coast from Florida to Maine. Contrary to their orders from The Holy Mother Church, they operated in secret, and thought of it as a radical duty to save girls in trouble whenever they could. Amanda was considered the engineer of the project; all who knew of her role in this work revered her, especially the young girls who grew into women and came back to thank her.

Before long more than fifteen religious communities were funneling girls to Canada and many more were providing safe havens along the way. Most churches in the surrounding areas harbored hidden rooms, used over the years for runaway slaves, suffragettes, radicals, even women fleeing violent husbands. When a new congregation wished to take part, Amanda had the Sisters poke around in closets and basements looking for concealed rooms, locked tunnels, barricaded bunkers. Nine out of ten times, the Sister found one.

There's a room in the basement with stacks of files, one astonished Sister from Rochester reported. *Hand-copied letters from Frederick Douglass to John Brown!*

Another, from Maryland, wanted to send photographs: *I think Harriet Tubman had one of her famous divine visions in the hidden wine cellar under our rectory!*

In no time girls were being sent up the coast routinely, each given her new identity, derived from the same name: Miranda Pax.

"The name means *Witness of Peace,*" the Ad Hoc Committee's Chair Sister said. "It links our radical orphans together forever as soldiers for peace wherever they go."

Each wayward child initially received papers for a new identity, and a hundred dollars spending cash from Amanda herself. As peace orphanages multiplied from Ottawa to Toronto to Montreal, the young women could choose to live in any number of communities with open access to good psychological treatment, nursing care, and schools. If this did not suit their needs, they could opt for a loving Canadian family to adopt them. And if all else failed, there was always emancipation. The Sisters of Peace owned real estate all over the provinces; they could set up graduated Peace Orphans in apartments and help find them clerical jobs. A few of the young women have even followed in the footsteps of the Catholic Sisters who raised and nurtured them, seeking their novitiates at orders involved in the cause.

The only payback any graduate of the program owed the Sisters was to participate in three peace demonstrations a year, and to vow to organize at least one passive resistance protest during her lifetime.

Amanda has managed mostly to keep her work secret, sparing Father Giuseppe all but the necessary details.

How goes the Nunderground, Mother? he sometimes asks.

Do you really want to know, Father?

He's always treated Amanda fairly: *Perhaps just the broad strokes.*

Swimmingly, Father, she answers. *We're making great progress.*

She prays for those who have joined her cause throughout the years. Those who willingly assisted: Brother Joe, Brother Ignacio, Sister Eugene, Sister John of the Cross, Sister Robert-Claude, and Little Sister Pius. Several of the others had a fairly good notion of what was going on, but chose not to intrude or get involved.

I pray for you, Mother, they said to her privately. *I pray for missing girls everywhere.*

The problem is that Amanda can never control how her colleagues understand the mission; she knows they speak to one another in shorthand, mentioning their work as *building peace armies* and *running an underground railroad.*

And only once has anyone ever outright questioned the good of the mission. Brother Ignacio and Brother Joe had taken her aside to express their concern.

Saving one or two children from a bad situation is one thing,

Mother, Brother Ignacio said. *But a crusade is quite another.*

The word upset her—a misunderstanding, in her estimation—but she kept to her point: *Need I remind you how long it's taken Congress to pass a simple protection against child abuse? Animals have more federal rights in this country than children do!*

Brother Joe bridged the gap gently: *There are local protections, Mother. We are bound by New York law to hand these children over to the state.*

And I am bound by God's law to save them! she said.

She'd wanted to ask where exactly they thought she should draw the line. At which child? Was not every single poor creature a part of the human family? Weren't those girls valuable too? Didn't she have a duty as a mother to save them if she could? She has saved children in circumstances so dire and so beyond repair that *not* helping would be unChristlike—cruel even.

People sought her out with hard luck cases, frantic relatives, troubled teachers, bewildered strangers asking for help.

These girls, every one of them, came to *her.*

BACK IN FATHER GIUSEPPE'S office, Cee-Cee breathes the warm air. Sister Amanda snaps the plywood board back into place.

"Is it legal?" Cee-Cee asks. "To save those little girls?"

Amanda gives her puzzled look. "Helping people is always the right thing."

"But what about their families?" Cee-Cee says. "Don't they care?"

"Girls go missing all the time." Amanda says. "Especially around here."

"Is it kidnapping?"

Amanda clears her throat. "Of course not. These are children who deserve a better life than the one they've been given. Now let's pray that our little travelers have a safe passage, shall we?"

They kneel behind Father Giuseppe's mahogany desk.

Trying to slow her excited heart, Cee-Cee concentrates, but feels unsettled. She taps on Amanda's shoulder for a final question.

"Don't they miss their mothers?"

"God gives each of us a hundred mothers, Cee-Cee." Sister Amanda opens her eyes. "Those little girls will have hundreds of mothers to love them, just like you will."

Cee-Cee feels her skin getting warmer as she thinks this over. A piece of gum might help her about now, but she forgot to grab a pack from her desk.

"I have an idea!" Sister Amanda says. "A couple of my graduates are coming from Canada tomorrow. Maybe they can tell you what happened to them."

"Where will they stay now?" Cee-Cee thinks about Nonna being gone.

"There are many wonderful women like your Nonna who will take them in for a night or two." Sister Amanda puts her cool hand on Cee-Cee's forehead, feeling the fever spiking under her skin. Cee-Cee wishes they could stay like this forever, with Sister Amanda holding her head.

"Let's get you back to bed."

Eyes closed, Cee-Cee floats in a reverie through all the places where girls are hidden and buried. She sees them alive, trapped, looking for escape. Instantly she gets a headache at the back of her neck.

Tomorrow six little girls will fly away and be free.

Through the window, Cee-Cee sees the tiny tree buds sprouting across Our Lady's property. Sister Amanda strokes her forehead. In the distance somewhere a hearse is driving Nonna up a hill to be buried in the ground.

AFTER THE FUNERAL, VINNIE waits around the church parking lot.

He is hoping he'll see his mysterious Sister. Yesterday after the coroner came and took the old woman's body, he found a note tucked under his windshield wiper: *Must talk soon! Saw the missing girl!*

Vinnie's partner Al folds his arms across his chest. "Again with the religious shit?"

Vinnie stuffs the note back in his pocket.

They are standing between two parked cars, uncomfortable in civilian clothing. A couple of feet away, Al's wife is chatting with a woman in a red hat.

"I never accused the priest, Al," Vinnie says. "I said he happened to own a blue jacket. That's all."

Vinnie had spent a few not unpleasant minutes with Sister Edward the previous week discussing a number of things. She was adamant about the priest's innocence, but Vinnie still wanted to run his theory by a few senior guys at the precinct to make sure he wasn't letting something important slip by.

"Accusing a *priest?*" Al shakes his head. "And now—what? You're solving crimes with one of the Sisters of Perpetual Motion?"

"She just wants to help, Al."

"A piece of tail in a black veil. Knock yourself out; it's your day off."

Vinnie watches his partner stalk off.

The churchgoers disperse. A line of cars—in one sits Glory Bianco—follows the hearse, Vinnie knows. He sits in his own car and reads the Sunday comics, then the *Romeville Sun* crime log.

The church is dead, not a soul around.

Where do nuns go when they're not praying at Mass?

Driving across the street to the Bianco girl's grandmother's house, he waits some more. He's glad to have the rest of the afternoon off to mull things over. After another half hour, he checks his watch and decides to go home.

He's hungry.

THE NEXT DAY, PULLING up to the Romeville diner, Vinnie takes out the nun's note and looks at it one more time, trying to decide what to do. He has a few minutes to kill before picking Al up for their morning shift. He could always drive over there, knock on the church door, and ask if Sister Edward is home. But maybe Al's right; maybe it's just a waste of time.

Before all the missing children, the Mohawk River Valley was a sleepy little part of New York State; he had plenty of time to sit and think. It was partly why Vinnie had picked Romeville, hoping for an easy time. But several tragedies had struck locally early in his career—a kid stolen here or there, a small body floating in the river, a husband bludgeoning his wife with a toaster. The kind of tragedy that makes a person want to change careers. Vinnie has always wanted to do something creative with his hands; plumbing, maybe.

Still, he knows the most valuable lesson a cop can learn: *Trust your instincts...no matter what.* They are really all you have when stepping into other people's messy lives. Forget guns and shields and bulletproof vests; instincts were the only real weapon.

Now, outside the diner in his patrol car, he notices a couple of longhairs making a racket in the parking lot.

Damn hippies. Just what he needs to start his shift.

He lays on his horn, hoping to break up the ruckus without having to leave his squad car. It's starting to rain. Technically, his shift hasn't started. He flashes his headlights.

He could drive away. He waits another half minute, watching the hippies wave a brown paper bag and something small and black: a gun? Vinnie can't be sure.

Suddenly he catches on: what's taking place is a crime.

"Two Caucasian suspects armed and dangerous on Utica," the police scanner buzzes. "Possible robbery in progress."

This kind of thing happens to Vinnie all the time now. His most peaceful hour of the day turns into a felony in progress. If he'd just chosen another place to pull over, he'd have missed this scene entirely.

Stay calm.

These are the moments he dreads.

The two criminals have made a clumsy dash for their car parked diagonally behind a dumpster. By the time he reaches their side of the parking lot, he's switched on his silent siren, a flash of blue and white light to indicate he's serious. The Pinto doesn't move, headlights on, engine revving. Vinnie pulls up along its right rear bumper, flashers pelting out a blinding light. He gets out of the car and unsnaps the gun-strap on his holster. Already he's made a mistake, leaving his squad car without calling it in.

Technically, he is still off duty.

"Hands up!"

The car door opens. A coatless figure steps out, hands in the air, long red hair flowing, mouth already in full gear, voice high and hollow.

"Don't shoot. Okay? Peace and love, man. All right? Just don't shoot; we don't mean any harm…"

"Shut up," Vinnie says.

The driver is short and stocky with a tuft of facial hair and too-white skin. Wearing sneakers with holes and tattered dungarees, his lips are unattractively large; his nose spreads unevenly across the center of an unfortunate face. There's something Vinnie can't quite place: apple cheeks, wispy red eyebrows, frizzy hair, pigmented freckles. Maybe he's mixed-race.

"Okay. No violence. I'm shutting up."

Vinnie slides him up against the hood of the car, checking for weapons. The second suspect in the passenger seat is more attractive, young—maybe fifteen. She reminds him of his oldest daughter in Syracuse, a pretty kid with a mouthful of crooked teeth he will someday have to pay to straighten.

Vinnie signals for the passenger to get out of the car. "Slowly, please."

In response, the girl exaggerates her movements, as if climbing through molasses. "Is this good?"

He can't help but smile, waving her over to his side of the Pinto. He pats down her jacket.

Cuffing the two suspects together, he leans them up against the car.

"You have the right to remain silent," he says.

The driver gives him the thumbs up. "Right on, man!"

Vinnie always feels self-conscious blurting out their rights. When he's done, the pretty one smiles at him. He starts to doubt that there was a gun.

"Mind telling me what you two are up to?"

"Scrambled eggs, silly!" The pretty girl nods toward the diner. "What else?"

The driver cracks up into strange birdlike laughter, and it occurs to Vinnie that this is no strange mulatto man with a high voice and slim build, but a girl! An ugly, flat-nosed girl.

Vinnie looks from one to the other. "What are your names?"

They answer in unison: "Miranda!"

"Both of you are named Miranda?"

Again, the answer is a duet, a strange boastful song: "Miranda!"

"Are you high?" Vinnie asks. "Doped up?"

This makes the ugly one double over in laughter.

Vinnie can't help still thinking of her as a man, or perhaps some other scrappy breed, neither female nor male. He wouldn't mind hauling off with a punch or two.

"I told you to shut your mouth."

Pretty Miranda intervenes. "Don't mind her. We're just happy, officer! Witnesses of Peace!"

"Your friend rubs me the wrong way."

Neither of them answers.

"Did you rob that diner?"

They stare at him.

Vinnie can't quite pinpoint what bothers him. Maybe they are just a couple of teenagers goofing around with him, putting him on. Pretty Miranda has green eyes that sparkle and a very pleasant nose, small and triangular like a tiny beak. She looks familiar.

"Are you two sisters?"

"In a way." Ugly Miranda hiccups.

A clammy layer of doubt rises off Vinnie's skin. He wants to send them on their way, to be rid of them completely. He's glad he hasn't called the incident in to dispatch. He can free himself easily, if he can just manage to let go of the unanswered questions.

"What about the gun?" he asks, remembering. "Didn't I see a gun in your hand when you came running out of that diner?"

They look at the ground.

"You're not from here, are you?"

"We're Canadian," Ugly Miranda says.

Maybe it wasn't a gun; maybe it was a transistor radio, a small purse or wallet. He should let them go with a warning and be done with it.

"I'm going to ask you again. Did you rob that diner? Because we can go find out."

Vinnie is nervous. He can't be late picking up Al again; can't go through another day of silence and sulking, accusations about how Vinnie doesn't really respect him.

Ugly Miranda opens her knit vest, exposing a patch on her shirt: the letters *B.L.A.* in tri-colored rainbows crossed by a lightning bolt. "Do we look like robbers?"

Vinnie gets into their Pinto and takes the key out of the ignition. Feeling under the car seats for drugs, he checks the mats and glove box for weapons. Nothing.

Somewhere across town, Al is probably lingering over a cup of coffee, the newspaper, looking out the front window for the squad car. The thought calms Vinnie. Everything is fine. There's plenty of time.

"Law's the law, ladies," he says. "May not be that way in Canada, but it's that way here."

Ugly Miranda looks worried. "Okay, okay. So, maybe we forgot to pay the bill, but we can give you a couple of bucks to make up for it. There isn't a law against forgetting, is there?"

"And the gun I saw?" Vinnie wants to believe.

"I swear we're not criminals." Pretty Miranda pouts. "We're just on our way to Seneca Falls for the Women's Peace March."

"You can't go around making everyone think you're up to no good. People get the wrong idea."

What Vinnie really means is *he* got the wrong idea. He can feel Pretty Miranda's eyes on him: fourteen years if she's a day. "Do your parents know you're attending a lesbian rally?"

"It's a peace festival!" says Ugly Miranda.

Pretty Miranda steps close to Vinnie, leaning into him. She smells of apples and soap. The gentle childlike pressure of her body makes it hard for Vinnie to think. "We're good girls, Officer. We stand for peace."

Agitated, Vinnie walks to his car, leaving the two suspects

standing in the rain. He gets in and turns up the dispatch radio, which is buzzing out details about the bank robbery on Utica Street downtown.

"Utica *Street*," Vinnie mutters. Through the drizzle, he watches something tangible pass between the two suspects—fear, maybe—or a secret. He rubs his face, takes a deep breath, and walks back over to their car.

"I'm giving you a warning." He unlocks their handcuffs. "Consider this your lucky day."

They smile at him.

He hands over their car key. They get in, rolling down their windows.

"Take it a little easy, then," Vinnie says.

Bank robbers on Utica Street, not peaceniks on Utica Avenue. He has to laugh: these girls are as harmless as they come.

Pretty Miranda smiles. Ugly Miranda makes a peace sign. "Thanks for the break, man."

"Don't go giving anyone else a heart attack today," he says.

Then, as if magically pulling a coin out of thin air, Ugly Miranda sticks a gun in Vinnie's face: "You mean like this?"

Vinnie flinches, ducking.

He is about to hit the pavement and throw his hands over his head to save his life when the girl pulls the trigger. A little orange flag inscribed with the words *FLOWER POWER* pops out of the barrel.

"Got you!" Ugly Miranda lets out a peal of laughter.

"Peace and love!" Pretty Miranda says as the car starts to move.

Vinnie tries to laugh at himself, ashamed of his paranoia. If you think everyone is a possible criminal, all you have is suspicion. What kind of guy walks around with that kind of dim view of the world?

"Give me that thing."

They hand it over, rolling slowly forward, waving out the

window.

At the edge of the lot the car squeals to a halt. "Death to the fascist insect that preys upon the life of the people!" the two girls shout out the window.

Vinnie shakes his head, thinking of the missing Iaccamo girl who's always on his mind.

He watches them drive away, as he turns the squad car around and hightails it toward Al's. He's only a few minutes late.

But then it dawns on him. How could he have missed it?

Shit, he thinks. *That was her.*

Vinnie no longer cares what people think. He is going to solve this case after all. He has smiled into the face of his own future.

Freckles, beautiful nose, pretty eyes.

And better still: His future smiled back.

SISTER EDWARD IS JUMPY.

Something big is about to happen, something special; the air is charged. Even Christ's Most Precious Wounds seem prickly with anticipation this evening, as they fast for Lent in earnest, starving themselves for the reparation of human sin and Holy Week, which is just around the corner.

Sister Edward is determined to solve the mystery of Amanda's activities. *Orphans:* she's sure it's some sort of code. But what? What kind of army is she training? What kind of military business is she up to?

Maybe the Bianco girl has something to do with the general nervous state of affairs. Maybe she knows more about Mother General's secret army than she's let on.

After school, when Sister Edward went to speak with the girl in her cell, she was intercepted. Sister Pius snatched Edward's pile of papers, homework for the week. "I'll deliver these."

"I'd like to see my student," Sister Edward said. "I need to explain the week's spelling list."

"Impossible, Sister. The girl's contagious, been sick all week."

"Preposterous!" Sister Edward blurts. "I saw her this afternoon walking in the garden with Mother General!"

"Yes, but she overdid it, and now she's feeling ill again." The Littlest Wound's smile is impenetrable. "I only know what I'm told, Sister."

Sister Edward has seen Brother Joe don his sunglasses and sweep the girl off Our Lady's campus. "Men are immune, I suppose?"

"Doctor's appointments. Plus the child insists on visiting her brother. We make Brother Joseph wear a mask. No need to expose the whole school."

Exasperated, Sister Edward slips off to the Manse, heading for Father Giuseppe's office to call the police station one last time. If the line is busy, she'll hang up. If Officer Golluscio is out, she will not leave another message. If he is there, she will ask to speak with him, the right of any citizen.

The switchboard operator sounds vaguely suspicious. "Whom may I say is calling?"

Sister Edward decides to remain cryptic. "A witness to a crime."

During a long pause, Sister Edward paces the length of the telephone cord behind Father Giuseppe's desk.

"Officer Golluscio." His voice is sudden and strong.

Sister Edward stutters. "Do you know who this is?"

"I got your note on my car after the funeral." Another pause. "Are you sure you saw her?"

"It was her, Vincent." Sister Edward likes how his name feels on her lips. "I saw her with my own eyes; I spoke with her, but she ran off like a scared rabbit."

"I knew she'd show up," he says. "I think I saw her too."

A charge of electricity runs through Sister Edward. "We must be the only two people on earth…besides the Bianco girl."

"What's she got to do with it?"

"Just happened to be there." Edward speaks carefully. "The Iaccamo girl came around asking for the Mother General on Saturday. I believe she's somehow involved."

"Involved in what?"

"I'm not sure: explosives, I think."

"What makes you think that?"

Sister Edward wants to tell him about the FBI and her years of suspicion: about the Mother General being up to no good. "There was mention of an army—also of orphans, but I think it was code for something."

"So your head nun is a criminal?"

Sister Edward smiles at his mistake: nuns are cloistered; Sisters are not.

"The Mother General receives a great many letters from antiwar movement leaders, especially that radical priest from Utica."

"I don't see how this involves the girl."

"There's a connection. Why else would the missing Iaccamo girl come here?"

"I don't know," Vinnie says.

"Can you come to Our Lady tonight? They're in a peace circle all evening; I can slip away."

"Outside the church?"

"Yes, seven o'clock."

"Okay," he says. "Tonight."

Our Lady Queen of Sorrows quiets down after the dinner bell.

Sister Edward's stomach growls, a reminder of her brothers and sisters around the world who are hungry every day, not just once a year, because Easter is coming. While the others gorge on two spoons of spicy rice, Sister Edward abstains. *I like to feel closer to God*, she announces, taking her seat but leaving her bowl empty.

Sister Edward says a quick prayer for the starving, watching as several of Christ's Most Precious Wounds stream into the conference room for their monthly peace circle meetings.

Others head off to the chapel.

Brother Joe is nowhere to be found. His car has been missing all day.

Sister Edward pokes around the main room. A newspaper's

front-page story hints at Nixon's precarious position; not sure what to think of him, she prays for his strength in leading the country.

After everyone has gone about her business, Sister Edward glides through the hall, trying to make as little noise as possible. Near the end of a long corridor, she taps three times on a door.

"Come in," Cee-Cee says.

Sister Edward finds her at the little desk, pen in hand, several cats perched on her desk. "Feeling better, Miss Bianco?"

"Not bad, Sister." Cee-Cee crosses her arms over her chest. "Thanks for asking."

"Shoo," Sister Edward tells the cats who skitter away. "Filthy animals."

"I'm kitten sitting for Sister James," Cee-Cee says. "I think they're actually pretty clean."

Sister Edward perches on the edge of the bed. "You've missed a lot of school. Perhaps some tutoring is in order."

"I'm all caught up."

"Are you now?" Sister Edward says. "Then what, may I ask, are you writing?"

Cee-Cee looks down at the open page. "Notes."

"On what topic, please?"

Cee-Cee stares, wide-eyed, thinking of something to say.

Sister Edward holds out her hand. "May I see?"

"I can't show you this one."

"Are you disobeying me?"

Cee-Cee closes the book. "You can look at one of the others if you want."

Sister Edward fingers the stacks of notebooks. Picking one off the nearest tower, she opens to a page in the middle, scanning quickly. It's mostly nonsense: the scribbles and doodles of a child, part of a memorized poem, several drawing of trees, a list of vegetables, spelling words, homework assignments, games of tic-tac-toe and hangman in Brother Joe's handwriting. Wads of discarded gum stick several pages together.

A note on one page says:

Magic Twenty-One: Separate deck into three piles, count to eleven.

Another says:

Please, please, please, please, please. Help me.

"*This* is what you write?" Sister Edward closes the notebook. "Not exactly *The Story of a Soul*, is it?"

Cee-Cee shuffles through a separate pile of notebooks until she finds the one she's looking for.

She rips out a page and holds it for Sister Edward, who takes it and reads the words. For a long moment, all Sister Edward can do is stare at the sentence in the child's scrawl. "You wrote this?"

Cee-Cee nods. "It came into my head and went down on the page."

"You copied it from a book?"

"No, I wrote it, but not all sentences turn out good like that one."

"*Well*," Sister Edward corrects. "They don't all turn out *well*."

Sister Edward feels an urgent need to be under the open sky, to breathe and wander, to mull over how a child of ten could have insight into the particular nature of her personal loneliness or the course of her vocation.

"So this is what you've learned?" Sister Edward asks. "Poetry and predictions."

"I learned a great new card trick called Double Cross. Also to pray."

"For yourself, I suppose?"

"For you, Sister." Cee-Cee pins her eyes on Sister Edward's face. "For people who are lost."

"And you've been assigned to do this? Pray for us poor lost souls?" Sister Edward says. "Why? As a demonstration of your great gift, so that God will appreciate your looming sainthood?"

"Praying doesn't help God appreciate me, Sister." Cee-Cee

bounces a rubber ball attached to its paddle a few times. "It helps me appreciate God."

"Anything else you'd care to share?"

"I can teach you to walk on your hands if you want."

Furious, Sister Edward gets up and leaves the room without another word. She slams the door behind her, feeling bewildered and yet slightly moved.

It's not until she's halfway down the drafty hallway that she realizes she's forgotten to ask the girl about the Mother General.

IN THE GARDEN OF Olives, Jesus shed 62,700 tears and 98,600 drops of blood to wash away the sins of the world. He received 607 strokes with the whip, 100 precious wounds by the thorny crown, and carried the cross 320 steps to Calvary—all so the world would be saved. And yet Sister Edward still feels she is owed.

Not lavish praise for her personal sacrifices, not public recognition, but a simple nod, a word of thanks, a sign that she's on the right track.

The terrible silence from within rises again. It makes Edward wonder if an unsmiling sixth grader in a plaid pinafore could in fact be a sign from God.

Despite the mildness of the night air, she wraps a shawl around her shoulders. A breeze kicks up from nowhere, hinting at a rainstorm. She crosses from the living quarters past the empty schoolhouse, across the parking lot and alongside the church, toward the stone path that leads to the Manse where she and Father Giuseppe often share an after-dinner tea together in his office.

When Father is out of town, Sister Edward usually feels a bit unmoored. But tonight she's glad he's in Albany.

The FBI wants bombs. The insistent young agent who has been her contact all these years keeps trying to convince her to sweep with a metal detector—*your duty to country!* She had to laugh: The only country Edward's ever known has been Our Lady Queen of Sorrows.

The grounds are peaceful, separated on the north side by an ancient curving wall. Edward runs her hands along the mossy surface, using the old stone structure to guide her way, touching the rough gray and yellow stones as a blind woman might. She tries to imagine all the nameless, faceless Wounds who came before her. A humble schoolteacher, Blessed Sister Rosalie Votarro, born in 1870, founded the order after suffering from stigmata. A silent-screen actress from Niagara Falls became famous for arriving by bicycle to answer God's calling; according to legend she was wearing only a strand of pearls and a pair of white bloomers. Countless humble souls once walked these paths anonymously—unknown, long-suffering women of devotion. Like Sister Edward.

The trail of spruce needles is worn, difficult to follow.

Sister Edward walks in her simple lace-up shoes as she's been taught: eyes down, hands inside her sleeves. Absently she pats the pocket of her modest skirt, feeling for the notebook page:

> *The person who carries the story forward is the sinner who is saved, the lost one who finds love. Your turn. Don't blow it.*

She reads the words and shakes her head, folding the page back up and putting it away.

Something about the evening feels different somehow— the soft air, the promise of a rainstorm, her purpose. And there's Officer Golluscio, too. Tonight goodness and rightness step with her. Reaching the end of the path, she crouches behind a bush to spy on the Mother General's peace circle.

Sister Edward hasn't felt this many strong emotions since her youth as a veiled postulant, when the very idea of chastity aroused her soul and scared her to death: the notion of an interior life detached from the body, severed from all things physical, pure and untouched and yet—what? Lonely. She's been so long dead—to her flesh, to her faith, to herself—that for a moment she doesn't recognize the sound of her own heart beating rapidly in her chest.

There is a faint rustling nearby. It fills her with panic.

Sister Edward throws herself down in the cool evening grass so as not to be seen. Being prostrate induces a calmer state. Christ's Most Precious Wounds used to require public humility, even for something as simple as dropping a fork at dinner. *Pray for me, my Sisters, that I receive penance for this unnecessary racket, this error in silverware.* Those days, things were clearer. Sister Edward had to kiss the floor, kneel down, say a prayer, lie before the community on the cold dining room tiles and ask forgiveness.

Even the sweet-smelling azalea bush cannot hide Edward's sudden defiance.

She stands, hoping the rustling is her officer, fearing that it is the FBI, dreading that it may be the Mother General.

How could she explain herself now?

But it is only Sister Pius carrying a plate across the courtyard. From the wafting air, Sister Edward suspects the Littlest Wound has been baking cookies for the peace circle again—a Lenten indulgence no Mother General should allow.

As Sister Edward moves out of the bushes, she sees the police officer striding toward her in the dark.

"Thank God," she says. "It's you."

"What's wrong?"

"I don't know...something." Sister Edward's heart thumps double-time. She stands close enough to smell his cologne.

A twitch of a smile crosses his lips. "Let's talk in the squad car where it's safer; I'd like my partner to hear your theories."

Following behind with her head bowed, Edward swallows her disappointment. What had she thought this was, a date?

At the far end of the parking lot, a police car sits in the dark. Officer Golluscio introduces Sister Edward to a smallish man with a square head.

"Al, this is the witness I was telling you about."

Sister Edward shakes the man's hand, admiring his uniform, the same one her own officer is wearing.

From the back of the squad car someone leans forward and rattles the mesh screen dividing the back seat from the front, startling Edward.

It's a boy, raging like a caged animal.

"This is your criminal?" she asks.

A second boy leans forward at the first boy's side; light from the parking lot shines on his familiar face. "We told you we haven't seen his sister."

Al Carpi leans in and shows the first boy his teeth. "Your sister's dead, Liam. You probably fucked her and killed her yourself."

"Watch your mouth, Al."

"Shut up! Shut up!" the boy shouts.

"Well, someone killed her. Who's to say it wasn't you and your buddy?"

"Don't talk that way about Eileena!" the boy screams. "She's not dead!"

Sister Edward doesn't like the other officer one bit. "The young Mr. Iaccamo is correct; I saw his sister very recently."

Everyone goes silent.

"I fucking told you!" Liam explodes. "She's not dead; she's fine!"

"Let us out of here," the other boy says. "We told you what we know."

"Shut your whiny asses."

The second boy is the brother of Cee-Cee Bianco. He waits for his sister every so often on the playground. Sister Edward starts to say so when her officer abruptly slaps the top of the car.

"Watch your mouths in front of the lady!" he shouts. "No more noise."

Sister Edward blushes. No one ever calls her anything but Sister.

"You're not prisoners," Officer Golluscio says somewhat officially. "I just need your help."

Liam sniffles. "Tell that asshole to shut up about my sister, then."

"Al," Vinnie says. "Shut up about his sister. She's not dead."

Al sighs. "Says who? You and the nun?"

"I saw the girl in a lime green Pinto myself."

"Lime green?" Sister Edward says. "That's Brother Joe's car!"

She and the officer lock eyes.

MARY MARGARET AND NORBERT see the distant lights of Romeville. They trudge past the high school and down the long hill to Our Lady Queen of Sorrows Junior High. They shuffle through the high grass in the soft evening air and stop outside the first old church building they see.

All week long, the Sisters have said Cee-Cee's been sick, but Mary Margaret knows better. Minimal snooping has revealed that her room is in one of the wings where the Sisters all sleep, but which room?

Sister Robert-Claude hasn't let anyone close enough to figure it out.

The Sisters are tight when they're keeping a prisoner, grouchy when they start fasting. So Mary Margaret has decided to take matters into her own hands. She's got Norbert with her for protection.

Holding Mary Margaret's crying baby brother, Norbert rocks back and forth from his good leg to his bad. For reasons unexplained, he has applied a large smear of purple lipstick to his mouth.

"Shhh! Brother-Boy, quiet down!" Mary Margaret says. "We've got to look in every window."

They peer into window after window, without seeing anyone, until at last, they find a room with something happening in it. Inside, the Sisters crowd around a table. Every surface is piled high with maps and papers, things Mary Margaret has seen pinned to the wall during detention. She has never seen the large poster of a blonde man with little round glasses, the word *Bonhoeffer* at the bottom.

Sister Robert-Claude is smoking a cigarette. Sister Amanda is shaking her head. Brother Ignacio throws his muscular arms in the air, flexing the veins in his neck.

"Poker game?" Mary Margaret guesses.

Norbert slumps against the cold bricks, sliding until he is sitting down in a pile of peat moss. "This baby is heavy."

Mary Margaret glances into the next window. "She's not in there."

"What if we never see her?"

Mary Margaret readjusts her stance. "She's in one of those rooms. We'll find her."

They cross the courtyard to look into a few more windows. Norbert leans so close he leaves a purple kiss stain on every pane of glass, accidentally squishing the baby, who falls silent under the comforting pressure.

"Not in there."

The next four windows are dark. A lone light shines near the far end of the building.

Mary Margaret leads the way.

At the window, she stands on tiptoes, Norbert breathing onto the glass from behind her. "Cee-Cee! There she is!"

Their friend sits at a small wooden desk, face set in concentration, surrounded by cats.

"I knew she wasn't sick!"

Norbert taps at the window, lightly at first, until Cee-Cee

looks up from her notebook. She brightens and goes to the ancient window, chewing her favorite pink gum. "What are you doing here?"

"Looking for you." Mary Margaret presses her lips through a small crack of window.

"Can I touch those kitties?" Norbert says.

Mary Margaret cuts him off. "I brought Norbert for protection."

A doubtful look crosses Cee-Cee's face. "Against what?"

"Kidnappers, of course!" Mary Margaret is exasperated.

Cee-Cee recognizes it. "Norbert, these cats sleep with me every night."

Norbert looks down at the baby, smiling and thinking about the kitties.

"No time for that now," Mary Margaret says. "Come out here, please."

Cee-Cee cranks the window closed and shuts off the light. Norbert and Mary Margaret wait in darkness.

Thrashing around to the end of the building, Mary Margaret ignores Norbert stepping on her heels. When Cee-Cee opens the emergency door, they pull her into the bushes with them. "The Sisters are up to something," Mary Margaret whispers. "We have to be careful."

Cee-Cee hugs Mary Margaret. "I have things to tell you: I saw the missing girl. I saw her right after Nonna died."

"Sorry about your grandmother, Cee-Cee."

"Do you like my lipstick?" Norbert jumps up and down on his good leg, jostling the baby a bit. "Do you like the color? Isn't it pretty? It's Heavenly Mauve!"

Cee-Cee bends him down to look at the wide band of purple he has painted over his mouth. "I love it, Norbert. You look handsome."

Norbert holds out the baby. "We've got Tiger with us tonight!"

"I see that," Cee-Cee says, holding the baby's little hand.

"Never mind that; we've got business." Mary Margaret leads them back to the front of the building. "You saw Eileena Brice Iaccamo for real?"

"Yes, in the chapel."

"What did she say?"

"She ran off before I could talk to her."

"What else?"

"That girl, lying on the forest floor?" Cee-Cee says. "I think she was me."

"That's bad." Mary Margaret mulls it over. "It could have been any of us."

Cee-Cee looks at her, grateful to not have to say another word.

"Let's go," Mary Margaret takes a deep breath. "It's time to save someone."

Just then, a violent sound of rubber crunching gravel slices the air—a car squealing into the parking lot.

Mary Margaret throws her arms out to keep her comrades safe. "Watch out!"

A second car screeches forward from the dark end of the parking lot, red light flashing.

"Cops!" Norbert shouts.

The first car's back doors burst open. Two girls jump out, taking off full throttle in separate directions.

Mary Margaret points at the car. "They're here!"

Behind them, six Sisters and a Brother press their faces to the Manse's main window, looking out into the night, blind as bats.

IN A MATTER OF seconds, the parking lot of Our Lady Queen of Sorrows erupts into mayhem. A crowd circles the cars: religious women, children, cops, and somehow a screaming baby. Vinnie sees nuns appearing from nowhere. They form a protective circle around the girl he's determined to rescue. Keeping his eye on her, he has already lost track of the second girl, ugly Miranda—not to mention the driver of the Pinto, a surprisingly large black man, who seems to have disappeared into the night.

Pretty Miranda is his missing girl, he knows: Eileena Brice Iaccamo. He can feel it in his bones. She is the person who can still save his botched career and his ailing pride; she can restore order to the world.

This is his one chance to make things right. No room for mistakes.

Vinnie must take hold of the situation.

The girl makes a sudden break for the woods behind the chapel, but Vinnie manages to dodge three nuns and grab hold of her arm, twisting her around to look into her face. He inhales her sweaty smell, salty and innocent as any daughter on earth. He's very happy she's not dead.

"I'm one of the good guys, Eileena," he tells her. "I'll get you home safely."

He cuffs her wrists together and smiles.

All around him nuns and children make noise, distracting

him, moving in closer. A large boy with a purple mouth shouts, pointing to the middle of the parking lot. *His* Sister—Sister Edward—moves steadily toward him, eyes down, hands tucked into her sleeves. Vinnie is so glad to see her he wants to call out her real name, but realizes he doesn't know what it is.

She says something he can't hear, pointing at a small shadow stumbling around in the middle of the parking lot gasping for air.

"Cee-Cee!" Sister Edward shouts. "Cee-Cee Bianco!"

Vinnie watches the shadow in the distance, trying to reconcile that this is Cee-Cee, the girl he knows, his guide of sorts. She seems to be performing a bad parody of getting shot in the neck.

Sister Edward insists. "She needs help! Something is wrong!"

Why is the girl everywhere Vinnie is? What does it mean? He should drop everything and go to her, but he hesitates. The rest of the nuns move into a tighter knot around him.

With a great clap of thunder, a flash of lightning brightens the sky.

Drawing his gun, he points at his captive, Eileena Brice Iaccamo. "Move back!"

The nuns back away, giving him room.

"Take it easy, Buddy," Al says from beside the squad car that holds Liam Iaccamo and the Bianco boy. "Everything's under control."

Is it?

As if miles away, Vinnie's partner talks loudly over the radio, reporting the situation. The Sisters' habits ruffle, their empty stomachs grumble, the soft April breeze rustles with moisture.

Vinnie swallows.

Out beyond his peripheral vision, Cee-Cee is collapsed in a heap on the pavement in the center of the parking lot. He should help her, but he cannot let go of the girl he has handcuffed, Eileena Brice Iaccamo, who is going to save his life. She just needs to let him save hers.

"Cee-Cee's not breathing!" someone shouts.

Vinnie's partner Al takes action, releasing Liam Iaccamo and the Bianco kid, who run across the parking lot toward Cee-Cee.

Vinnie's focus returns. Iaccamo and Bianco will take care of Cee-Cee, and he, Vinnie, will take care of Eileena. This is the kind of understanding he and Cee-Cee have always had, mutual. He will bring Eileena Brice Iaccamo back to the station and find out what happened, why she ran away. He will unravel all the mysteries of all the girls gone missing in Romeville. He will find out who hurt Cee-Cee Bianco out there in the woods.

"Officer, I am Mother General at Our Lady," a woman says. "We met the other day under unfortunate circumstances."

"I know who you are," Vinnie says.

"I can vouch for the young woman in your custody."

"I don't think so. I don't think you can."

"The girl you have handcuffed is named Miranda Pax White. She's an orphan from the Holy Child Parish in Ontario, Canada, which is run by an affiliate order of Sisters. Miranda is here with another young woman, who is also considering joining our religious community. Our very own Brother Joe has been showing these unfortunate orphans around."

"I don't know how you're involved in this, lady," Vinnie says. "But I think you're dead wrong."

"How come I've never seen them before?" Sister Edward is standing nearby, addressing her superior defiantly. "If they've come to join our community, how come I've never met them?"

"They've only just arrived," the Mother General tells Vinnie. "You can check the registration of the car if you'd like; it belongs to Our Lady. We use it for official church business—to run our errands and do good deeds."

"Like robbing diners?" Vinnie's throat tightens. "Like carrying guns?"

"No, Officer Golluscio, you are mistaken."

"I know all about your radical activity, lady. And I know who this girl is."

"I don't think you do. Let's go inside and talk this over."

Done with talking, Vinnie points his gun at Eileena Brice Iaccamo again.

Her angelic face, now shaded with fear, matches the photograph he's carried in his wallet since her disappearance.

True, maybe her hair is shorter and dyed a different color. And maybe she's grown a few inches in the time she's been missing. But that's normal, isn't it? That's what girls do: they dye their hair, they grow taller.

His own daughters are barely recognizable to him when he visits.

"Strange how she shows up here with you." Vinnie's voice sounds hollow. He's clammy now, unsure of himself. What if this isn't Eileena Brice Iaccamo? What if he's made a terrible mistake? "Seems like she's gotten in deep with you radicals."

The religious women around Vinnie start to murmur.

"Officer Golluscio, how can I impress upon you that this poor orphan is our friend?" The head nun is standing so close that she could reach out and touch his face. "This girl has come in peace from Canada to find out if she'd like to devote herself to teaching the catechism and living here with us as a member of our community."

The Sisters separate slightly; whispers travel around their circle.

Vinnie begins to sweat. "Stop talking."

He needs to think. What if he's gotten it wrong?

Two stocky Sisters flounce their skirts loudly. Miranda White—this girl he has captured, this person he's sure is Eileena Brice Iaccamo—twists from his embrace, letting loose a string of obscenities as she tries to get free, but fails.

"I've got you," Vinnie says. "It's all right. Calm down."

Defenseless in handcuffs, she spits in his face.

Across town at All Saints Rehabilitation Center, Frank knows what he is going to do the minute he walks into the sour-smelling hospital room.

"It's time."

"Frank, don't," Moonie says.

Human being. The words pop into Anthony's head. Something bad is about to happen.

Frank feels strangely light, optimistic; he's not completely powerless, not a loser. All he has to do is stop the machine from pumping life into his dead son. All he has to do is take control of his family, his future.

He bends to the electrical outlet, putting his hands on two enormous black plugs.

"Glory will have a fit," Moonie warns.

Fuck Glory. Frank pulls as hard as he can.

The ventilator goes silent; the monitors no longer beep: Baby Pauly is free. He lies without moving, eyes taped shut like a baby bird's, as if the nurses didn't want him to see what he has become. There is no stirring, no air, no life. Just the stillness of his ribs. Whatever existed inside his body seems to have fallen out of its frame.

He is nothing now.

Frank holds the electrical tails of the terrible machines, stunned that he has taken this step. He misses their noise, their comforting presence.

Anthony quivers, fingers jerking like minnows leaping out of water. He stiffens, relaxes, stiffens again.

"Is he dead?"

Frank takes on the somber mood of the room. "He's been dead for three and a half months."

According to their noisy machines, only the three other coma patients in the room are alive.

A nurse walks by briskly.

Down the hall, on the other side of the white curtain and

half-closed door, a phone rings. All three Bianco men have the same thought: Glory calling to check up on them.

Frank will find a nurse and deliver a story about the machine plugs coming loose from their sockets. But when he turns to go, it's worse than he expected: Glory is standing there.

She looks around, suspicious. "What?"

Frank, Anthony, and Moonie stare at her.

In less than a heartbeat, Glory understands what's happened, and lets loose a sound so broken that all three men have to look away.

"What have you done to my baby!?" she howls.

LYING FLAT ON HER back in Our Lady Queen of Sorrows' parking lot, Cee-Cee opens her eyes. Beneath her the pavement is a hard surface that smells like fresh tar. Her cheek absorbs the heat stored there from the day's sun and the humid air.

A voice in her ears whispers, *Enter me and you shall...*

She lifts her head: "Baby Pauly."

Roadie touches her shoulder. "He's in the hospital..."

Without warning, Cee-Cee's diaphragm expands sharply, and Roadie shrinks back. Cee-Cee's lungs fill with air until she feels the pressure like a stabbing pain. In her chest, intercostal muscles tighten like she is going to explode. But then everything loosens. Tissue and muscles and matter go lax, vessels grow spongy with blood, bright and red with oxygen.

Her jaw unhinges in a long noisy exhale. "I'm breathing for him."

One complete breath: the difference between life and death.

Across town Frank and Moonie lean in as Glory lies on the hospital bed sobbing. The nurses have come running. They have untaped Baby Pauly's eyes, called for an attending to pull out the breathing apparatus to deliver mouth-to-mouth with a hand pump.

Wait! Anthony says.

As if on cue, Baby Pauly's tiny chest heaves.

Glory lifts her head.

Baby Pauly breathes in, and miles away, in a church parking lot, Cee-Cee breathes out. Roadie reaches for Cee-Cee's hand. "What's happening?"

Baby Pauly sucks in another plug of precious hospital air, and Cee-Cee pushes it back out through her own mouth into the wet spring evening.

Glory is amazed. "Is he breathing on his own?"

Moonie puts an ear to Baby Pauly's lips, which exhale the gentle evening breeze of springtime, the smell of grass and the April moon.

"He is," Moonie says.

Anthony counts eight inhales per minute, each breath stronger than the last. It's not quite enough to make Baby Pauly pink, but it's enough to erase some of the blue in his lips.

Life in its most basic form: one breath, and then the next, and then another.

"Shit," Frank says.

"Thank you!" Tears slide down Glory's face. "Thank you. Thank you!"

BACK ACROSS TOWN IN the parking lot, Cee-Cee bolts upright like something out of a horror movie.

She opens her mouth and draws in a long ragged breath, greedy for oxygen. The nervous crowd gasps and takes a collective step backward. Sucking in with a rattling inhale, she expels her next breath with a hiss.

"Are you okay?" Roadie says.

"Air," Cee-Cee says.

"Move back!" Norbert pushes Roadie aside. "Cee-Cee needs to breathe."

Norbert crouches beside her, smelling of meatloaf and dirty diapers.

The sky emits a burst of lightning, so close that the crowd around Cee-Cee flinches. From above, a second great light breaks; this time, miraculously, it's a vision. A beautiful lady appears, wearing a white shimmering gown and a gossamer veil. There are so many bright stars around her head that Cee-Cee has to shield her eyes.

She rolls three perfect somersaults away from the crowd and lands on one knee in a sweeping gallant motion. *Ta-da*, she thinks so the lady can hear.

But the lady is sad. She doesn't even smile at Cee-Cee's acrobatics.

Like a dream then, the snowy afternoon returns: A circle of trees. A circle of brothers. The choir of teenaged virgins are there. And Jesus too, holding her up above the shit of the world.

It comes back like a movie.

Everything is silent. The trees stand still. In the thicket overhead, the branches are picked clean as bones, no longer swaying.

Anthony pushes Roadie toward the oak. "You go first."

"Leave her alone!"

There's a scuffle. "Faggot."

Roadie is paralyzed. Jeremy Patrick can't help him get up off the ground. Tears stream down both their faces.

The little girl is there, but not there. She steps back, butting her heels against a fat oak tree. Above, the sky is flat and gray.

Anthony grabs Jeremy Patrick. "What about you? Or are you one too?"

Jeremy opens his mouth and starts to shout at Roadie.

"Do something!" he cries.

Roadie covers his face.

Prying the little girl's fingers loose from the bark of the tree, Anthony pushes her onto the watery ground. He lifts her dress and pulls down her tights. He unzips his pants and breaks the little girl in two.

Part of her floats up to the trees; part of her dies right there. Something tumbles and hits the ground, scattering into a million pieces on the forest floor.

Off to the side, Roadie and Jeremy Patrick are still as statues: Jeremy Patrick turned away. Roadie making a terrible choking noise.

The trees absorb his echo.

"I DON'T LIKE THIS GAME!" Baby Pauly leaps onto Anthony's back, tightening his arms. "STOP! YOU KILLED HER!"

Anthony twists Baby Pauly's wrist, batting him away.

Jesus and the hundred virgin martyrs weep and sing.

Amen, *concludes the heavenly choir.* It is done; you're one of us!

Who will put her back together? No such thing, *the choir sings.*

"THE MAILMAN IS COMING!" Baby Pauly catches sight of a blue uniform. "THE MAILMAN WILL SAVE US!"

"Shit!" Anthony closes the little girl's coat and pulls up his zipper.

The girl watches from above, floating with the angels. She suffers from below, shattered and mostly dead. She will never be whole again. The beautiful separate floating girl slides down from the trees into the little broken body on the forest floor.

Kneeling in the parking lot of Our Lady Queen of Sorrows, Cee-Cee screams. Her voice startles everyone standing there watching.

The lady holds her hands and comforts her. It is clear that Cee-Cee will spend the rest of her life trying to piece herself together; that will be her task. Tears slide down her face.

"I like my version better," Cee-Cee says.

All around, everyone is still watching. She can hear them breathe.

A few Sisters fall to their knees, crossing themselves and bowing.

"Do you see that light?" someone whispers.

The lady soothes Cee-Cee with caresses so sweet she is almost consoled.

"Peace, my little flower," the lady says. *"You are like a path to the blind. You are loving and pure. Your life is the prayer."*

The lady tells Cee-Cee three secrets.

Six children who live very far away will someday transmit the lady's messages for the rest of their lives. This is God's plan for saving the world, she says.

That's *the plan?* Cee-Cee says.

The lady nods. *To touch every heart. To have the whole world believe in miracles, pray for peace and follow the light. Love is simple, but it is not easy.* The sign flashing above the lady's head is a long word that Cee-Cee doesn't know, *Medjugorje.*

Cee-Cee feels sorry for the six children, who don't have any idea what's about to hit them, but also she feels a little spark of envy.

Probably no one will listen to them anyway.

She feels sorry for a world that's so dumb.

The lady has to leave, she says, and kisses Cee-Cee good-bye.

Cee-Cee stands and stumbles inside the circle of Sisters and cops. She is struck by a head-splitting vision that lodges at the base of her skull: all the missing girls in New York State piled up, tied down, cowering, whimpering, shouting, scratching.

Cee-Cee's blood pressure drops.

She has to hope the lady knows what she's doing, because Cee-Cee cannot possibly find them all.

Al now circles the Pinto, calling for reinforcements. Everyone turns to watch him. The car doors are wide open on both sides, a June bug about to take flight.

"Check for explosives," Vinnie calls across the parking lot to his partner.

Al opens the hatch and searches. "Nothing here!"

"Confess your crimes, Mother General!" Sister Edward

shouts. "Repent your sins! What exactly are you up to? I demand to know."

"Shut up!" Vinnie's captive bursts out unexpectedly. Vinnie can feel her fury. "If Mother Amanda is guilty, it's only of helping girls like me—girls nobody cares about until after we disappear."

Twisting into a sort of half gainer, Vinnie's captive manages to free herself at last. She shoves him away and heads for the tall grass in a full-out sprint.

"Halt!" Vinnie aims his weapon into the sky and fires off a round of ammunition.

In the distance, sirens sound. Everyone freezes, waiting for bullets to fall from heaven.

AFTER THE STATE POLICE round up all the children in the parking lot, Mary Margaret's parents show up, steaming mad.

"Jesus!" Mary Margaret's stepfather says. "What happened here?"

"They arrested the Sisters," Roadie says. "It took the State police and a S.W.A.T. team to get them all in handcuffs."

"Good God. What for?"

Roadie shrugs.

A state cop steps in and answers the question: "Conspiracy, kidnapping, and four counts of endangering a minor."

Cee-Cee and Roadie watch Blanche drive Norbert Sasso away. Through the window, he waves at Cee-Cee, and she waves back. You can tell by the way Blanche hightails it out of the parking lot that Norbert is in big trouble.

Unable to reach Frank and Glory, the cops discuss what to do with Cee-Cee and Roadie. Someone suggests calling protective services, but Mrs. Cortina pipes up, "We'll take the Bianco children home with us."

Her husband groans and shakes his head.

"You can take us to All Saints," Roadie says. "That's where our family is."

"Get in the car—all of you!" Mary Margaret's stepfather says before addressing the cop: "I'll take these children to their parents."

In the back seat, Roadie and Cee-Cee sit with Mary Margaret, who seems exhausted.

"Did you see them dragging the Sisters away?" Mary Margaret says. "All this time they've been recruiting girls and teaching them to be soldiers in some kind of underground army!"

"Not exactly," Cee-Cee says. "But close."

"They have bombs, don't they? They're going to burn things down!"

"No."

Mary Margaret looks disappointed. Her baby brother dozes safely in the crook of her arm, diaper wet and sagging.

Driving like a maniac, Mr. Cortina turns around at every stoplight to yell at them: "I don't know what the hell you kids are thinking, pulling a stunt like that, disappearing with the baby!"

In the passenger seat, Mary Margaret's mother smiles oddly, humming softly. "Ooh, Russ! I love this song! Turn it up!"

"I should haul the lot of you off to prison myself!"

Roadie leans forward to take the brunt of it. "Sorry, sir."

"The lady had a message for you," Cee-Cee says.

Roadie looks around the car. "For me?"

Cee-Cee nods: "She says one day the world will say God despises you and God wants you dead, but it isn't true, so don't believe it. God loves you most of all."

Roadie's eyes are big. "Me?"

"Hey, that's Luke!" Mary Margaret says, reciting the passage by heart. "*Blessed are ye, when men shall hate you, and when they shall separate you from their company, and shall reproach you, and cast out your name as evil, for the Son of man's sake*—Sister Edward drills that crap into our heads."

Cee-Cee adds her own message: "Also, Roadie: Don't be such a coward."

Roadie bites his nail, turning to face out the window without answering.

Mary Margaret leans back against the seat, looking out the

window on her side. "What about me? What's my message?"

Cee-Cee puts her head on Mary Margaret's shoulder. "Can't tell you yet."

"Later?" she says, hopeful.

"Maybe."

Mary Margaret squeezes the baby closer to her. "What about Tiger? Isn't anyone going to save him?"

"Already done."

Mary Margaret whispers urgently. "We have to keep him away from that lunatic."

Cee-Cee runs her hand across the sleeping baby's head. He smells like urine. "Your stepfather's not the problem, Mary Margaret."

They both watch Mrs. Cortina sing with the radio: *We had joy, we had fun, we had seasons in the sun…*

Mary Margaret sinks back into her seat. "No way."

"Sister Amanda says we each get a hundred mothers to care for us," Cee-Cee tells her. "Imagine that—a hundred each."

Mary Margaret closes her eyes. "Sister Amanda is going to jail."

They ride in silence the rest of the way, hurtling down Main Street toward Baby Pauly—as if the past never happened, as if the future were merely an eye blink away.

IN THE ROMEVILLE HOLDING tank at the police station, Amanda paces. She will either be sent upstate, or released to Father Giuseppe, who is contacting the church lawyers in Albany. He was her first and only phone call.

"We've been discovered," she said into the phone.

"Uh-oh," he said. "Where are you?"

"Jail with most of the other Sisters. It's kind of a long story. The girls from Canada got spooked and spilled the beans."

Despite the seriousness of the situation and the fact that

this pretty much means the end of his bid for Archbishop, Father Giuseppe laughs. "Okay, sit tight. We'll have you back home by midnight."

Amanda walks in circles around her cellmates, mostly the other Sisters and a couple of prostitutes from Geneva, New York.

"How far, Mother General," Sister Edward hisses from a bench on the other side of the cell, "how far you have strayed."

Sister Eugene growls. "Saving children in the name of peace is hardly straying, Edward! At least she *tried* to save someone."

Sister Pius sticks her face through the bars. "Not just someone. How about dozens of girls all up and down the East Coast? Many from right here in Romeville who would probably otherwise be dead by now! How many people can say that? Who have you saved, Sister Edward?"

"She stole those girls!" Sister Edward says. "Your Mother General is no better than the Romeville Snatcher…Maybe that's exactly who she is! A kidnapper and liar!"

There is frightening silence; the Sisters shuffle closer together.

"I never retrieved a single girl," Amanda says. "They came to me for help."

Sister Edward rolls her eyes. "That's not what your little protégé said. That's not what the police say."

If in the end what Amanda has done is indeed wrong, she will confess and repent and be redeemed. It is all any of God's shepherds ever needs to do: admit to doing wrong, avoid doing it again.

"I have only followed my heart," she says, the final word on the matter.

The outer office of the police station is abuzz with activity. Processing the night's arrests, Vinnie fills out papers at his desk.

"You'll probably get a medal," Al says. "Cracking a ring of underground radicals trafficking in children. Wow!"

Al has become a believer. To him, it's as if Vinnie has been investigating anti-government nuns all along, just pretending to fumble around with small-potatoes missing-person cases.

Al spreads the new version of their story around the precinct.

"The FBI guys are pissed," he says. "They've been following those Sisters for years, trying to pin all sorts of crimes on them: two Nixon assassination attempts, a Kissinger kidnapping plot, a plan to bomb the Library of Congress."

"There'll be a team of church lawyers from Albany," Vinnie says. "Bail will be posted and they'll probably get off scot-free. Anyway, I don't know about all that. There were no explosives."

"One of the Feds said he found gasoline and rags in the church's garage." Al smiles. "They call that shit a Molotov cocktail."

"Every garage has rags and gasoline. It'll be hard to get charges to stick."

Vinnie is worried about his own personal nun: Sister Edward. He let her get arrested along with the rest for appearance's sake, but he's made certain she will be the first one released. Lucky for Vinnie, Al hasn't mentioned the business of his mistaking the young girl in the Pinto for Eileena Brice Iaccamo.

Shortly after it became clear that neither Miranda was actually the one he was trying to save, they simply let the girls go. The two of them ran off into the fields near the school. No use getting innocent teenagers involved, no use having to deal with the mess of mistaken identity and false arrest. Anyway, there weren't enough restraints to go around for all the arrests they needed to make.

"I don't know," Vinnie says. "An officer can get fired for discharging his weapon without cause."

"It was a warning. Besides, no one got hurt. They'll go easy on you...you're a hero!"

Vinnie's not so sure. A panel will have to consider the matter of where his warning shot landed. Weird thing is, no one seems to have found any bullet casings on the first sweep of the church's grounds.

Vinnie wonders if maybe the tide has turned for him.

It's not often a person's life gets turned around, whether by fate or God—whatever you want to call stupid blind luck that alternately ruins or redeems lives. You're in the wrong life at the wrong time, and presto! you get a second chance. Years later, looking back, Vinnie will see how everything conspired to open the doors of his future happiness.

"Lucky bastard," Al says, reading his mind.

"I guess."

"Some of those nuns said they saw a light in the sky," Al says. "You know, when the Bianco girl was choking."

"Yeah?"

"You didn't see anything, did you?"

Vinnie had seen lightning in the clouds. "Nope."

Al points to a bench where Liam Iaccamo, unwilling witness to the entire evening, sits slouched, half asleep. "What about him?"

"We sent everyone else home."

Al shrugs.

Vinnie looks at the sleeping kid, then away. "Free to go."

Al shakes the boy. "Go on home now! Party's over!"

Liam Iaccamo sits up abruptly. Startled, he looks around, sees Vinnie across the room.

"Hey!" His voice cracks. "Hey, Officer, you know that girl you caught?"

Vinnie grunts, struggling with the typewriter; he's never been very good with machines. He's only got an hour to process the night's arrests.

"She wasn't even my sister, asshole!"

Eventually Vinnie will close the Iaccamo file for good. Permanent status: case unsolved.

STANDING OUTSIDE THE POLICE station, Sister Edward has no regrets.

A person has to do what's right, even if it means betraying a friend, or a Sister. While they are in jail, the story comes out piecemeal: underground safe rooms, secret night runs to snatch children out of their homes and send them to orphanages in Canada.

How was Edward to know that the Mother General's bombs were actually abused children? They'd left her completely in the dark, the only one. When they release her, a sarcastic guard steers her around her police officer in the hallway. *Watch out, Sister... you don't want to bump into Super Cop.*

She is hoping to get a moment to speak him.

"You better scat," he tells her. "The others are on their way out too. I'll find you when I get out of here."

Sister Edward hurries into the parking lot, uncertain where to go. There's the diner where she met with agents from the Federal Bureau. There are churches that would take her in for a night or two before word gets out about the arrest. She has a cousin in Buffalo, but no money for the train.

Outside, her young FBI agent waits in an unmarked car with tinted windows. He unlocks the door and she gets in the passenger seat.

"You shouldn't have told anyone about the bombs," he says. "FBI business is confidential."

"What bombs?" Sister Edward should be thanked, not scolded. "Besides, the police have as much right to arrest a criminal as you do."

The young agent sighs, then shows Sister Edward a photograph of his wife and kids. "It's lousy spying on people all day."

Through the foggy glass Sister Edward watches Christ's Most Precious Wounds as they are released into the custody of Father Giuseppe. She feels a twinge of jealousy as he hugs each one of them.

"I've always been an outsider," she says, watching several *Il Duce* cabs whisk them away in groups of three. "A loner."

Finally the Mother General emerges from the station. She gets in the back of a cab with Brother Joe and Father Giuseppe. Sister Edward imagines the three of them will go back to the Manse and have a glass of wine.

The FBI agent slams his hands on the dashboard. "I knew they'd let her go."

"She probably knows I was the leak."

"Put it this way, Sister: I wouldn't go back to Our Lady tonight if I were you."

"My given name is Kathleen McDunna." Sister Edward wonders how hard it is to get a driver's license. She sighs. "I guess you might as well call me Kathleen."

"Okay, then. Kathleen."

"How long can you stay here with me?" Sister Edward doesn't know how late police officers work.

She doesn't know anything.

It turns out the FBI agent has hours to sit in the dark car with her, drinking coffee from a thermos and nursing his pride. They turn off the engine.

"So he's your boyfriend, this cop?"

"How should I know?"

Years later, after Kathleen McDunna marries Vincent Golluscio and bears four children, she calls this her first night on Earth. She tells the bedtime story dozens of times for each of her eleven grandchildren, so that they will tell their children, and their children's children.

The story always ends the same: *And that's how your grandfather became the finest plumber in all of Romeville.*

OUTSIDE ALL SAINTS REHABILITATION Center, Cee-Cee makes up her mind. She tells Roadie what she plans to do when they get up to room 404.

Roadie stares at her. "They'll kill him."

Cee-Cee twists her lips and shakes her head. "That's what you think."

Inside the hospital it's an entirely different climate: stale, sealed air and nothing but the vague smell of decay. The change in the atmosphere is uncomfortable, almost more than Roadie and Cee-Cee can bear.

They hold their breath, staying silent in the lobby and all the way up the elevator.

They walk down the fourth floor corridor until they get to Baby Pauly's white curtain. They pull it aside and find Frank, Moonie, Glory, and Anthony standing around the bed.

Everyone turns and looks.

"Where have you been?" Frank says.

"Cee-Cee, what are you doing here?" Glory says.

Roadie and Cee-Cee have no words to explain the police, the FBI, the S.W.A.T. team from Albany, the canvassing of Our Lady for bombs and bullet casings. They don't even try.

Standing next to Roadie, Anthony makes a demand. "Well?"

"Cee-Cee breathed for Baby Pauly," Roadie says. "I saw it happen."

Anthony looks around the room nervously. "What are you talking about?"

Frank watches Baby Pauly's chest rise and fall. "If she could really help him, he'd be walking and talking by now."

Without the chugging machines, Baby Pauly seems small, as if the coma has compressed his little body.

Squeezing in, Cee-Cee pulls off her shoes and climbs on the bed.

"Time to wake up," she says, nudging her brother gently.

Baby Pauly's dark eyelashes flutter.

"Did you see that?" Glory whispers. "He moved his eyes."

Moonie grabs Glory's hand. You can hear a pin drop, which means you can hear the machines above the other beds in Baby Pauly's room, as well as the beeping and talking and footsteps in the hallway, all sorts of distant clanking sounds—as close to silence as a hospital gets.

And just like that, Roadie sees his moment approaching. Why has he spent so much time worrying over nothing, he wonders, when here it is, so amazingly clear? Redemption!

He clears his throat: "I have something to say about what happened in the woods."

"Shut up!" Anthony says, twisting a knuckle into Roadie's arm.

"What are you talking about, Roadie?" Glory says.

"There was no man in a blue ski jacket," he says. "We made it up—I made it up—to cover for what really happened."

Everyone keeps half an eye on Baby Pauly's chest.

"Liar!" Anthony says. "Why would anyone believe you?"

Cee-Cee looks at her family, a sad little huddle of ruin; they will never understand what has happened, or what is about to happen.

"Anthony did it," she says. "There's something wrong with him."

Glory tries to decode Cee-Cee's face, the words she is saying.

"She's not lying," Roadie says. "It was Anthony."

"Cee-Cee's crazy," Anthony is shaky. "And you're…"

Glory brings her hands up to her trembling mouth. "But that would mean that he…"

Frank grabs Roadie by the neck. "What's the matter with you? Why are you saying this?"

Frank looks like he's going to kill Roadie.

Then, on second thought, he lets go of his son's neck, patting him on the back. He walks over to Cee-Cee and bends down, saying in her ear: "Honey, you know I love you, but this goes too far."

Cee-Cee looks at him, feeling his sadness. "I'm telling the truth."

Resigned, Frank walks out of the room, a lost man in an unfamiliar place.

Moonie crosses his arms. "You need to be careful what you two are saying. An accusation like that could ruin a person's life."

Anthony blinks so many times in a row that he decides in the end it's better just to keep his eyes shut.

Glory throws herself across the bed desperate to get ahold of Roadie. "Why are you saying this terrible thing? Why can't you let just one of my children be okay?"

Roadie lets her hang on him and cry.

A part of Glory would like to stand up and walk over to her oldest son, to slap him hard across the face with the back of her hand. She would like to see the small welt from her wedding ring rise on his cheek. She would like him to stand there, not rubbing away the sting, not crying at all. She would know that he has waited his whole life for a slap to stop him from becoming a terrible person.

"I should kill you for this, Anthony Gerard," she would like to say and send him to military school. But she cannot do any of this. She just stands very still trying to make herself believe that such a thing could never be true. This is the reverse act of faith

Glory will perform every day for the rest of her life. Until Cee-Cee is old enough to make her own escape.

There are places other than here, Cee-Cee thinks. *Places for girls like Mary Margaret and me.*

She wonders what Canada looks like.

She hopes Sister Amanda will help them.

After all, at this point, what are two final missing girls?

THESE ARE THE THREE stages of Baby Pauly's coma: shock, rage, surrender.

Shock is pain, raw nerves—an eyeball exposed to light. Pauly's body clamps down, eyes go blind. There is lung-fire and people in a blur like a flock of birds. They peck at his organs, threading their wires. They flock by his pond: black as crows. They blot out the sun, their voices an overwhelming crescendo.

Inside, where no one can reach, Baby Pauly is screaming. The worst part of rage is the thirst. Luckily, it only lasts for a second.

Then, without warning, the brain shuts down. The self goes into hibernation: a swollen frog, asleep, untouched, tucked into the mud, all that's left of him. Which is not much. There's no ruffle, no whisper, no sister, no light.

Surrender is a straightjacket. If he could form a word, it would not be *Yes* or *Me*, or even *I*. It would be—*What?*

What is a person who has no thoughts?

The only option in sleep is to be relinquished. Not whole. Nobody's twin. Nobody's brother.

What's weird about waking up, it turns out, is that the stages of entering the coma are the same as leaving the coma, only reversed: surrender, rage, shock.

Baby Pauly bursts to the surface and opens his eyes. He sees her first, the prettiest bright light he's ever seen.

He makes a signal to indicate he'd like to stop screaming

now. He listens to the air. He isn't screaming at all; he is making exactly no sound. He has moved exactly no muscles except his eyelids. His brain is sluggish, not exactly awake and not the same as before. It is difficult to understand what is happening until he sees himself reflected in a pair of eyes, his sister's.

"I've been waiting for you," Cee-Cee says.

ACKNOWLEDGMENTS

THANKS TO THE W.K. Rose Fellowship Committee, the Fine Arts Work Center Summer Program, the MacDowell Colony, the Sherwood Anderson Foundation Fiction Prize Committee, and the good Sisters at Genesis Spiritual Retreat Center and Wisdom House for fellowships, grants and quiet places to write.

I am grateful to the following people who offered encouragement, fodder, and good advice: Rosemary Ahern, Laurie Arbeiter, Claudia Ballard, Ginger Barber, Cynthia Bargar, Diane Bartoli, Sally Bellerose, Nancy Blaine, Maryanne Bragg, Blanche McCrary Boyd, James Cassese, Meryl Cohn, Mark Collins, Karin Cook, Frank Carbin, Beverly Coyle, Sally Cooper, Risa Denenberg, Andy Dollard, Martha Ertman, Ann Imbrie, Leigh Feldman, David Freudenthal, Amy Gallo, Marti Gabriel, Ellen Greenfield, Evan Harris-Hamada, Marie Howe, Jezra Kaye, Dan Kempton, Diane Lederman, Eric Lee, Sharon Lerner, Max Lewis, Anne Lopatto, Kirstin Manges, Lourdes Mattei, Judy Nichols, Toby Olson, Maureen O'Neal, Carolyn Patierno, Robert Sydney Phelps, Paula Pressley, Susan Ramsey, Rose Rubin-Rivera, Paul Russell, Alice Ruvane, Ralph Sassone, Ira Sharkey, Christopher Schelling, Oona Short, Jean Stafford, Kate Stafford, Mark Taylor, Mary Newman Vasquez, Nancy Warren, Erin White, Henry Williams—and each member of all the writing groups I've had in Manhattan, Brooklyn, Provincetown, and Northampton.

I am indebted to my friend Helen Eisenbach who edited this novel for fifteen years and never stopped believing in it. I thank Risa Denenberg for all the stories and for passing the St. Cecilia relic along to me. I am in awe of what Victoria Barrett and Engine Books manage to accomplish so whole-heartedly on behalf of writers and fiction and literary publishing. And I rejoice every day for the grace of having an amazing, literary spouse, Meryl Cohn: thank you for all your love, guidance, patience, and support.

ABOUT THE AUTHOR

MB CASCHETTA IS THE recipient of a W.K. Rose Fellowship for Emerging Artists, a Sherwood Anderson Foundation Writing Award, and a Seattle Review Fiction Prize. Her work has appeared in the *Mississippi Review, Del Sol Review, 3:AM Magazine, New York Times,* and *Chronicle of Higher Education,* among others. This is her first novel.

BOOK CLUB DISCUSSION GUIDE

To whom does the title refer? Who are the Miracle Girls and how are they miraculous?

Miracle Girls is a book filled with gritty reality as well as magical realism. How do the magical moments in the book serve to offset the brutality of the world in which the novel is set? When does the magic occur? What purpose does it serve narratively, metaphorically, and literally?

The book is divided into three parts: The First, The Second, The Third. What do the section titles refer to? (The first what? The second what? The third what?) What do you suppose the author meant to suggest?

What miracles are performed in this novel? How are they perceived? Are all miracles good ones?

How are matters of spirituality viewed in the book? Which characters believe that Cee-Cee is a miracle girl? Which characters are skeptical? How does each character's faith (or lack thereof) relate to his or her redemption?

How does Cee-Cee use her visions to survive her childhood? How does she interpret them? How do some of the other characters in the novel interpret her visions? Do you suspect that she is a traumatized child, or a visionary, or both?

Glory reports that the shrink thinks Cee-Cee's religiousness is her attempt to create a perfect family by conjuring up the Holy Family: an all powerful father (God), a loving mother (the Virgin Mary), and a self-sacrificing brother (Jesus). In what way is this true? In what way is this not true?

What do you think the author is trying to say about religion? How should it be viewed? How does it give hope to the hopeless? How does it give power to the already powerful? How is it simply part of the mix of the flawed humanness of the characters?

How does Cee-Cee's family act when they are confronted with the truth about Anthony? What does this mean for Cee-Cee's future?

What do you think will happen to Cee-Cee and Mary Margaret? What is the plan Cee-Cee hatches on the last page or two? Do you think she will succeed in escaping? Do you want her to?

What do you think of Glory and Frank as parents? What do you think of Nonna? How are the adults in the novel portrayed?

Roadie believes he failed his family by not saving Cee-Cee and Baby Pauly from what happened in the woods behind the house. Why does he feel it's his responsibility to save them? Was it? Does the narrative arc of his character indicate that Roadie is ultimately redeemed? How?

Is Anthony an evil character, or just a screwed up kid? What do you make of a boy who rapes his sister? Why is he so confused? How do Roadie and Jeremy Patrick become complicit in the crime against Cee-Cee?

Who is the stranger in the blue ski jacket? Who is the Romeville Snatcher? How is it true that in fact that entire community is as responsible for the missing girls of Romeville as a single criminal would be?

Does Cee-Cee save Pauly in the end? Or is it a coincidence that seems filled with meaning given the Bianco family's Catholic surroundings? Who in the book is ultimately redeemed?

How do certain historical events in the backdrop of this novel set the stage for the larger thematic issues? What significance does the Vietnam War have to the Bianco family? How has it personally affected Uncle Moonie? Sister Amanda?

What about the breaking of Watergate? How does Nonna react to the news from the radio?

What impact do NASA discoveries have on Vinnie? How does it encourage his belief in the idea that even a screwed up investigation can be made right?

Cee-Cee Bianco is deeply connected with several characters. For instance, she is "twins" with Baby Pauly. How does this play out in the novel?

How is Cee-Cee connected to Eileena Brice Iaccamo? Though she is but a ghost of a character, is Eileena Brice Iaccamo a shadow self of Cecelia Marie Bianco? In what ways? (Hint: look at their names if you are good at anagrams).

Why do you think we never find out what happens to Eileena Brice Iaccamo? What do you hope is her fate? What do you suspect has happened to her? Why?

What is Cee-Cee's connection to Mary Margaret? What's happening in Mary Margaret's family? How does this parallel the other tragedies in the novel? What is the state of child welfare at this time and in this world of the novel? Do you think Cee-Cee has saved Tiger?

Sister Amanda defends her "Underground Orphan Peace Army for Girls" as her duty to God. Do you agree with her? Was she right to undertake such a radical act? In the 1970s, certain bombings and kidnappings were sometimes justified as essential to furthering peace. What do you think of that idea with the benefit of an historical lens?

What do you end up thinking about Sister Amanda and her mission? Do you think she has a moral imperative to do what she can to save girls? Or is she a criminal caught up in a time of radical politics and subversive activism?

What is the significance of Sister Amanda telling Cee-Cee that everyone gets one hundred mothers? Is it an excuse to justify her actions? Or is it in some way true that we get more mothers in our lives than just the ones we are born to, or the ones who raise us?

When Glory asks Sister Amanda if she believes that God speaks to Cee-Cee through angels and visions and messages, Sister Amanda answers that God speaks to all of us, but some are better at listening. Do you believe that? Is that the point of view of the novel, or merely the character?

Is Vinnie a good cop? Is he competent? How does his romance with Sister Edward unfold? How does their love change them both?

The epigraph at the beginning of the novel suggests that the book is based on Chaucer's "Second's Nun Tale," which tells about the life of St. Cecilia. What do we learn about the saint in the novel? How is Cee-Cee like her namesake saint, "a virgin martyr who survived a burning bathtub and three bloody whacks to the neck"? How does the novel compare and contrast to Chaucer's classic poem structurally and thematically?

If Sister Amanda is the first nun, and Sister Edward is the second nun, how could Miracle Girls be seen as a tribute to Chaucer's "Second Nun's Tale: The Life of Saint Cecilia?"

What does Cee-Cee's written message to Sister Edward mean? How can Sister Edward "mess it up"? What is her mission according to the note? Does she fulfill it by carrying the story or telling the tale? How do we know?

Which characters are redeemed by the events of the novel? Which characters stay the same? Which characters defy redemption?